Slippery Slope

EMILY HARVALE

Emily Harvale lives in East Sussex, in the UK.
You can contact her via her website, Twitter, Facebook or
Pinterest

Author contacts :
www.emilyharvale.com
www.twitter.com/emilyharvale
www.facebook.com/emilyharvalewriter
www.facebook.com/emilyharvale
www.emilyharvale/blog
www.pinterest.com/emilyharvale
www.google.com/+EmilyHarvale

Scan the code above to see all my books on Amazon

Also by this author:

Highland Fling

Lizzie Marshall's Wedding

The Golf Widows' Club

Sailing Solo

Carole Singer's Christmas

Christmas Wishes – Two short stories

Acknowledgements:

Thanks, as always, to my fabulous friends for their support and friendship.

Thank you to the wonderful staff and my fellow members of the Ski Club of Great Britain.

Grateful thanks, once again, to Christina Harkness for editing this novel and for never saying, 'How many times do I have to tell you this?' Her input is much appreciated.

Heap of thanks to David of DC Creation, for all the clever things he does with my website and everything else to do with my technological needs. He is always at the end of a phone or email and never gets annoyed when I say, 'David, what's this button for?' for the thousandth time or 'David, could you just ...?' I honestly don't know what I'd do without him. www.dccreation.com

Thank you so much, Karina, for the gorgeous cover.

Thanks to my Twitter friends, Facebook friends and fans of my Facebook author page. It's great to chat with you.

And to you, wherever you may be, for buying this book – Thank You.

Love,

Emily xx

ISBN 978-1-909917-04-0

Published by Crescent Gate Publishing

Print edition published worldwide 2014
E-edition published worldwide 2014

Editor Christina Harkness
Cover design by Miss Nyss

This book is dedicated to all search and rescue (SAR) teams and their amazing dogs, across the globe. They save many lives each year – and not just in avalanches, of course. But none of the dogs come with a small keg of brandy around their necks ... unfortunately.

CHAPTER ONE

'Please don't tell your father about this yet,' Verity Lambert said, switching off the car ignition and casting a conspiratorial glance at her daughter, Lucy. 'I think he's planning a big surprise for my birthday and I don't want to spoil it.'

'My lips are sealed.' Lucy swiped her forefinger and thumb across her mouth in a zipping motion and got out of the car.

'Although come to think of it,' she added, grinning at Verity across the car roof, 'He's going to go ballistic when I tell him my news. Perhaps I should tell him yours, first, and quickly sneak in the bit about me going off to spend five months in the French Alps as a chalet girl.'

'I don't think that'll work,' Verity said, walking towards the boot to retrieve their shopping. 'And he'll probably have an apoplexy if he's told both things at once.'

'I'll check his life insurance is up to date before I tell him,' Lucy teased.

'Check mine too because he may well kill me when he finds out I've encouraged you to become a chalet girl. Although I thought you said they're called chalet hosts these days and not chalet girls. Host sounds more professional so tell your father that.'

Lucy sighed and pulled a face. 'It may sound more professional but it also sounds *really* boring. They only do it to be 'politically correct'. Chalet girl sounds much more fun.' Her blue eyes twinkled with mischief as she joined Verity, and gave her a little nudge with her elbow.

'Which is precisely *why* you should tell him you're going to be a *host* and not a *girl*.'

'Boring!' Lucy flicked back her long blonde hair in a dramatic gesture before placing one gloved hand on her chest. 'I may call myself a host, but in my heart I'll always be a girl.'

'You and me both, darling,' Verity said, mimicking Lucy's gestures. 'I may be a forty- year-old woman on Sunday, but in my heart I'm still a sixteen-year-old girl, with dreams of living in the Alps.'

'And you still look sixteen, Mum. Well not quite sixteen but certainly no older than twenty-one. All the shop assistants today said that we could pass as twins.'

Verity smirked. 'People will tell you all sorts of lies when they want to sell you something.'

'Well it worked,' Lucy said, grabbing the handles of several store bags and nodding towards the remaining bags Verity was gathering. 'Anyway, I hope I look as good as you when I'm your age.'

'Hmm. Thank you. I think.'

Avoiding one of many large puddles, they headed towards their Victorian terraced home. The month of November had brought nothing but rain and Dunclutha Road was rapidly turning into a stream with stepping stones, rather than a pavement.

'So ... when are you planning on telling Dad your news?' Lucy asked as she leapt across another pond-sized puddle.

Verity skirted around it. 'After the weekend. And unless you have a particular reason for telling him yours today, couldn't that wait until after the weekend too? We've been keeping it a secret for the last few weeks so a few more days won't make much difference.'

Lucy shrugged. 'I suppose so. I just wanted to get it over and done with to be honest. He'll be furious when I tell him I'm leaving next week.'

'True. But he'd be furious whenever you tell him. At least this way he won't have time to talk you out of going. And he'll calm down as he always does. You know his bark is much worse than his bite. He still believes that because his mother is Italian, it's his filial duty to uphold the Latin temperament.'

'And he does it so well,' Lucy quipped. 'Actually, as much as I'm dreading telling him about mine, I'd quite like to be here when you tell him yours.'

'I don't think you would. Even I don't want to be here! Perhaps I should text him.' Verity shot a look at Lucy and they both sniggered.

She was referring to the fact that her husband, Tony seemed to have adopted texting as his favourite means of communication of late. He texted to ask her to do something for him; texted to let her know he'd be working late at his restaurant; he even texted in response to her telephone messages. She was beginning to wonder if he'd text her to tell her he'd like to have sex – but as she couldn't remember the last time they'd had any, she thought that was probably an unlikely scenario in any event.

The whole thing had become an ongoing joke between her and Lucy, although if she were honest, it wasn't really that funny. It was rather disappointing, and not in the least bit romantic. But she couldn't remember the last time they'd any of that either. Romance was something she only found in books or on television these days.

'Perhaps you should,' Lucy agreed. 'Or you could break it to him in the same way you did to me. Short, sharp and to the point! I still can't believe that you let me prattle on about France all afternoon, only choosing to tell me about this on the way home.'

'Well I am only five feet three inches tall, darling, with a bit of a temper so I couldn't be anything other than short and sharp could I? I do have rather lovely, naturally blonde hair though.' She tossed her head from side to side like a model in a shampoo ad; her thick, satin-smooth hair falling back into its stylish, shoulder-length bob.

Lucy smiled and Verity continued, 'Seriously though, I didn't want to rain on your parade, and I love it when you "prattle". It means you're happy and excited, and that means the world to me.'

'Aw thanks, Mum. But you should have told me earlier. I mean it's not every day you find out that your mum has decked her boss and got the sack. I need more details! And it all sounds so unfair. Why should you have to leave instead of that lecherous sod? You loved working at the bank.'

'I did. But to be honest things have changed so much since my previous boss retired and I began working for Alfie. I was wondering whether to move on anyway. And for the record, I wasn't sacked and I didn't *deck* Alfie – although I wish I had. I merely kneed him in the groin. The fact that he stumbled backwards into the coffee table, lost his balance and fell flat on his back, ripping two of the seams of his designer suit in the process, had nothing to do with me. Although that was no more than the pervert deserved. Champagne breakfast in his office to celebrate my upcoming birthday, indeed! I think the entire twenty-fifth floor heard where I told him he could shove that.'

'I'd love to have seen his face! So what happened after that, exactly?' Lucy asked, pushing their front gate open with her bottom. 'You obviously reported him to Human Resources.'

'I didn't have to. Fortunately, Georgina the head honcho of HR, was in the office next door at the time. She heard the commotion and came to investigate – and she takes such things very seriously as well she should. She went straight to the top. I'm pretty sure it's not the first time Alfie's done this sort of thing – there have been rumours. Anyway, to cut a long story short, they realised I was defending myself against what, legally, could amount to a sexual assault. There've been some redundancies lately because they're in the middle of a big merger so, after several hours of to-ing and fro-ing, we reached a mutual agreement. They would pay me a considerable sum to leave, and I would do so ... quickly and quietly. They really didn't want any potentially bad publicity.'

'And that's what you're going to tell Dad, is it? I don't think you can text that. It's incredible though. This morning you left for work as normal and just a few hours later, you're telling me you've been sacked – sorry, you've been made redundant – after almost twenty years! I can't believe how quickly it was all done and dusted.'

'I can't either, but those guys can move like lightning when it's in their interests to do so. It wouldn't normally have been settled so quickly but things are far from normal there at the moment. Anyway, compared to Alfie's annual salary and contractual bonuses, what they've given me is a drop in the ocean, but this couldn't have happened at a better time.'

'A better time?' Lucy queried, stepping onto the front door step and taking as many of her mother's shopping bags as she could manage. 'Because you didn't like working with Alfie, you mean?'

'Not just because of that.' Verity looked Lucy directly in the eye. 'I didn't mention it, and I only found out myself a couple of weeks ago because your father didn't tell me – or even text me – but he's thinking of selling the restaurant. He says it's been losing money and that's why he's been working all hours – just to keep his head above water.'

'What? Why didn't you tell me? You paid for me to go on the chalet hosting course! I wouldn't have gone if I'd known.'

'I didn't know at the time, but it wouldn't have made any difference. You wanted to go and I wanted to pay. End of story,' Verity said, rummaging in her handbag for the keys. 'But remember, your father doesn't know it was a chalet hosting course – or that I paid. He still thinks it was a cordon bleu cookery course and that Grandma paid, and he made enough of a fuss about that. "What can they teach her that I, Antonio Lawton, cannot?" he asked me – amazingly not via text but in person – and I had the devil of a job trying to think of something.'

'But you could've used the money for the restaurant.'

5

'No. And it wouldn't have made the slightest difference in the scheme of things, darling. We agreed before he opened it that it would be an entirely separate business, which had to support itself and pay him a good salary or he wouldn't continue with it. The restaurant is his 'baby', remember, and it always has been. He wanted it that way.'

'Yeah, but I've never really understood that. It's like you lead two separate lives, sometimes. Anyway, are you and Dad going to be okay then? Financially, I mean. Oh, you will be now, won't you, with your big pay-off?'

'We would've been okay without it. Your father would've found a position at another restaurant and I ... have some ... money I think I could fall back on. But he does love *Antonio's* and the fact that it's his own place. Or he used to. I was surprised when he told me he was thinking of selling. Anyway, now he has the choice, so my ... windfall, we'll call it, really is a godsend. We can use it to clear the balance of the mortgage, pay everything else off, and still have enough to live on for the foreseeable future. So if he wants to keep the restaurant going, he can. Where on earth are my keys? I didn't leave them in the car, did I?'

'No. I saw you lock it and throw them in your bag – although why you didn't keep them in your hand is beyond me. Are you losing it, Mum ... now that you're so old?' Lucy teased.

'Very funny. This is bloody ridiculous! How can a set of keys go missing in a handbag?'

'That's not a handbag, it's a suitcase! You *really* need to get a smaller bag, Mum.'

In frustration, Verity bent down and tipped the contents of her bag onto the tiled doorstep. A few moments later, she held the bunch of keys aloft like a prize in a treasure hunt. 'Ta dah!'

Lucy shook her head, deposited the shopping bags on the doorstep, and knelt down to help her mother retrieve her belongings.

'What I don't really understand though, bearing in mind what you've just told me about the restaurant, is why you don't want to tell Dad about your pay-off, immediately. Surely knowing he doesn't have to sell *Antonio's* or work such long hours, will make him happy and stop him worrying? He's been even grumpier than normal over the past few months. Now I know why.'

'Yes, and I'll tell him after the weekend but as I mentioned, I'm certain that he's got a big surprise for me. I think he's planning to take me somewhere special because I heard him on the phone the other day. He must have been talking to that guy he knows who's a travel agent because he said, "We can't leave until after Verity's birthday. Lucy has organised a party for that weekend." If I tell him now that I'm rather well off and we can do anything we want – within reason – go anywhere we want, it may make him feel that his surprise trip isn't that special after all. If you see what I mean?'

'I think so,' Lucy said. 'Dad does get into a strop if he's not given the appreciation he thinks he deserves. I suppose if he has been arranging a special surprise, he would feel a bit peeved. But it seems that you keep a lot of secrets from each other, Mum.'

Verity straightened up. 'Not a lot of secrets, darling and every marriage has secrets, believe me. Sometimes with the best intentions.' At least, that's what she'd told herself over the years.

'I suppose so,' Lucy said. 'And the only reason we didn't tell Dad about my plans to be a chalet girl was to save him having one of his lengthy strops. Although I think that was more for our benefit than his.' She grinned at Verity and stomped her booted feet on the doorstep. 'Open the door will you, Mum? It's getting really cold and I'm gasping for a cup of tea.'

'Sorry darling,' Verity said, pushing the key into the lock. 'But if you think this is cold, spending almost five months in the snowy Alps may not be such a good idea after all.'

She eased the door open and stepped inside but instantly stopped in her tracks as a shrill voice cried out from above:

'God! Oh God!'

Verity and Lucy exchanged startled looks. They both knew they should be the only ones in the house at five o'clock on a Thursday afternoon.

Recognising her husband's voice and fearing something dreadful had happened, Verity dropped her belongings to the floor and the pair of them raced up the stairs, their footfalls silenced by the deep-pile stair carpet. Verity reached the guest bedroom – where the voice was coming from – in just a few seconds and although the door was open, she felt as if she had charged headlong into a brick wall.

Her jaw dropped open and her lips formed the word 'Oh!' but she was too stunned to speak and she wasn't sure which thought crossed her mind first.

That she was staring at her husband's naked bottom – and it wasn't her panting and sighing beneath him as he called out repeatedly, 'God! Oh God!'

Or … that this wasn't quite the big surprise she'd been expecting for her upcoming fortieth birthday.

CHAPTER TWO

Lucy reached the bedroom door just a second after her mother.

'Dad!' she shrieked over Verity's shoulder.

Tony's head shot up. 'Shit!' he exclaimed tearing himself from his partner's embrace and yanking at the duvet in a lame attempt to cover them both.

'It's a bit bloody late for that, Dad!'

Verity swayed and grabbed the door frame for support. She took a deep breath and tried to focus on the face of the woman in her guest bed. It was Daniella: a waitress at the restaurant. Verity had only met her a few times but she recognised her instantly. You don't forget someone that beautiful – or that young. Daniella was only eighteen.

'I ... we ...' Tony began, guilt written all over his face.

Daniella didn't say a word but the expression on her face certainly wasn't guilt. If anything, it was triumph.

'How could you?' Lucy hissed.

'This explains a great deal,' Verity said calmly, although she felt far from calm. She felt she wanted to do to her husband what she'd done to her ex-boss, Alfie, several hours earlier. 'I need a drink,' she added, turning and heading back towards the stairs.

'Verity!' Tony called after her. 'We need to talk.'

'Shut up, Dad!' Lucy snapped, and slammed the bedroom door so hard that the brass doorknob came off in her hand.

Verity glanced back and saw Lucy staring at it. 'Your father will fix that,' she said, before realising the absurdity of such a comment after what she had just witnessed.

Lucy cast tearful eyes to Verity's face. 'How can you be so calm, Mum?'

'I don't feel calm, believe me,' Verity said, making her way downstairs, 'but I can't do this now.' She could hear Tony calling her name, and Daniella's raised voice garbling something in Italian. 'I need to get out of here. I ... I'm going to my mum's. Do you want to come with me?'

Without waiting for an answer, she headed towards the half-open front door. She almost tripped over her discarded handbag in the hall and picked it up, hesitating for just a second over her shopping bags before shoving them into the corner beneath the coat rack.

Lucy grabbed the keys that Verity had left in the lock and followed her mother out, slamming the door behind her. 'I'll drive. You're in no fit state to. Mind you, I'm not sure I am.'

'We'll get a cab,' Verity said. 'We can afford to take a cab to your grandma's, now.' She glanced across at Lucy before bursting into a fit of manic laughter.

Lucy quickly dialled the number of the local minicab firm. Seconds after ending the call, her phone rang, and seeing that it was her best friend, Joanna, she gave her mother an apologetic look, linked her arm through hers, and answered the call.

'This isn't a good time, Jo,' Lucy said into her phone. 'Can it wait until later?'

'Not really,' Joanna said so loudly that even Verity could hear her. 'I'm afraid I've got some bad news. I've bloody well broken my ankle! Can you believe it?'

'What? How on earth did you do that?'

'It's those new shoes I bought last week. The bloody heel snapped and over I went. Flat on my arse! It was *so* humiliating. Although a hunky builder did come to my rescue – and yes, I got his number. Anyway babe, I won't be going to Meribel next week, and unless we can find someone to step in pretty bloody sharpish, you'll be going on your lonesome.'

'Shit! You are kidding me? I can't do that! What will your uncle say? This'll be my first season. I have no idea what I'm supposed to do. You told me yourself he has high expectations of his staff. And we've never even met. I only got the job because of you!'

'Calm down and don't talk crap. You'll be fine. You've done the chalet hosting course. You just do what they taught us. You cook, clean, keep the punters happy, don't blow the food budget – and have a good time. That's it. It's not rocket science, babe.'

'No but–'

'Please don't back out! Mum's already had a go at me for being ... irresponsible. As if I had any control over my bloody heel snapping! I'm going to sue that sodding shop. And the manufacturers. I could have killed myself! Although I did meet Rich, the hunky builder because of it, so it's not all bad. He's gorgeous. Anyway, you've got to go. Uncle Josh will kill me if no one turns up. He can be a bit of a miserable git sometimes.'

Lucy had a bewildered expression on her face as though she wasn't quite sure exactly what was going on. 'Great!' She glanced at Verity. 'Actually, Jo ... I'm not sure I can. We ... we've just had a nasty shock. And Mum's lost her job too. Well, not lost exactly but she's not working at the bank any more and–'

'I've just found my husband shagging one of his waitresses, Jo!' Verity shouted at Lucy's phone.

Lucy gave her mother a startled look. She obviously hadn't expected her to share that piece of news.

'And she may need me around for a while, as you can imagine,' Lucy told Jo, anxiously eyeing her mother.

'Shit!' Jo said. 'Er ... which one? I bet it was that tart, Daniella.'

'It was,' Lucy confirmed.

'I knew it! I didn't like the look of her from the start. Far too pretty for my liking. And tits the size of China. No wonder she's a waitress. She could balance plates on those things.'

'Jo! That's not funny. Mum and I are devastated and–'

'Sorry! Of course you are. What a bastard! Is your Mum leaving him? Or is she chucking him out?'

'I don't know what's going to happen. We've only just ... found out. We need time to get our heads around it. Mum needs time to think. We're going to Grandma's now but ... I suppose we'll come back here later. After that, who knows? We both just want to be as far away from Dad as possible right now.'

Verity nodded in silent agreement.

'I understand,' Jo said. 'Well, this is a right turn up for the books, isn't it? Me with a broken ankle and you – and your mum – with broken hearts. I'll get Mum to call Uncle Josh and tell him he's stuffed. He'll have to make other arrangements and ... wait a minute! I've just had a brilliant idea. You said your mum needs time to think and that you both want to be as far away from your dad as possible. Well, Meribel is pretty far away. And it's the ideal place to sit and think. It's so pretty, and what could be better than sitting in front of a roaring fire with a bottle of wine, watching snow fall as you ponder your future? It's perfect. Why doesn't your mum take my place and you can go together? Uncle Josh won't mind. He's a really great guy and–'

'Hold on a minute, Jo. You're getting a bit ahead of yourself, aren't you? And I thought you just said that he's a bit of a miserable git.'

'Sometimes. I said he's a bit of a miserable git, sometimes. Most of the time he's really lovely ... and cool ... and understanding.'

'I think the last thing Mum wants at a time like this is a man around – understanding or not.'

'What was that?' Verity asked. 'I didn't quite catch that bit.'

Lucy shook her head. 'Nothing. Don't worry, Mum. Just one of Jo's dumb ideas.'

'It's not a dumb idea! It's a brilliant idea,' Jo said defensively. 'And you'll hardly ever see him. He keeps himself very much to himself plus he has loads of other chalets in the Alps that he has to go and check on.'

'Whatever. Oh, the cab's here, Jo.'

The cab pulled up and Verity and Lucy hurried towards it as Tony came running down the path after them, still zipping up his hastily thrown-on jeans.

'Verity! Lucy! Wait. We need to talk.'

'Jo,' Lucy said into her phone. 'I'll call you later. Dad's about to cause a scene.' She ended the call and opened the cab door so that Verity could get in. 'Wilderness Road in Chislehurst,' Lucy instructed the driver as she climbed in beside her mother. 'As fast you can, please!'

Tony reached the cab and grabbed at the door handle.

'Go!' Lucy yelled at the driver.

With a wheel spin any Formula One racing driver would be proud of, the cab sped away, yanking Tony forward before he could let go of the handle. He lost his balance and ended up on his knees in the gutter.

Verity twisted round on the back seat of the cab. 'Best place for him,' she muttered, staring at her husband until the cab turned the corner and Tony was out of sight.

Then she burst into tears. And so did Lucy.

CHAPTER THREE

'What in God's name has happened?' Laura Tennent asked, seeing her daughter and granddaughter in tears, on her front doorstep. 'Come in! Tell me what's wrong!'

'It's Dad!' Lucy cried.

'Has he had an accident? Is ... is he dead?'

Lucy and Verity stared aghast at Laura.

'You'd ... like that, wouldn't ... you?' Verity said between her sobs.

'No! Of course I wouldn't. How can you think such a thing?'

Verity wiped her nose with a sodden tissue. 'Well. I think I'd rather like that right now. In fact, I may very well kill him myself!'

'Let me guess,' Laura said, ushering the pair into the sitting room. 'He's having an affair and you've only just found out.'

'How do you know that?' Verity snapped, rummaging in her handbag. 'Did you suspect something? Why didn't you tell me? I need a tissue. Have you got any tissues?'

'Boxes of them, darling,' Laura replied, grabbing two boxes from a drawer and handing one to Verity and one to Lucy. 'I'll pour us some drinks and you can tell me about it, but no, I didn't know. He's a man though, and that's what men do.'

'Not all men, Grandma!' Lucy protested.

Laura shrugged. 'Perhaps not all, sweetheart, but the vast majority.'

Verity blew her nose rather loudly. 'Well, that's the pot calling the kettle black! At least two of your divorces were due to *you* having affairs behind *your* husbands' backs.'

'That's true,' Laura admitted. 'And possibly another, although we won't go into that now. But that's because I wasn't getting what I needed from those husbands.'

Verity glowered at her mother. 'Is that a roundabout way of telling me that *I'm* not giving Tony what *he* needs?'

'No! Women only have affairs if they're unhappy at home. Men have affairs because it stokes their egos. It's a completely different mindset.' Laura handed Verity and Lucy large glasses of wine and poured herself an even larger one.

'That's a rather sweeping statement, Mother,' Verity said, a little calmer now. 'So you're saying that Tony's having an affair even though he's happy with me! Humph! In the end it all comes down to sex in your opinion though, doesn't it?' She gulped down the contents of her glass and held it out for a refill.

'Yes, sweetheart it does. Help yourself,' Laura said, passing the bottle to her daughter. 'So have you just found out about it then? How? Did he tell you?'

'We just found him and ... Daniella having sex in the guest bedroom,' Verity said, refilling her glass and knocking that back too.

'Good heavens! Er ... who's Daniella? Do I know her? She's not a friend of yours, is she? Or yours, Lucy?'

'No! She's a waitress at Dad's restaurant.'

'And she's younger than Lucy,' Verity added.

'The dirty old sod.' Laura dropped down onto the sofa. After a few moments of silence, she asked. 'But ... why were you home so early today? Did you suspect something and left work early hoping to find him in the act?'

'No!' Verity said, pouring a third glass of wine. 'I had the afternoon off to have lunch with Lucy and go shopping.' She wasn't in the mood to explain to her mother that she'd also lost her job. She'd tell her about that later.

'So Tony thought he'd be safe then? He expected you to be out until late?'

Verity shook her head. 'No. He thought I was at work and he knows I usually get home around seven. I didn't tell him about our plans. We were shopping for Lucy's trip and ... we still haven't told him about that, either.'

'I don't blame you,' Laura said. 'He'll have one of his hissy fits when he finds out. Sometimes I wish the man would just smash something and have done with it. Instead, we get weeks of sulking, snarling, shouting and weeping. Well, perhaps not quite weeping but as good as damn it. Were you trying to postpone telling him until after the party on Saturday?'

'We were but ... Oh! The party! I'd completely forgotten about it after finding ...' Verity's voice trailed off. She couldn't say it again.

'Good heavens! Yes of course. Well it can still go ahead – if you want it to, that is,' Laura said. 'What would you do about Tony though? I suppose you can tell him to stay away. Or are you considering adopting a 'stiff upper lip' approach and pretending this hasn't happened, until after the weekend?'

'No way!' Verity said. 'And I can't go through with the party after this. I couldn't bear it.' She raised tearful eyes to Lucy and Laura. 'I'm really sorry. I know how much work you've done to organise it but I can't pretend to be happy and excited when I feel so ... so bloody miserable!'

'We can cancel it, darling ... can't we?' Laura glanced across at Lucy to check, and when Lucy nodded she continued, 'Don't worry about a thing. I'll get a couple of my pals on to it.'

Verity heard her phone beep, announcing an incoming text and she automatically rummaged in her handbag to find it. It took her some time and when she eventually retrieved it and looked up, she saw both Laura and Lucy frowning at her.

'You really need a smaller handbag, darling,' Laura advised.

Verity shrugged and read the text. It was from Tony. It read:

I'm in love with Daniella. Sorry.

'Is it from Dad?' Lucy asked angrily.

Verity nodded. She couldn't believe her eyes and as she struggled for words, it felt as if they were barbed wire ripping at her throat and strangling her at the same time. 'He ... he says that he's ... in love with her!'

'What!' Lucy clearly couldn't believe it either.

Verity stared at the phone as it beeped again and another text from Tony appeared.

And I'm leaving you. I'll stay until after your party.

Verity blinked several times. 'He ... he says that he's leaving me! After the party.'

'We'll see about that!' Laura said, her pale blue eyes flashing with anger.

A third beep heralded a third message.

But we need to talk.

Verity repeated the texts over and over in her head as Lucy and Laura berated Tony. What was there to talk about? He'd told her everything she needed to know, and far more brusquely than she could ever have imagined possible.

Not that she had ever imagined this scenario. She knew they had been drifting apart over the years – married couples often did that – but it never occurred to her that she and Tony would split up, in spite of her mother's opinion on the subject.

Verity had intended to talk to him to see what they could do to regain the magic they once shared. But she couldn't actually remember the magic, or when they had lost it, and she wasn't really sure what to say or do about it.

It never crossed her mind that one of them would fall in love with someone else. Although perhaps it should have; her mother did it all the time. But Verity wasn't her mother – and neither was she the one who was having an affair.

Another beep and this time a longer text.

I'm sorry. I was going to tell you after the weekend. We have to decide about the house and stuff. Text me. We really need to talk. And soon.

At least he hadn't used abbreviated text, she thought, somewhat ludicrously, but she wasn't sure she understood. "Decide about the house and stuff." What did that mean? She thought about it for a second.

'Oh shit!' she said, suddenly realising that her life would never be the same again. She glared at the text and took a deep breath. 'No we bloody well do *not*!'

She threw her phone across the room with such force that it hit the wall and smashed in two – a bit like her marriage just had.

CHAPTER FOUR

'Mum, we're here,' Lucy said, gently shaking Verity.

'How long have I been asleep?' Verity asked, not quite sure where 'here' was, exactly.

'You fell asleep a few minutes after we left Chambery airport, so about an hour and three- quarters. Etienne said we should've been here at least half an hour earlier but after the heavy snowfall today, some of the traffic was struggling up the mountain roads and it's taken a lot longer than normal. I'm surprised his swearing didn't wake you. Even I learnt a few new words.'

Lucy grinned and glanced towards the man in question as he retrieved their luggage from the roof of the minibus.

'Well I'm almost sorry I slept through that,' Verity said. 'I knew he couldn't be quite as perfect, or as angelic as he looks.'

She stretched her aching limbs, got to her feet and was about to clamber out of the minibus when Etienne appeared in front of her: fair haired, muscular bodied, deeply tanned, hunk of gorgeousness that he was.

He held out his arms and lifted her down as if she weighed no more than a snowflake, and although it was evening and the sky was dark, she wished she'd kept her sunglasses on. She was almost blinded by the radiance of his smile.

'If you ever tire of being a ski guide-come-instructor-come-minibus driver, Etienne, you could earn a fortune working for a toothpaste company.'

He winked at her. 'Merci bien, Vérité,' he replied in a perfect French accent, although he'd already disclosed that he was raised in Kent by his English mother after his French father had taken a dislike to married life. He'd spent long holidays with his dad though, he'd said, who'd taught him how to ski and had encouraged him to move back to Meribel, several years later.

'I'll make sure you two are settled in,' Etienne continued, reverting to English as he lifted Lucy down from the minibus with equal ease, 'then I'll get the rest of this bunch to their various haunts.'

Verity and Lucy weren't the only seasonaires Etienne had met at Chambery airport. There were eight others, all of whom were regular employees of the conspicuously absent, Joshua Calder. They would be working at various resorts in the Three Valleys in one of several, *Calder Chalets*. Verity had discovered this much before she had succumbed to her much needed sleep. She and Lucy were the only 'virgin seasonaires' this year.

'Did I hear you say that Mr Calder is out of the country at present?' Verity asked, hoping she hadn't imagined it.

Despite Joanna's assurances that her uncle was very grateful when Verity stepped in to take her place, Verity was feeling apprehensive. She wondered how her new employer really felt about having her foisted on him at such short notice.

Throughout her early teens, she'd dreamt of becoming a chalet girl and living in the Alps. But life had other plans for her – and she met Tony. Now that she was actually here, she wondered if it would be a disappointment. Or worse – if *she* would be a disappointment. Her cooking was more *bleurgh* than cordon bleu, as Tony had told her. Repeatedly.

'Yeah,' Etienne said. 'He's spent Thanksgiving in the States with friends, as always, and he probably won't be back for another day or two. We don't usually open 'til mid-December. We're opening a week early because there's been so much snow this November and a group of his regular guests asked him to. He's done it before when conditions have been as good as they are now. I often help him out so it's no big deal and he'll be back before the first guests arrive next weekend. That you can count on.'

Verity almost sighed with relief. She had a few days' grace to improve her cooking, she thought. That should be okay. After all, how hard could it be to make crème brûlée?

Etienne grabbed the luggage from the snow-covered forecourt where he'd deposited it a few minutes earlier.

'Back in five,' he told the rest of the seasonaires seated in the minibus.

'Goodbye and good luck,' Verity wished them.

But as she linked arms with Lucy and walked across the crisp, white snow towards the front door of the chalet which would be their home for the next five months, she had a strong feeling that she was the one who would need the luck.

The chalet was 'picture-postcard perfect'. Made of wood and stone, with heart-shaped cut-outs breaking up the balustrades of the wrap-around wooden balconies, it was the epitome of most people's *dream* chalet.

There were shutters at the windows, which matched the deep, warm oak of the balcony balustrades and the imposing double front door. The roof and every exposed metre of balcony, windowsill, window box and bench-seat, were covered with at least six inches of snow, some of which had fallen today.

The chalet was in darkness but Verity could picture the windows bathed in a warm, golden glow of light and a roaring fire with smoke billowing from the big, square chimney. She couldn't wait to sit in front of a real log fire again. It seemed like an eternity since she'd done that.

'Welcome to *Chalet Marianne*,' Etienne said, opening the massive door into an expansive wood-framed hallway and depositing their bags near the foot of a large wooden staircase. He led the way into a vaulted sitting room. 'I'll light the fire and give you a quick tour. Then I'll leave you to get settled. Josh has a welcome slash instruction slash information pack to explain everything and I've left that in the kitchen. Have a read of it and I can go through anything you're unsure of, tomorrow.'

'Wow!' Verity said, following Etienne, her head turning from side to side like a child in a toyshop, marvelling at the many delights on offer. 'This place is really something! And this sitting room is about the same size as my entire house!'

'Size isn't everything,' Etienne replied, flashing his pearly white teeth in a wide smile.

'It is sometimes,' Verity said, her eyes scanning the room.

The fireplace to the right was at least six feet across and made of stone with a raised hearth and a heavy wooden beam for a mantle. The walls of the room were wood, which had mellowed over the years to a dark honey tone but the oak floor was clearly reclaimed from a much older building and was a deep, rich brown. Two six-seater sumptuous leather sofas sat either side of the fireplace and a large oak coffee table in the centre of a colourful rug, stood between them. A couple of armchairs and an odd, red, heart-shaped designer-looking chair completed the seating arrangements.

Heavy curtains hung stylishly at the sides of several French doors that opened out onto one of the wrap-around, snow-covered balconies. Through the strategically placed, large picture window, Verity could see a large cluster of brightly lit buildings just a little way off. Earlier, when they were outside, faint strains of music and the noise of people partying had wafted through the alpine air from that direction.

'Is that Meribel Village?' she asked, pointing towards the lights.

'Yes and no.' Etienne moved closer to the window. 'That's the main village and the heart of the resort where most of the nightlife et cetera is, but it's called Meribel or Meribel Centre, not Meribel Village. You'll find Meribel Village on the road heading out of town towards Courchevel. That's mainly chalets and hotels and you can't see it from here. Many people get the two places confused

22

and find they're not staying where they thought they were. Further up the valley in the opposite direction is the higher resort of Meribel Mottaret. It's not as pretty as Meribel but there's some great skiing up there. Can you ski well?'

'I haven't been skiing for years,' Verity said, peering out into the darkness at the welcoming lights of Meribel, 'but Lucy is an expert snowboarder. She goes every year. I used to ski when I was younger but then I got married and had Lucy and ... we couldn't really afford skiing holidays.'

'Yeah, I really screwed things up for you didn't I?' Lucy said, only half joking as she joined them at the window.

Verity wrapped her arms around her daughter and hugged her tightly. 'You're the best thing that ever happened to me and don't you ever forget that.' She planted a long, lingering kiss on the side of Lucy's head.

'Okay! Mind the hair,' Lucy joked. 'So ... the tour, Etienne. Forget about lighting a fire, we'll do that. Where's the bedroom?'

Etienne raised honey-blonde brows. 'You're a fast mover. We've only just met but if you're offering ...'

'Oh, very funny. I meant for Mum and me, as if you didn't know that.'

'Follow me,' he said, grinning like a Cheshire cat.

He collected the bags from the hall and, turning in the opposite direction to the stairs, led the way through a spacious kitchen. Verity was amazed to see that this also had a fireplace, similar to the one in the sitting room but somewhat smaller. The kitchen led into a short hallway and that, to a room, which could only be described as compact. There were two single beds, two wardrobes, two chests of drawers and hardly any space left to move in. A door on the left led into an en suite bathroom and a door to the right opened on to one of the balconies.

'I see Mr Calder keeps the hired help away from the guests,' Lucy remarked. 'Although that's probably a good thing.'

'It's not exactly the Grand Hotel, I agree,' Etienne said, 'but I don't suppose you'll be spending much time in here anyway. Meribel's après ski is second to none.'

Verity glanced around the room. 'Hmm. I think I'm a bit too old for après ski.'

'Bullshit! You don't look a day over twenty-one. Anyway, you're never too old for après ski. I'm almost thirty and I can still party like an eighteen-year-old.'

'Preferably *with* an eighteen-year-old, no doubt. I'm ... a bit older than that,' Verity said, suddenly remembering that exactly seven days ago she was forty; along with other memories she didn't want to deal with tonight.

She was a little disappointed that she didn't have a room of her own. As much as she loved her daughter, it felt a little odd to be sharing a room with her. She'd have to keep her nightly sobbing to a minimum so as not to disturb Lucy. Either that or she'd have to pull herself together and put a stop to the tears once and for all. But it had only been just over a week since she'd discovered her husband in bed with someone else. These things take time, she reminded herself.

She rubbed her eyes as she felt the familiar pricking sensation of threatening tears. Etienne misread the gesture.

'You're tired after the journey. I'll leave you to it and I'll see you tomorrow.'

He smiled, deposited their bags on the few feet of available space and wished them a good night. 'I think you'll love it here,' he said, suddenly serious and looking directly at Lucy. 'I'm ... I'm looking forward to getting to know you ... both.'

'I'll see you out,' Lucy replied.

Verity dropped down onto one of the beds and flopped back, stretching her arms behind her head. She still wasn't entirely convinced that she'd made the right decision to take Joanna's place and join Lucy as a chalet host – or girl as they had both decided to call themselves in an attempt to harness a spirit of adventure.

It had been a monumental decision, and a rather hasty one, but so had leaving her job after almost twenty years. And her husband of more than twenty-one – although that one wasn't her choice and neither was it her decision. Tony had made it clear from the texts he'd sent, that he was leaving her. She'd had to summon up all her courage to borrow Lucy's phone – after her own was smashed to smithereens – and text him to say that she needed time to think before they could "talk".

She needed even more courage to text him just a few days later, to tell him that she was going to France – and that she may be some time. Amazingly, for the first time in months, he actually called to speak to her but as it was via Lucy's phone, Lucy told him that neither of them had anything more to say for the present. If he wanted to get in touch with them, he should contact Laura. They all knew he'd only call Verity's mum in a dire emergency.

'Well,' Verity said, 'I'm here now and I'm going to make the most of it.'

'I think you've already got an admirer,' Lucy said, racing back into the room and diving headlong onto the other bed.

Verity turned to face her. 'I think it's you he's interested in, not me.'

'Bullshit – to quote the delectable Etienne. He was asking lots of questions about you on the way here whilst you slept soundly.'

'Oh God! In front of all the others! You didn't tell him about your father and Daniella did you? He'd probably think I'm some lonely, desperate old woman and I'm gagging for it!'

'I didn't say a thing, don't worry.' Lucy lifted her head from the pillow. 'Well, that's not quite true I suppose. I did say that you and Dad were going through a bad patch and that, as Jo couldn't make it here, you stepped in to take her place because a bit of time and space would enable you to think about your future.'

Verity grinned at her daughter in spite of herself. 'Thanks! Yep. Basically a lonely, desperate old woman, gagging for it.'

Lucy giggled. 'I didn't say you were old! I could have told him you hit the big four-0 last Saturday ... but I didn't. Besides, forty is *not* old!'

'It feels old, especially when it creeps up on you as it has me. And Etienne knows you're my daughter so he doesn't have to be a genius to work out that I'm a few years older than he is – unless he thinks I was a child bride.'

'You were. Eighteen is pretty young.'

'I was nineteen by the time I actually married your father. I was already pregnant when he asked me, don't forget.' Verity sat bolt upright. 'Anyway, I'd rather not talk about your dad, and it doesn't matter what Etienne or anyone else thinks. I'm not planning on getting involved with anyone. I'm here to think about my future, that much is true, and to work of course.'

Lucy jumped to her feet and pulled Verity to hers.

'But there's nothing to stop us from having a bit of fun too,' she said. 'It's part of the job description. Just because Dad has behaved like a total scumbag, it doesn't mean we have to shut ourselves away and sob our hearts out. We'll show him that our lives don't revolve around him. Let's go and find our nearest bar and have ourselves a little welcome drink. Everything else can wait.'

CHAPTER FIVE

Verity felt as if the *Hounds of Hell* had taken up residence inside her. Her stomach growled, her brain barked, her chest was on fire and her tongue definitely had a fur coating. Her breath, she was sure, would smell of dog.

'Good morning!'Lucy enthused from somewhere in the bedroom.

Verity gingerly lifted a hand in response. She didn't dare try to lift her head, or open her mouth for fear of what might come out of it. As for opening her eyes – forget it.

'That bad?' Lucy asked. 'Here. I've made you some coffee. It's a beautiful day out there.'

'Please,' Verity mumbled. 'Stop!'

Lucy dropped onto the edge of the bed and gently brushed several matted strands of hair from her mother's face. 'Is there anything I can do?'

'Leave,' Verity said but she managed to squeeze Lucy's fingers in a gesture of affection.

'Okay, I'll go for a walk. I've got a bit of a fuzzy head this morning too. Perhaps we could nip to the ski shop later and sort out our ...' she stopped mid sentence and stood up. 'Sorry, I'll leave you in peace. I'll be back in an hour or so. Call me if you need me. Um ... Etienne said he'd pop by this morning, don't forget.'

'Uh huh.'

Verity wasn't concerned by that prospect. She thought she'd probably be dead by the time he arrived.

***

'I see you've settled in comfortably. I do hope I'm not disturbing you.'

Verity opened her eyes, wondering if she had indeed died and gone to heaven. The room was flooded with a blinding light and she knew that Lucy was considerate enough to leave the curtains closed when she left.

But was that Etienne's voice she could hear? She turned her head towards its direction but before she could focus on anything, beams of sunlight hit her eyes like white-hot lasers, and she had to close them. She lifted her head from the pillow and raised a hand in front of her eyes but the sun shone directly on her face; even though she shifted her position, she couldn't move out of its glare. She was wearing nothing but a skimpy T-shirt, which she must have thrown on for some reason last night, so she didn't want to get out of bed and expose her body to anyone's scrutiny.

'No,' she said, 'you're not disturbing me. 'But if you'd turned up an hour or so earlier it would have been a different story.'

'Really? You do look like death warmed over.'

'Thanks!' she said, thinking that Etienne's voice sounded different today. It was still deep and sexy but a little more gravelly than before and somehow, less friendly. 'Er ... could you do something about that sun, please? It's shining directly in my face.'

'Certainly. I'll use my super powers and shift it to a different hemisphere.'

She wondered why he was being so facetious. Perhaps he'd heard about last night. She re-opened her eyes a fraction and squinted at him, tilting her head to one side. All she could see was his frame, although even that didn't seem quite as muscular as it had the day before. He looked slightly taller and possibly more agile this morning. She was clearly still hung-over.

'I meant, could you close the curtains or something? I'd do it myself but I'm still feeling a bit the worse for wear and I'm not dressed yet.'

'I can see that,' he said, making no attempt to move.

'Er. ... Perhaps you would at least pass me my handbag. I've got some headache tablets in there. It's on the chest of drawers behind you ... I think. They should have me up and about in no time. When I woke up this morning I thought my head would explode.'

'By the look of this room, it did.'

'Er. You don't sound very happy today.'

'That's probably because I'm not.'

'Is something wrong?'

'Yes, and I'm surprised you need to ask.'

She shifted position again but she still couldn't see his face.

'You've heard about last night, is that it? Although why that should make you cross is beyond me. I thought chalet girls were supposed to have fun. I'll admit I'm a bit old to be getting drunk and dancing on tables, but I've been going through a shitty time lately and I really needed to let my hair down. And you were the one who told me that the après-ski here was second to none. You were right on that score. Although I wish you'd warned me about the toffee vodka. I was like a woman possessed after a couple of those! Are you worried that Mr Calder might find out? Are ... are you planning on telling him?'

'I think you have me confused with someone else. Last night's ... antics are news to me. I was just surprised to arrive and find you still in bed at eleven o'clock in the morning, to be honest. Now that I know why, I think we can safely say I'm a little annoyed.'

How dare he speak to me like that, Verity thought. He's not my keeper. She swung her legs out of bed, completely forgetting that her white T-shirt was virtually see-through and that it barely covered her bottom.

'You've changed your tune,' she said, stumbling towards her handbag. 'Yesterday, you were the life and soul of the party. Today you sound like a Grinch. I assure you it won't happen again, but you can tell Mr Calder if you want. I really couldn't care less. I had a good time and I couldn't give a damn what you, or he, have to say about it. I know he's a bit of a miserable git, but frankly I'm surprised by your attitude and ... Oh! You're ... you're not Etienne! *Who* the hell are you?'

The dark-haired man towering over her didn't answer immediately. He was too busy staring at her legs. His eyes travelled upwards as his bottom lip travelled down. 'I ... I ...' he stammered.

'You have two seconds to get out of here before I deck you and call the police,' she said, although she had no idea how to do either. He looked as if he could pin her down with one hand – unlike her ex-boss, Alfie. And she didn't know the number for the French emergency services, even if she could make it past him to her handbag and her new mobile phone.

'Verity? Lucy? Are you here?'

That definitely *was* Etienne and his voice was coming from the hall.

'Etienne, help me!' she screamed at the top of her lungs. 'There's a strange man in my room!'

The stranger gave her a bewildered look. 'I'm not a strange man!' he insisted before Etienne burst into the room, almost careering into him.

'Josh!' Etienne said, slapping the man on the back and grinning with relief. 'What are you doing here? I thought you were still in Boston.'

Now it was Verity's bottom lip that dropped. Josh. This man was Josh. Josh Calder ... her new boss! Dear God, it couldn't be.

'I was. I mean ... I've just got back. This morning. I took the red-eye.' He turned back to Verity with an odd look on his face. 'Do you think you could put some clothes on? It's pretty distracting having a semi-naked woman standing so close to me.'

Verity could feel her temper rising, partly because Josh's eyes kept lingering on her thighs and partly because she wanted to die of sheer embarrassment.

'Well! Excuse me!' she snapped. 'But this is *my* bedroom and I thought you were Etienne.' She saw the look of surprise on both men's faces and realised how that sentence may be misconstrued – possibly in different ways by each of them. 'No. That wasn't what I meant. I meant ... I thought you were someone I knew. ... As opposed to a total stranger, that is. No, that's not exactly–'

'Take this,' Josh interrupted, removing his all-weather jacket and holding it up in front of her like a screen.

She glanced at it as a hint of aftershave wafted towards her.

'I have a better idea,' she said. 'Why don't you both get out of my room?'

Something flashed in Josh's eyes as they met hers and she looked at him properly for the first time now that the sun wasn't blinding her. He was rather good looking. Extremely good looking in fact.

He was taller and marginally leaner than Etienne but clearly a man who kept himself in shape. His dark brown hair was just a fraction too long to be considered 'tidy' and his face had the look of a man who loved the outdoors, with a clean-shaven jaw and those slightly chiselled features that always made Verity look twice. Dark brows sat perfectly above piercing, blue-grey eyes framed by lashes she would die for and edged by the finest of laughter lines. As she studied his face, she saw his generous mouth twitch at one corner and she felt the colour rush to her cheeks. Was that a twinkle of devilment in those blue-grey eyes? Or possibly a challenge?

'Technically, it's *my* room,' he said, 'as I own the chalet ... and everything in it.'

She tipped her chin up and held his gaze with some difficulty; her heart was pounding. 'But you don't own me,' she said, attempting a sultry edge to her voice although she had no idea why. 'And a gentleman would leave.'

Josh hesitated for just one moment, as if he had something more to say but he bowed his head in an old-fashioned gesture and left the room, pushing Etienne out in front of him. When he'd gone, Verity collapsed on the bed.

'Bloody hell! It's been a long time since I've had a man as gorgeous as *that* in my bedroom,' she said in a raised voice, suddenly gasping as she realised they might have heard. Two gorgeous men, she thought, counting Etienne. But he didn't hold a candle to Josh in her opinion.

In truth, she reminded herself, the only gorgeous man she'd ever had in her bedroom – or anywhere else for that matter – had been Tony. She wondered, not for the first time, whether she'd been missing out and then she wondered if she'd ever have sex again now that Tony was gone. No! She must *not* think about Tony. Or sex. But it's funny how you miss things once they're gone. Although she wasn't sure which she missed more right now: her husband or sex.

She wondered how old Josh was. Etienne was thirty and they were friends but Josh looked older than that. She would have said around the forty mark. Was he single? Had his niece, Joanna mentioned that? She couldn't remember. Hmm, she thought, perhaps I'll enjoy working here more than I expected.

Working here! Josh had found her in bed at eleven o'clock in the morning – and he clearly wasn't happy about it. Was she about to lose another job? This time it would be her fault she realised, suddenly remembering what she'd said to him.

She wasn't sure what to do. She needed a shower but should she just throw on some clothes and face the music? She could have a shower later – if he didn't send her packing. Perhaps he'd just give her a warning.

She dashed into the bathroom and almost died when she saw her reflection. Tufts of hair were sticking out at odd angles and her mascara was smudged. She looked like a cartoon burglar ... with jaundice ... and she'd have to pay excess baggage on the bags under her eyes. What must he have thought?

Her stomach made unpleasant gurgling sounds and she could feel the bile rising in her throat. She stumbled back into the bedroom and searched through her handbag. Where were those tablets? Why hadn't she listened to her mother and Lucy and bought herself a smaller bag? Taking several deep breaths, she waited until the queasiness passed.

A few minutes later, feeling slightly better, she returned to the bathroom and washed her face, brushed her hair and tidied her make-up. She threw on a pair of jeans and a sweater, slipped on a pair of shoes and mustered all her courage to face Josh. She made her way into the sitting room via the kitchen and dining room, just as Lucy entered from the hall.

'Hi Mum. You're feeling better I see. Is that Etienne's car outside? It's–'

'It's mine,' Josh interrupted, getting to his feet. He and Etienne had been sitting by the fire.

'Oh!' Lucy said, clearly surprised. 'And you are ...?'

He shot a look at Verity. 'A bit of a miserable git, according to your mother.'

Verity wanted the earth to open up and swallow her. Yep, she'd definitely lost her job. She met Lucy's bewildered look with a wry smile.

'This is Mr Calder, darling. We ... we had a bit of a misunderstanding.'

'To say the least,' Josh said.

His eyes raked over Verity's body as if she were still wearing just her T-shirt – or even less, and she could feel her temper rising again.

'Well perhaps if you'd introduced yourself instead of just barging into my bedroom, sorry, *your* bedroom, things might have been different. I thought you were abroad and I wasn't expecting you for another few days. If I'd known you were going to travel overnight so that you could check up on us today, I wouldn't have gone out last night, obviously.'

Josh looked as if she'd just slapped his face. 'Check up on you! I did no such thing. Although clearly someone needs to. I just came to say hello and to welcome you on

33

board but I didn't expect to find you in bed! Are you trying to say that this was my fault in some way? I wasn't the one pouring ... toffee vodka down your throat last night.'

'I didn't say you were!'

'So surely it's your fault, not mine? You got drunk with absolutely no assistance from me.'

'Well, you wouldn't have been much help anyway. You couldn't even manage to close the curtains or pass me my handbag this morning.'

'Forgive me! But I was under the misguided impression that *you* worked for *me*, not the other way around.'

Verity was seething. 'And *I* was under the misguided impression that *you* would be a gentleman, not some lech who couldn't take his eyes off my body!'

Josh glowered at her. 'Well you shouldn't have flaunted it in front of me if you didn't want me to look at it. And now I'm a lech too, as well as a miserable git – although how you could decide I'm a miserable git before you'd even met me is baffling. I can't believe Etienne told you that.' He shot Etienne a questioning look. 'Did you?'

'No! I'm not sure what's going on here or why you're both so cross, but I'd never call you a miserable git, Josh. You're not as laid back as you used to be and you can be a bit of a perfectionist but–'

'Thanks,' Josh butted in. 'That's good to know. No takers for membership of my fan club, it seems.' He scowled at Verity. 'I gave you a job, didn't I? How does that make me a miserable git?'

'It doesn't. But don't make out you've done me a big favour. Jo told us you were really grateful when I agreed to take her place. If that's not the case, I can leave right now. I don't need to be here, you know. Nor does Lucy for that matter. We can afford to stay in Meribel without working for *Calder Chalets*, believe me. Just say the word and we'll go. And for your information, it was your niece who said you were a miserable git, not me!'

'Mum!' Lucy finally intervened.

Josh looked astonished. 'Joanna? Jo told you I'm a miserable git? Well, so much for being the loving uncle. That's put me in my place. Although what the fuck I've done to ... Sorry. That's irrelevant.' He ran a hand through his thick, dark brown hair, shook his head and sighed loudly. 'You can go or you can stay. At this point in time, I really couldn't give a damn. I'm going home. I'm knackered. See you later, Etienne.' He marched towards the door, stopped and turned to face Lucy. 'I'm glad I've finally met you, Lucy. Jo has told me a lot about you over the years. And don't worry, she said much nicer things about you to me than she told you about me, it seems. I'd like you to stay but if you want to leave, I'll understand completely.'

Lucy cast Verity a pleading look but before she could reply, Josh Calder had gone.

CHAPTER SIX

'Can someone tell me what the fuck just happened?' Etienne said, sounding utterly bemused.

Verity shook her head. 'I lost my temper and I've screwed up my daughter's life ... again.'

Lucy's head shot round. 'What do you mean "again"?' She dashed to her mother's side and threw her arms around her. 'You've done nothing but help me until now. I'm ... I'm not really sure what all that was about, but surely we can sort it out? It's ... it's not like the thing with Dad. And that wasn't your fault either. That was his. Dad's an idiot. And it hasn't ruined my life, I can assure you. How many times do I have to say that? It's ... not ... your ... fault!'

'Er ... I think I'll go and catch up with Josh,' Etienne said. 'Lucy's right, this can be sorted, I'm sure. I don't know why he was so mad just now, or why Jo told you he's a miserable git, because he isn't. He's a great guy and he's usually very friendly. I expect he's just jet-lagged. Yeah, he's a perfectionist and he likes things done a certain way, and he is far more serious than he used to be, but there's a reason for that which I won't go into. You don't really want to leave, do you Verity?'

Verity sighed and kissed Lucy's cheek. 'I don't know, Etienne. We've only just arrived so it would be stupid to turn around and go all the way home again. Besides, I don't really have a home to go to ... as such. I ... I'd like to see if I can do this but ... well, to be honest, I'm not really sure what just happened either. I can't believe that he could get so cross just because he turned up and found me still in bed at eleven o' clock. It's not as if any guests are arriving until next week so I can't see why it's such a big deal.'

'Is that what started this?' Etienne asked. 'Josh finding you in bed?'

'I think so. That's what he said anyway. And when he found out that I'd been out, got drunk and was dancing on the tables, he was even more annoyed.'

Etienne nodded. 'That explains it a bit.'

'It does?' Verity wasn't convinced. 'Does he have something against alcohol then? Or just women consuming alcohol and behaving like idiots? I'll admit I did go a bit overboard last night. I'm not normally like that.'

'I don't think this was really about you. It was the situation. He's jet-lagged and clearly not thinking straight. It just stirred up bad memories. Look, if I can get him to agree which I'm sure I can, will you stay?'

'Mum, please!' Lucy pleaded.

Verity nodded. 'Okay, but I didn't like what he said about me working for him. I know that's true, but he made it sound as if I'm some skivvy or something. Well, I suppose I am, technically, but that's not the point. I'm not his slave! I can't work for someone who doesn't treat me with at least a modicum of respect.'

'He didn't mean that,' Etienne said. 'I'll go and have a chat with him and pop back this afternoon. I'll ... I'll see if I can get him to apologise.'

**

'Apologise!' Josh said thirty minutes later when Etienne turned up at his home to discuss it. 'I most certainly will *not*, Etienne. Who does the woman think she is?'

'It's only a word, Josh. You don't have to mean it. Just say you're sorry and everything'll be okay.'

'I won't say something I don't mean. Not again. Never again. Not after ...' Josh let his voice trail off. He didn't want to drag up even more of those memories. He ran a hand through his hair, flopped back into the armchair and crossed his ankles as he stretched his legs out in front of the fire.

Etienne let out a long sigh. 'You said some things today which I'm pretty sure you didn't mean.'

Josh glanced at his friend. 'I was angry. I still say things I shouldn't when I'm angry.'

'Then just apologise for being angry. Or say something you do mean. Say that you'd like her to stay. That's true, isn't it? Where are you going to get two new chalet hosts in time for the arrival of the first guests of the season next week? If you really don't like Verity, you can stay out of her way. I'll check in on them and make sure the chalet is running the way you want it to. You know you can trust me.'

'It's not that I don't like her ... exactly. We've only just met so I don't even know her. But she did make me angry and I don't like her attitude. I have certain standards and ... but of course, you know that. I may not be a miserable git but I am a bit of a perfectionist and I'm not as laid back as I used to be, isn't that what you said?'

'Don't take that as a criticism, Josh. You want things done a certain way, there's nothing wrong with that. As for the rest, even you know that's true. I wish you'd lighten up again but I guess you still need time.'

Josh screwed up his eyes and frowned. 'Okay. If she wants to stay, she can stay. But I'll have to make her understand that I have certain rules. I'll talk to her later. To both of them. Lucy seems reasonable and Jo thinks a lot of her. Mind you, I was under the impression that Jo thought a lot of me and look how wrong I was about that.' He yawned suddenly. 'I can't believe I'm so tired. I think I'm going to have to go to bed for an hour or so.'

Etienne grinned. 'During the day, Josh? It's a good thing you don't work for *Calder Chalets*. The boss wouldn't be happy about that.'

Josh smirked. 'Very funny. Okay, I'll admit I may have over-reacted. I may apologise about that. We'll see.'

'Why don't we meet at the chalet this evening? That way you can see what her cooking's like and you can explain that you're just concerned about standards being maintained once the guests arrive. She'll understand that, I'm sure. And she did say that last night was a one-off and she doesn't usually behave like that.'

'Hmm. Where have I heard that before?' Josh said sarcastically. He got to his feet and forced a smile. 'Fine, I'll see you later. I'm going to have a shower. Perhaps that'll make me feel better.'

'I'll tell them we'll be there at seven,' Etienne said, standing up and walking towards the door. 'I'm sure everything'll be fine after a few drinks, a good meal, and a friendly chat.'

'If her cooking's as good as her body, I'll probably be willing to forgive her anything,' Josh said, surprising not only himself but also Etienne.

'Bloody hell! Is that a trace of the 'old' Josh returning?'

Josh shrugged. 'Perhaps.'

'Then you shouldn't just apologise to Verity, you should thank her!'

'It's got nothing to do with her,' Josh snapped. 'If my niece is telling people I'm a miserable git, I think I need to consider the possibility that I have become one, and do something about it. She used to call me her Funcool, instead of Uncle because she used to think I was. I didn't realise I'd changed quite so much. You're obviously not the only one who thinks I need to lighten up.'

'You can start tonight by showing Verity you're not the tyrannical, obnoxious, slave-driver of a boss ... and miserable git she seems to think you are.'

Josh raised his brows. 'You left "lech" out of that list.'

'I said, show her the things you're *not*. Didn't you just say something about her having a good body?' Etienne said, grinning broadly as he closed the front door behind him.

***

'He wants to have dinner? Here? Tonight?' Verity said when Etienne told her the news.

'Yeah. You'll see he's not the person you seem to think he is and he'll see that you're going to be the perfect chalet

39

host. He's just concerned about the guests' wellbeing. You can't blame him for that. They are his livelihood, after all.'

'I understand that completely.'

'Then why the worried look? It's simple, Verity. Josh really loves good food so all you have to do is cook something nice tonight and he'll forget what happened earlier. He may even apologise.'

'There's just one little problem,' Verity said without thinking it through. 'Lucy's gone for a walk and I'm not sure when she'll be back.'

'Why is that a problem? Are you still hung-over?'

'A little. But that's not it. Even when I'm not ... I'm a really crap cook.'

CHAPTER SEVEN

'Something smells delicious,' Josh said, strolling into the kitchen of *Chalet Marianne* at precisely seven o'clock.

'And someone looks pretty delicious too,' Etienne added, following closely behind him.

Verity was bending over, checking the contents of the oven but she straightened up and forced a smile. She was still feeling apprehensive and she thought it would require a supreme effort on her part to get through the evening without getting sacked, but she decided to start as she hoped to go on. Fortunately for her, Lucy's walk had been a short one, and together they had shopped, prepped and Lucy had cooked a meal even Josh would have to approve of.

'Thanks, Etienne. People often say my rear is my best feature,' Verity joked. 'And thank you Mr Calder. I'm sure it'll taste as good as it smells. It's beef casserole.'

Etienne winked but Verity could see by the expression on her boss's face that Josh Calder wasn't amused. Had she put her size four feet in it already?

'Beef casserole?' he queried, looking as if he'd never heard of it before.

'Yes. Oh! Are you a vegetarian? I'm so sorry it didn't occur to me to ask. Lucy can–'

'No, I'm not a vegetarian,' he interrupted, 'but I was hoping for something a little more ... interesting than beef casserole.'

Verity could feel her temper rising but thankfully, before she could respond, Lucy appeared from the dining room.

'Mum's teasing you Mr Calder.' She threw Verity a warning look. 'Think ... *boeuf bourguignon* – but even better. We've used a very old and very secret, family recipe, made a few tweaks and come up with a dish we're calling *boeuf à la spéciale de Marianne*. It's accompanied by *potatoes boulangères*, followed by *tarte tatin*. Oh, and *oeufs en cocotte* to start. I hope that's okay. I'm not trying to make excuses or anything but we only arrived yesterday evening and I ... we haven't had a chance to plan the menus or stock up properly yet.'

Boeuf à la spéciale de Marianne! This was news to Verity but even with her basic command of the French language, she knew that just meant Marianne's Beef Special. And there was no old or secret, family recipe that she knew of. Lucy simply said: 'We'll chuck these veg in that pot with some beef and those herbs and stuff it in the oven for a couple of hours,' when Verity asked what they could cook. It did smell divine though, so clearly Lucy knew what she was doing.

Lucy gave Josh her sweetest smile and Verity could almost see the ice melt from his eyes. His mouth curved into what she could only describe as a sensuous grin. He glanced from Lucy to her, raked a hand through his hair and gave a little cough.

'That sounds perfect,' he said enthusiastically, his gaze fixed firmly on Verity. 'And naming a dish after the chalet is a particularly nice touch. Food is a passion of mine I'm afraid, and also one of my priorities. It's very important that my guests enjoy good quality, well prepared and perfectly cooked meals. If this all tastes as good as it sounds, I won't have anything to worry about on that score.'

'Let's start, shall we,' Lucy said, 'and we'll soon find out. Why don't you go and pour the wine, Mum? I'll finish off in here.'

'Oh. If you're sure,' Verity replied, grateful to Lucy for the 'get out of jail card' – or in this case, the 'get out of the kitchen before Josh realises you're a fraud' card.

Josh took off his jacket, held out his hand for Etienne's and walked back into the hall to hang them up.

Verity winked at Etienne in grateful thanks for not exposing her. He'd promised he wouldn't tell Josh about her lack of cooking skills and clearly he'd kept that promise. She hugged Lucy and sauntered happily into the dining room to do something she was good at: playing the hostess.

Years ago, when she and Tony held dinner parties at their home, long before he opened his own restaurant, Tony had done the cooking and she had been the hostess. Keeping people happy and their glasses full was a talent that had come naturally to her. It was one of the things Lucy had used to persuade her to go to Meribel.

'I can do all the menu planning and cooking, Mum,' Lucy told her. 'You can keep the punters happy. You're really good at that. We can share the shopping and cleaning. And we need to be together right now. If you don't want to come to Meribel with me, I'll stay here with you. I'm not leaving you to face this without me. But perhaps it would do us both good to get away. We'd make the perfect chalet hosts ... as a team.'

'Lucy's right,' Laura added. 'And you always dreamt of being a chalet girl when you were young. Now's your chance to fulfil that dream and give yourself some breathing space from Tony. It's almost as if it were meant to be.'

Verity hadn't taken much convincing. Tony was bombarding them with texts and phone calls and, as Verity hadn't yet replaced her broken phone, he was contacting Lucy instead. They'd been home only twice – when he was out – to collect some things, including their recent purchases and were staying with Laura and her latest husband, Bertie. After the third day, Lucy ignored her father's calls. When he started calling Laura's number, Verity realised she had to get away.

She knew she'd have to talk to him eventually but she also knew she couldn't face him, or the fact that their marriage was over, without bursting into floods of tears. She wanted to delay the inevitable for as long as she possibly could.

'May I help you with that?' Josh's voice brought her back to the present.

She turned to find him standing directly behind her, so close that she could smell his subtle aftershave and feel his breath on her face. Unwittingly, she took a step back.

'I think I can manage to pour wine without any help, Mr Calder.' She saw his eyes narrow and his jaw clench. 'But thank you for the offer,' she added hastily. 'Red or white?'

'Red, please. And stop calling me Mr Calder, will you?' He dragged a hand through his hair.

He seemed to do that a lot Verity noticed, wondering what his thick and rather unruly, dark hair felt like. Would it be soft to the touch? Would it be coarse? It needed a trim, being just an inch or so too long; it brushed against the collar of the white shirt he was wearing beneath his navy blue jumper. She shook herself mentally, took a deep breath and poured the wine.

'And what exactly would you like me to call you?' She held the glass of wine out to him.

'Certainly not a miserable git! Call me Josh. Everyone does,' he said with a smile hovering on his lips.

She smiled in return and feigned an air of friendly indifference but as he took the glass and his fingers brushed hers, she felt as if she'd been stung by a bee and she snatched her hand away so quickly that the glass tipped up, spilling wine onto the floor.

'Shit!' she said, meeting his eyes momentarily before hurriedly depositing the bottle on the table and dashing towards the kitchen. 'I'll get a cloth.'

Verity shoved the kitchen door open and Lucy stepped away from Etienne with a half guilty, half disappointed look in her eyes.

'What's up?' Lucy asked, her voice an octave higher than usual.

'I've just spilt wine all over the floor,' Verity said, wondering if she had interrupted something between Etienne and her daughter. She wet a cloth under the tap, and

44

with another quick glance at her daughter's flushed cheeks, she headed back towards the dining room. 'If I'm not on the next plane back to the UK by the end of this evening, it'll be nothing short of a miracle!'

Josh was wiping the front of his jumper with a handkerchief and Verity realised that it wasn't just the floor she'd spilt wine on. Had it soaked through to his white shirt? She hoped not. She watched, almost mesmerised as his hand travelled down to his charcoal grey trousers and she saw three large, deep red splashes just below his waist and down his right thigh.

'May I help you with that?' she asked, realising too late exactly what she'd just offered to do.

She wondered what on earth had come over her. Was it the alpine air? Was she suffering from some sort of delirium-inducing altitude sickness? Had she suddenly turned into a lonely, desperate woman who was gagging for it? Something had happened to her because as she stood there watching Josh Calder, that's exactly how she felt!

He raised his head and as his eyes met hers, she wasn't sure if she saw surprise, amusement or anger in them. The corners of his mouth twitched and lowering his head again, he continued dabbing at the stains.

'I think I can manage, thanks. Perhaps another time.'

'There won't be another time, I assure you. I'll be more careful in future.'

She could feel him watching her as she knelt at his feet mopping up the wine and silently telling herself to stop acting like a besotted sixteen-year-old. She was irritated that he hadn't stepped back. If she raised her head now, her face would be ...

'Are you okay down there?' Josh asked, bending down and taking the cloth from her hands. He stood up and held out a hand to help raise her to her feet.

She ignored the proffered hand and leant on the table instead, grabbing the cloth back from him and heading towards the kitchen, more annoyed with herself than with him.

'I work for *you*, remember,' she said.

'You could have fooled me,' he mumbled.

Verity took a breath and entered the kitchen, relieved to see Etienne leaning against the worktop farthest away from Lucy.

'Can I help in here?' she asked. 'I think it's best if someone else pours the wine.'

'I'll do that,' Etienne said, grabbing another two bottles.

When he'd gone, Verity turned to Lucy.

'Was there something going on just now between you and Etienne?'

'No. He was just ... being silly.'

Verity studied Lucy's face. 'He seems extremely nice, Lucy and there is no denying he's incredibly handsome, but he is nine years older than you, he works as a ski guide and he lives in a ski resort.'

'I'm well aware of that, Mum. And your point is ...?'

'Nothing. Sorry. You're old enough to make your own decisions and a lot wiser than I am, in all probability. I just don't want you to get hurt, that's all.'

Lucy smiled and, removing the ramekins from the oven, placed the first course on a tray.

'Don't worry, I'll be careful. Besides, who says I'll be the one getting hurt?'

She winked and nodded towards the door, which Verity opened to let her pass into the dining room.

Josh and Etienne were standing by the fireplace. It was smaller than the one in the sitting room but the heat from the fire had less space to fill. This room wasn't vaulted, so even though the floor space was comparable, it was as warm as toast within about fifteen minutes. Which was just as well; Verity had forgotten to light the fire until ten minutes before Josh arrived. She wondered if he'd realised and would mark her down on that score too. Lucy had told her how important ambience was in a ski chalet and they'd agreed that Lucy would cook whilst Verity prepared the dining room. She almost failed at that.

'It's very cold tonight, isn't it?' she said, hoping that would cover her lapse.

'If you think this is cold, just wait until January,' Josh replied. 'The temperature often drops several degrees then. More of a 'beach bunny' are you?'

'A beach ... bunny?' Verity could feel herself scowling and tried very hard not to. Every time Josh opened his admittedly kissable-looking mouth, he either infuriated her ... or made her think things she definitely shouldn't be thinking.

'As opposed to a ski bunny,' Josh clarified.

'Oddly enough, Mr Calder–'

'Josh,' he interrupted, with that sensuous smile hovering on his lips.

She attempted to match it. 'Oddly enough ... Josh, I have never thought of myself as either type of ... bunny. I'm an all weather, all conditions, woman. I think you'll find that many women are ... nowadays.'

'Let's eat,' Lucy suggested with a definite edge to her voice.

Verity was surprised when Lucy and Etienne sat opposite one another. She was even more surprised when Josh held out a chair for her before taking his. He was clearly determined to irritate her. She studied the ramekin containing her egg.

'Do you know much about Meribel?' Josh asked.

Glancing up, she saw he was looking directly at her.

'Um. No. I've never skied in France. Only Vail in Colorado and St Anton in Austria.'

'Really? Why just those two resorts?'

Verity sighed. 'One of my mum's husbands lived in Vail and another had a chalet in St Anton.'

'Past tense? She's no longer with either of them? And neither one was your father, clearly. You didn't refer to either as 'Dad'.'

47

Trust him to pick up on that, she thought.

'No. Mum and Dad divorced when I was very young. He died a few years ago. Mum's on her fifth marriage now – or is it her sixth? I lose count.'

'Fifth,' Lucy said, 'but she ...' Her voice trailed off and she took a mouthful of her food.

'I'm sorry,' Josh said.

'Why?' Verity asked. 'Because my dad's dead or because they divorced when I was young? Or did you mean because my mother's like a moth when it comes to relationships? Always attracted to a brighter flame.'

'Mum. Not the time or place.' Lucy threw Verity a 'remember he's our boss' kind of look even though she was smiling.

'I meant, I'm sorry I asked something that clearly upsets you,' Josh said.

'It doesn't!' Verity snapped, annoyed with herself for letting her guard down and bringing up the subject of her mother's numerous marriages, but she caught Lucy's glare from the corner of her eye and forced a smile for Josh. 'I mean, not really. Sorry. Please tell us about Meribel.'

He gave her an odd look. 'Okay. Well, there's a large British contingent here. I'm not sure if you've read that Meribel was established as a ski resort in the late 1930s by a British Colonel, Peter Lindsay and, unlike many other resorts, Meribel still has that quaint 'chocolate box' charm. That's one of the reasons it appeals to so many of us Brits. And the skiing is superb. Meribel's in the heart of the Three Valleys as you no doubt know, so it's part of the world's largest ski area. It's also got plenty of shops, restaurants and bars and the nightlife is great. But you've already sampled the nightlife, haven't you?' His eyes held hers.

'We're planning,' Lucy said before Verity could open her mouth, 'to nip down the valley to the old spa town of Brides-les-Bains when we have a chance.'

Etienne smiled. 'That's another great thing about Meribel, isn't it, Josh? There are tons of other places to see, some better than others, but all worth a visit if you're here for a few months.'

Josh merely nodded in agreement, his gaze still fixed on Verity.

'I'll take you on a few guided tours to the ones we can ski to if you like,' Etienne offered.

'That would be good, wouldn't it, Mum?'

'It would,' Verity said, glancing up at Josh from beneath her lashes. She'd been trying to avoid looking at him for the last few minutes but she'd felt him looking at her. 'Assuming we have the time that is. We are here to work, after all.'

Josh sighed, pushed his empty ramekin to one side, ran a hand through his hair and grabbed a bottle of wine.

'We appear to have got off to a bad start,' he said, topping up Verity's glass. 'I'm not the tyrannical, slave-driver you seem to think I am. You'll have plenty of free time to ski or do whatever else takes your fancy, and you do get one day off a week. I'll admit I have certain standards but as long as the guests are happy, the chalet runs smoothly and the food is good, I really don't mind what you do – within reason. I'm afraid I do draw the line at sleeping with the guests though. It can cause all sorts of problems.'

Verity could feel her jaw drop but she quickly recovered her equilibrium.

'Damn,' she said, smiling at Josh as provocatively as she could. 'I suppose we'll have to cross that off of our 'how to keep the punters happy' list then.'

The look Josh gave her in response wasn't at all what she'd expected.

'I'll serve the main course,' she said, desperately needing to get away from his deeply unsettling eyes.

Lucy followed Verity into the kitchen. 'I think it's going well. If you can manage to keep your temper and the facetious remarks to a minimum, we may still have jobs this time tomorrow.'

She was grinning but Verity realised her daughter was only half-joking. Lucy had been looking forward to working this season in Meribel from the minute her best friend Joanna had mentioned the possibility.

'I promise I'll behave,' Verity said, 'and no matter how much the man annoys me, I'll remain cool, calm and collected from now on.'

'Hmm. Why do I think that's about as likely as Grandma deciding to become a nun?'

But Verity was true to her word – for a few hours at least – and each time Josh said or did something irritating, she drank her wine and held her tongue, which was probably why she was beginning to feel rather tipsy.

'Are we keeping you?' she asked when Josh yawned and glanced at his watch for the second time in ten minutes.

'Sorry. I think I'm still a bit jet-lagged but it is getting late. It's almost midnight.'

'And is that when you turn back into a frog?'

For a split second, Josh's eyes narrowed but he grinned and stood up. 'Does that mean that you think I've been a prince tonight? Or are we both getting our stories confused? This has been a wonderful evening, thank you, but I'm afraid I must go home to bed.'

'I'm so glad you've enjoyed it,' Lucy said, getting to her feet and gathering the plates.

'Let me help you with that,' Josh offered.

'No, I'm fine thank you,' she said, heading for the kitchen.

Etienne followed behind her, carrying the empty wine bottles and Josh grabbed the glasses and turned towards the kitchen whilst Verity gathered up the *Chalet Marianne* photographic placemats.

'We work for you, remember?' she said sarcastically when she thought Josh was out of earshot.

'You're not going to let me forget that, are you?'

She almost dropped the placements on the floor. Her voice must have been louder than she'd realised.

'I think I may owe you an apology,' Josh continued.

'Oh?' She tried to sound indifferent but her heart was thumping in her chest as she turned to face him.

'When Joanna told me that you would be taking her place, I didn't know what to expect. My chalet hosts are usually ...'

'Young?' she suggested as he was clearly struggling for the right word.

'No. Well ... I suppose they often are but that isn't what I was going to say. Experienced. They've usually worked at least a couple of seasons for other companies before they work for me. I was taking a chance on Joanna and Lucy but at least they'd done a chalet hosting course and I knew they wanted to be seasonaires, whereas you .... Well, let's just say that this was a last-minute decision on your part, and when I found you in bed this morning, I–'

'You thought I wasn't going to take this job seriously, is that it?'

Josh nodded. 'I suppose so ... in a way. Yes.'

'And sarcasm is always a useful motivator, isn't it?'

'What?'

'Never mind. I assure you that I'll do my very best – assuming I still have a job, that is. But whether my best will meet your high standards is a question only you can answer.'

'If this evening is anything to go by, I think we can safely say that answer is yes.'

'So ... are you saying you want me to stay, in spite of the fact that I threw wine all over you this evening?'

'I don't think you did that on purpose. ... Did you?'

She grinned. 'No. But I apologise for that anyway.'

'Just for that?' he said with the oddest look in his eyes.

'Are you suggesting I need to apologise for something else?'

He laughed, and Verity thought she'd like to hear that sound more often. He had the sort of laugh that lifted one's spirits and made one want to laugh with him. She suddenly realised that it seemed a very long time since she had laughed at all.

'No, Verity, I'm not suggesting that. You can call me a miserable git, a lech ... and a frog, amongst other things, any time you want.'

She blushed. 'Oh. Yes, okay. I also apologise for that. But you haven't answered my question. Are you saying you want me to stay?'

His blue-grey eyes looked iridescent as the firelight reflected in them.

'Yes, Verity. I most definitely want you to stay.'

CHAPTER EIGHT

Verity wasn't sure whether she should be pleased or concerned. For the second night in a row, she hadn't shed one single tear over Tony and the breakdown of her marriage.

Of course, the first night didn't really count. She'd been so drunk that she could hardly remember her own name let alone anything else, but last night ... she could remember almost everything about last night. And she hadn't given Tony a second thought from the moment Josh Calder walked into the kitchen. In fact, she'd hardly thought of Tony all day. She'd been too busy thinking how infuriating her new boss was. Now she couldn't stop thinking how attractive he was.

She was being ridiculous and she knew it. This was obviously some sort of reaction to the breakdown of her marriage. Some sort of rebound. Her husband had betrayed her with a young and beautiful woman, now she was 'betraying' him with thoughts of Josh. It was ludicrous.

She didn't even particularly *like* Josh.

She liked the way he laughed and his deep, gravelly voice; she liked his blue-grey eyes, his sensuous smile and his chiselled features; she liked his tall, agile frame and his lustrous, dark brown hair. She liked the way he seemed so sure of himself most of the time and yet, just occasionally, gave a hint of vulnerability. She liked his hands and the way he raked them through his hair and she wondered, once or twice, what it would feel like to run her hands through it. She also wondered what it would feel like to have his hands touch her – caress her ...

Apart from that, she didn't really like him at all.

She definitely *didn't* like the way he looked at her at times. It was the type of look that said he was thinking things he shouldn't. Things that involved touching and exploring; things that involved kissing; things that involved taking and giving. Things that she instinctively knew would make her knees turn to jelly and her insides to melted ice cream.

Her stomach already felt like a butter churn every time he added one of his smiles and last night, when he'd said that he wanted her to stay, there was something in that look that almost had steam coming out of her ears.

It was definitely her hormones. Since finding her husband and Daniella together, her emotions had been all over the place. One minute she hated Tony, the next, she loved him. She never wanted to see him again or she wanted to see him immediately. She wanted him back or she wanted him to die a very slow and painful death, without her. She alternated between tears of sorrow and tears of anger. She couldn't eat; she couldn't sleep. She drank far too much. She wanted to get as far away from him as possible; she wished he were by her side. Her brain and her heart were in turmoil.

No wonder she felt so confused. That was all this was. She couldn't bear to think about Tony, so her subconscious had focused on Josh. That was it. That must be it. She knew there had to be a rational explanation. And there was no real harm in that, surely?

Now that she understood what was happening and why, she felt much better. Relieved almost. For one dreadful, totally insane moment, she had actually wondered if she were falling in love! And with a man she'd known for less than a day. And more importantly … with a man she didn't even *like*!

***

Lucy leant back in her chair as Verity returned to the kitchen. 'I've designed the menus and made a list of the things we'll need for next week,' Lucy said.

'Excellent, darling. And I've checked the bedding and towels for the eight guest bedrooms. Did I hear Josh say that they had to be colour co-ordinated with the rooms?'

'Yeah. It said so in the information pack too.'

'How quaint. I suppose I ought to read that,' Verity said, grinning. 'Does it also say that staff must obey their lord and master at all times and in all things? I'm making coffee. Would you like some?'

Lucy nodded. 'I don't think he's that bad, Mum. You two just got off on the wrong foot but he seemed pleasant enough last night and you were both smiling when he left.'

Odd little goosebumps popped up on Verity's arms as she remembered that smile and she rubbed them away, thinking that she must put on another jumper: she was obviously feeling cold.

'He's okay, I suppose. He's very handsome I'll give him that and he did seem to be making an effort to be friendly. Although he may not be quite as happy when he discovers I can't cook!'

'He doesn't need to find out. Last night went off without a hitch and it's not as if he'll be here every day. Jo said that we'll probably hardly ever see him – unless there's a problem with the chalet or we need his help in some way.'

Verity wondered why she found that news disappointing. Surely she should be pleased?

'So what's the plan for today?' she asked. 'The rooms will only need a quick dust and polish and the beds made, and we can do that the day before the guests arrive. Perhaps we could go for a walk and get to know Meribel. That way we can tell the guests exactly where certain places are and how they get to them.'

Lucy grinned. 'Particularly the bars. We do need to know where all the best places are. There's lots of info in this pack Josh left us – the one you haven't read, but it's best if we see for ourselves.' She waved the five-page, plastic covered pack in the air before taking the cup of coffee Verity handed her.

'And then I think I'd like to see if I can still ski after all these years,' Verity said, taking the pack, flicking through it and tossing it onto the worktop opposite. 'Although perhaps I should do that *before* we check out the delights of Meribel, bearing in mind what happened on our first night. And that was in just one bar. These days you can get arrested for being drunk on the slopes! Or should that be pissed on the pistes?'

***

Not only could Verity still ski; after the first few blue runs she found she could still ski well. The snow conditions were perfect, the air was cold and clear and the sky, a beautiful, shimmering blue around a warming golden sun.

Together, Verity and Lucy explored some of the superb pistes Meribel had to offer but after a few hours of virtually non-stop skiing, they were both exhausted. The only 'rests' they'd taken were when they travelled back up to the top of the next run via the various draglifts, chairlifts, gondolas and cable cars.

'I hadn't realised how unfit I am,' Verity said as they headed to one of a choice of restaurants in Meribel for a well-earned lunch. 'My legs feel as if they're on fire!'

'You're not the only one!' Lucy exclaimed, virtually collapsing onto a chair at a table positioned at the front of a surprisingly empty sun terrace. 'And I've been boarding every year so I haven't even got the excuse of being out of practice.'

They had just completed the descent from the top station of Mont du Vallon at a height of 2,952 metres, down the red run of *Combe Vallon* on to the blue, tree-lined *Ours*, through part of Meribel Mottaret and finally, the green *Truite* into Meribel.

A waiter brought a menu, followed by the two large glasses of red wine they ordered, and they sat back, closed their eyes and soaked up the sun as they waited for their lunch.

'Well! Fancy seeing you here. And why may I ask, aren't you back at the chalet slaving over a grubby shower tray?'

Verity recognised the voice immediately and despite the question, she opened her eyes and smiled up at Josh.

'Because there aren't any grubby shower trays to slave over. But don't worry, we were hard at it for at least ... oh, half an hour before we came out this morning.'

'I was teasing you,' Josh said, a hint of concern evident in his blue-grey eyes. 'Are you having a good day?'

'I know you were. I could tell by your tone. And we're having a lovely day, thank you. We've just skied down Mont du Vallon. The views were stunning and the pistes really are superb. But we're exhausted now. Where have you been?'

He was dressed in ski pants, ski jacket and ski boots so he'd clearly been taking advantage of the terrain and the glorious weather. He removed his skis and Verity wondered if she should invite him to join them for lunch – or a drink at least.

'I've been over to Val Thorens this morning. I've got a couple of chalets there. All my chalets – except *Marianne* – have been run by the same teams for the last four years so I know they're in good hands. I just wanted to pop over and say hello. I like to catch up with all my teams the week before the first of the guests arrive but if I can get in some skiing at the same time, that's even better.'

'So it's only Lucy and I that you have to worry about then?'

'After last night I don't think I have anything to worry about – as far as the chalet is concerned at least.'

'That's good,' Verity said, seeing that strange look in his eyes. 'What happened to the team at *Marianne*? Why aren't they back this year?'

The smile immediately left Josh's face and he raked a hand through his hair. 'I ... one of them moved on ... to better things and the other … moved away. I have to dash. Enjoy the rest of your day.'

'I'm beginning to feel invisible when you two get together,' Lucy said as they both watched Josh march off.

'I don't know what you mean,' Verity replied. 'That was a little odd though, don't you think? One minute he's all sweetness and light, the next it's as if he's been encased in ice. His demeanour completely changed when I mentioned the previous team and his entire body stiffened. I wonder if there's more to that than he's saying.'

'I wasn't studying him that closely. He did seem in a hurry to get away though. Ooh! Perhaps he murdered them for failing to keep the chalet up to his standards and he's buried them in the cellar.' Lucy laughed and shook her head. 'Honestly, Mum. One of them obviously got a job with a rival company and the other left too. He's pissed off about it, that's all. Mind you, have you been down to the cellar yet? It's seriously creepy down there. It runs the entire length of the chalet and there're lots of nooks and crannies. I couldn't wait to get out of it. Maybe there is something buried down there … apart from the crates of wine and all the old furniture.'

'Maybe,' Verity said, still staring at Josh's back and foolishly wishing he'd look round and smile. He finally disappeared into the crowd and Verity glanced at Lucy. 'We'll have to find out where they went, won't we?'

Lucy shrugged. Clearly, she couldn't care less and as the waiter brought them their lunch, she turned her attention to her food.

'I don't think it matters, does it? As long as they don't decide they want to come back that is. Let's eat. I'm starving!'

CHAPTER NINE

Verity was beginning to think she'd hit a nerve by asking Josh about the previous team at *Chalet Marianne*. They hadn't seen him since that day. She was going to ask Etienne about it, but they hadn't seen him either and that surprised her even more. She was sure that he was attracted to Lucy and she wondered again whether something had happened between the two of them on that second evening.

'I'm surprised Etienne hasn't stopped by,' she said as she and Lucy were making the last of the beds. 'We haven't seen him since they came for dinner on Sunday night.'

Lucy shrugged. 'He's probably busy. I'm more surprised we haven't seen Josh since Monday at that restaurant. But I know he said he wanted to visit all his other chalets so I suppose that's why. I did think he'd come to check everything was okay before the guests arrive tomorrow though.'

'What happens about that? And yes, I did read the info pack where it said that the guests are dropped here on Saturdays around four in the afternoon, depending on flight times and traffic, but by whom? Etienne? Josh? Or are the chalets booked via package companies? It didn't mention that.'

Lucy shrugged again. 'Jo told me that Josh has deals with a few exclusive ski holiday companies but that some of the guests come independently. It does say in the pack that we'll be notified of alternative arrival times so we'll have to wait and see.'

'At least everything's ready for when they do arrive,' Verity said as they made their way downstairs. 'I'm a little nervous to be honest. What if they're all lager louts or stuck up snobs or worse still, miserable gits.'

'I hope you're not referring to me.'

Verity nearly jumped out of her skin and even Lucy was surprised when they turned the bend of the stairs and found Josh standing in the hall.

'No. But we were talking about you a few minutes ago,' Verity said, blushing. 'We were wondering how the guests would be arriving tomorrow. You'll be pleased to hear that everything is ready. Lucy has planned some wonderful menus. Would you like to see them?'

'Lucy? Oh, you're the cook Verity, and Lucy is the planner, is that right?'

'Um ... not exactly.' Verity wondered if she should simply own up. It was too late for him to sack her now, with guests arriving in less than twenty-four hours.

'We share all the duties,' Lucy added, smiling sweetly. 'We were just about to make some coffee. Would you like some? I've ... we've made a delicious chocolate and orange cake.'

Josh looked tempted. 'I can't stop now, I'm afraid. I just dropped by to check you were both okay and that you didn't need anything. I'll be dropping off the first batch of guests tomorrow. They're all regulars and Etienne will be taking them out every day as they're all expert skiers. It should be a pretty easy first week for you.'

'You don't know how pleased I am to hear that,' Verity said. 'I was just saying to Lucy that I feel a little nervous – but I suppose I shouldn't have told you that, should I?'

Josh laughed and Verity wished she could think of something to make him stay, even if only for a few minutes.

'I have complete confidence in both of you, and from what I've seen so far, Verity, I'd be amazed to find there was anything that could faze you. Anyway, call me if you need me. My home and mobile numbers are in the info pack. I assume you've read it?'

'Were we supposed to?' Verity teased. She could see by the look in Josh's eyes that he was joking. He obviously took it for granted that they had.

'Yes. And there'll be a test later. I must dash.' He turned and walked towards the door, hesitated, and looked back. 'Actually, talking of later, Etienne and I could pop round for a quick drink this evening to sort of, launch your chalet hosting season – unless you have plans.'

'No. We have no plans, do we Lucy? We were just going to have a quiet night by the fire so yes, please do pop in. That's okay, isn't it?' Verity glanced at Lucy.

'Yes. That would be great. We haven't seen Etienne for days. I'll cook supper if you like. Just something simple.'

'It's a date,' Josh said. 'Oh, I don't mean *a date* kind of date. I ... I just ... you know what I mean. Bye.'

'He actually blushed!' Lucy said with a grin when he'd shut the front door behind him. 'And he's not the only one!' She cast a worried look at Verity. 'Is there something you'd like to tell me, Mum?'

Verity sighed. 'Unfortunately not,' she said, strolling into the kitchen for her well-earned coffee break.

***

'I'm sorry I haven't seen you all week,' Etienne said. 'I've been helping Josh with some stuff at one of the chalets, and showing a new ski guide the ropes.'

'Don't you mean pistes?' Lucy joked, grabbing glasses from the shelf for the champagne Josh had brought.

Etienne beamed at her. 'Mais oui! How's your week been? You've been hitting the slopes every day, haven't you?'

'Good, thanks. Yeah, we've done quite a bit and Mum's skiing is brill so we've marked a few trails off piste too, which–'

'You shouldn't go off piste without me!' Etienne snapped. 'Or without one of the guides anyway.'

'No, you shouldn't!' Josh agreed. 'Next time you want to do that, please ask one of us to go with you.'

'But we did have a guide!' Verity said. 'Mathieu ... something or other. I forget his surname. Tall, muscular, fair-haired – a bit like you, Etienne.'

Etienne and Josh exchanged anxious looks.

'Mathieu Deschamps?' Josh asked.

'That's him!' Verity said. 'Is he a friend of yours?'

'No!' Josh and Etienne said in unison.

'Why did you ask him to guide you? Did he know you are working for Josh?' Etienne asked.

'We didn't,' Lucy said. 'He came and talked to us the other day. That day we saw you actually, Josh. Monday. Anyway, he offered to take us out the next day.'

'And he did,' Verity added. 'He ... he seemed very nice.' She noticed the temperature in the room seemed to have dropped a few degrees.

'He may seem it but he's not,' Josh said. 'If you'll take my advice you'll stay away from him.'

'Why? What's he done?'Lucy asked but Josh just shook his head as if the subject were closed.

'He ... reckless,' Etienne said. 'And he's got a bad reputation where women are concerned. Let's leave it at that.'

'Thanks, Etienne,' Lucy said, 'but I think Mum and I can look after ourselves. And the last man who tried it on with Mum seriously regretted it – once he got up from the floor, that is.'

'What's this?' Etienne asked, his mood lightening considerably. 'Don't tell me you're a black belt in karate or something, Verity?'

Verity felt the colour rush to her cheeks. 'Nothing of the sort. But I can handle myself and so can Lucy.'

Etienne grinned. 'We'd better be careful then hadn't we, Josh?'

Josh merely nodded. He had a far-away look in his eyes.

'Let's eat,' Lucy said in an obvious attempt to change the subject.

Nothing more was said about Mathieu Deschamps. Etienne told them about the new ski guide, François, and Josh went over the procedure for getting guests settled in. Most of it was in the information pack so it was just a matter of confirming that they were both on the 'same page'. Verity noticed Josh glancing in her direction several times but he seemed rather aloof and she wondered if it was because of the outing with Mathieu. She tried to bait him more than once, in a friendly manner, but he just smiled and let the comments go.

This time, it was Verity who yawned.

'We're keeping you up,' Etienne said. 'We'd better go and let you get some sleep. You've got a busy day tomorrow, girls.'

'Is something the matter, Josh?' Verity asked when he stood up to leave.

'No,' he said distractedly. 'We should be here around four tomorrow but I'll call if we're delayed. Call me if you need anything.'

'We will,' she said as they all walked to the front door.

Josh followed Etienne out but he seemed to hang back as if he had something else to say. He finally reached his car and Verity was about to close the door when he spoke:

'I can't tell you what to do or who to spend your time with, obviously, but please take care with Mathieu. Things aren't always as they seem as I'm sure you're well aware. Goodnight.'

'We will, Josh, but …'

There was no point in continuing. Josh had got in the car and started the engine. He drove off without a backward glance.

'What the hell was that about?' Lucy asked as Verity shut the front door. 'You'd think they'd give us a better reason than "He's reckless. And he's got a bad reputation where women are concerned." We're not bloody Victorians. And as for "Things aren't always as they seem," what does that mean?'

'It's all very odd,' Verity said. 'And Josh seemed really concerned. They both did. I bet Mathieu 'stole' their girlfriends or something and Josh and Etienne are still upset about it. You know what men are like.'

Lucy shrugged. 'I suppose so. The silly thing is though, by sort of telling us not to see Mathieu but not really explaining why, it just makes me want to see him all the more to find out.'

Verity sighed. 'I know exactly what you mean. And I'd still like to know why the previous chalet girls left. I'm sure there's more to that story than Josh is saying. Perhaps the two things are connected in some way.'

'I bet we'll be disappointed when we do find out,' Lucy quipped. 'It's probably something really silly and totally unconnected. I'm off to bed. It's going to be a *really* long day tomorrow.'

CHAPTER TEN

Verity opened the curtains and wished she could go back to bed. Every day for the last week, the view from the bedroom window had been breathtakingly beautiful. Snow-covered pistes, chalets and trees surrounded by stunningly white mountains, set against a perfect, cerulean sky lit by a warm, golden sun. Even on the few occasions it had snowed, the sun had shone through shortly after. Today, she couldn't even see the neighbouring chalets. This was officially a white-out.

'Good morning, Josh,' Verity said, answering her phone after seeing his name appear on the screen. 'Although that's a bit of a misnomer this morning.'

'Tell me about it,' Josh replied. 'Not a good start to the first day of your season, is it? I'm calling to tell you to expect severe delays. Chambery airport is closed due to the weather and flights are being diverted. It's snowing in the UK too so some flights are being cancelled. We think the flight our guests will be on will be diverted to Geneva so that means we'll be at least two hours later than expected, but we'll have to wait and see. I'll let you know as soon as I have any more news. Everything okay your end?'

'Fine, thanks, apart from not being able to clear a path to the door yet. Partly because we can't even *see* the door once we get more than two feet away from it and partly because the snow is falling so thick and fast that it would be a futile exercise. I'm surprised planes are flying at all. What will the roads be like?'

'There'll be a few problems but they clear the roads pretty quickly out here so it should be okay. It'll just take longer, that's all. You'd better cook something for dinner tonight that can either be cooked quickly or be left simmering for hours on end. God knows what time I'll get the guests to you.'

'Assuming you *do* get the guests to us.'

'I'll get them there ... eventually.'

Verity sighed. 'And there was I hoping I'd get an extra day or so to sit in front of the fire and do nothing very much. You're a slave-driver, Joshua Calder. I knew it the moment we met. Have a safe journey.'

Josh burst out laughing. 'And you, Verity Lawton, are nothing but trouble. I knew *that* the moment we met. I'll deal with you when I get back.'

There was something in Josh's tone that had Verity imagining that comment was more of a promise than a threat, and the tingling sensation running up and down her spine as she rang off had nothing to do with the snowstorm rattling the shutters outside.

***

Verity stood at the door to greet the guests as they clambered from the minibus and made their way towards the warmth and comfort of *Chalet Marianne* via the hastily dug path. Thanks to the blizzard, both she and Lucy were still shovelling snow when Josh phoned to tell them that he and the guests were about half an hour away. Despite the weather, the delays and the plane being diverted to Geneva, he managed to arrive by seven-thirty: only three and a half hours later than originally anticipated.

'Come in. Welcome to *Chalet Marianne*. I'm Verity. Take off your coats and hang them on the rack. There's a fire in the sitting room and Lucy has a glass of warming *vin chaud* and a plate of hot canapés for each of you.'

Josh deposited the luggage in the hall whilst Verity and Lucy chatted to the sixteen guests. He joined them for a drink but only stayed for fifteen minutes and it wasn't until he'd gone, that Verity felt herself relax.

As much as she'd been looking forward to seeing him – and she most definitely had been – those blue-grey eyes of his seemed to burn all rational thought from her brain and tie her tongue in knots. She hardly said more than two words to him from the moment he arrived and he must have noticed that every time he walked towards her, she scurried away to talk to another guest.

'I'll leave you to it,' he said when he finally managed to catch her off-guard. 'You seem to have it under control and I'm clearly in the way. Call me if you need me.'

After saying his goodbyes to all the guests and giving Verity a last, lingering look as if he had something else to say, he left.

When he closed the door behind him, Verity concentrated on the guests.

'We'll be having dinner in an hour so you've got a little time to settle in. Josh tells us that you've all been here before so you know where everything is and how it all works but do please ask one of us if you're unsure or if there's anything you need. We're here to look after you and ensure you have a good time, so don't feel shy.'

'There's no chance of us being shy,' Rupert, one of the younger men in the group, said. 'Didn't Josh also tell you that we'll be conducting your *initiation ceremony*?'

'No,' Verity replied as the others laughed. 'He obviously forgot to mention that.'

She knew Rupert was joking and was relieved that the entire group seemed friendly and clearly intended to enjoy themselves. They varied considerably in age but were equal in enthusiasm and she quickly realised that being a chalet girl may turn out to be just as much fun as she always thought it would – once all the chores were done, of course.

***

Verity and Lucy were up by six-thirty the following day and after just one cup of coffee and a slice of toast, they began their first full day of the season.

Verity was shovelling a fresh path through the snow by seven-forty five, having lit the dining room, sitting room and kitchen fires. She'd also drawn the curtains, plumped up the sofa cushions and done half a dozen other little things to ensure everything was ready. She was glad she'd set the long, oak table for breakfast before going to bed last night; something both Lucy – and Josh's info pack – had said was a wise thing to do to save time.

'I think I'd better learn to cook,' Verity said, collapsing on a chair and nursing the second cup of coffee Lucy had poured for her. 'That way you can shovel snow in the freezing cold and I can stay in the warm and bake.'

Lucy grinned. 'I can teach you how to make a yoghurt cake. It's really easy and the yoghurt guarantees the cake will rise. High altitudes make cakes flop when you take them out of the oven. The yoghurt combats that problem. It's just a basic mix, and there's no weighing of ingredients because you use the yoghurt pot to measure. I'll show you, and tomorrow you can stay in and make the cake and I'll shovel snow.'

'A yoghurt cake! Hmm. I'm not sure.'

'Honestly, Mum, it's simple. And I asked Josh if it was okay because apparently some of the chalet owners don't like their staff making it, but he was fine. He said that as long as it tastes good and there are no complaints, we can do anything to make our lives easier. You know, the more I see of him, the more I like him.'

Verity couldn't help thinking that unfortunately, she felt exactly the same.

***

Breakfast was served from eight until nine and guests had a choice of cereal, cooked breakfast, fruit, toast and jams; fruit juice, coffee, tea and hot chocolate. After breakfast, once the guests had gone skiing, Verity and Lucy loaded the dishwasher; emptied bins; made the beds; cleaned the bathrooms; washed the floors; dusted the furniture; vacuumed the rugs; prepared for afternoon tea in the sitting room and peeled the vegetables for dinner.

'I can't believe we've finished everything we need to do and it's still only noon!' Verity said.

'And after a few days, I think we could cut the time it takes by half an hour, if not more. It's just a matter of routine. Let's go and have lunch, Mum. And a couple of hours on the slopes.'

'I think I need a couple of hours in bed! I can't remember the last time I worked this hard. In fact, I don't think I've *ever* worked this hard!'

'You can go back to bed if you like,' Lucy said, grinning, 'but it's a glorious day and wouldn't you rather be out in the sunshine – even if it's just to sit in a chair and soak up some rays?

Verity couldn't argue with that; she certainly would. And that's exactly what she was doing less than an hour later.

***

They were back in the chalet by four-thirty for afternoon tea. Josh's info pack instructed them that they only needed to be there on the first day. After that, they could just leave the beverages in the catering-sized flasks, and the cakes, biscuits or buns, bread and jam, out and covered, on the coffee table.

There were canapés at seven-thirty and dinner was at eight, accompanied by tales of the day's skiing, sharing of photos via phones and digital cameras, raucous laughter, jokes and copious amounts of wine. Coffee and petit fours followed and were served in the sitting room to allow Verity and Lucy to clear the dinner things and set the table for breakfast.

After that, around ten o'clock, the evening was their own, and as all the guests had either headed to Meribel's bars and nightclubs or gone to bed, Verity and Lucy curled up in front of the fire in the sitting room with mugs of brandy-laced hot chocolate.

They heard the front door open and footsteps in the hall. Moments later, Josh and Etienne appeared.

'We just wanted to see how your first full day went,' Josh said. 'Oh! You both look exhausted.'

'Thanks!' Verity replied. 'Although to be honest, we are. Well, I am. It's just a matter of getting used to it though. You'll be pleased to hear there were no disasters and so far, no complaints. We went skiing for a couple of hours too.'

'No wonder you're exhausted. You've no intention of breaking yourselves in gently then? And I didn't think there would be any disasters, or complaints – although it is only the first day.' He grinned mischievously before raking a hand through his hair. 'Um ... Etienne and I are going for a couple of beers and we wondered if you'd both like to join us but you look as if you've settled in for the night.'

Lucy jumped to her feet. 'I'm up for that. Just give me five minutes to change. What about you, Mum?'

'I ... I don't think I'm up to it. As much as I'd like to say yes, I think I'll have to pass. You go though Lucy, and have a good time.'

She thought she saw a flash of disappointment in Josh's eyes but it could just have been the reflection from the fire.

'Are you sure?' Lucy asked, looking doubtful. 'I don't want to leave you here on your own.'

Verity chuckled. 'I'll be fine on my own, darling. Please don't worry about me. Go. Have fun.'

Lucy hesitated but Verity waved her away and Lucy raced off to get changed.

'You won't change your mind?' Josh asked as Etienne hovered in the doorway.

Verity shook her head. 'No. But thank you.'

'Maybe later in the week?' Etienne asked. 'Josh and I often go for a beer.'

'Yes. I'd like that.'

She watched as Josh ran his hand through his hair again. She was still trying to decide if he did that when things didn't go to plan, or whether it was a sign of nervousness or doubt. It did seem to be a habit. She'd seen him do it several times since they'd met.

'Um ... what about if Etienne and Lucy go out on the town tonight and I stay here with you?' Josh suggested. 'If you don't mind, that is. I'm a bit old to be going out at this time of night too. Unless you'd rather be on your own? Oh, I didn't mean you're old. I meant–'

'I'll stop you before you dig that hole any deeper,' Verity interrupted, laughing. 'I *feel* old, today but I'm sure that won't last. And no, I wouldn't rather be on my own. But please don't feel you need to stay on my account. I'm happy either way.'

'You don't mind, do you, Etienne?' Josh asked.

'Nope. I'm happy to spend the evening with Lucy.' He winked at Verity and added, 'I'll have her home at a reasonable hour ... by Meribel standards.'

'I think you may find that Lucy will dictate when she comes home, not you, Etienne,' Verity said, grinning at him.

Lucy appeared at the sitting room door. 'I'm ready.'

'It's just us,' Etienne said. 'Josh is staying with your mum.'

For a moment, Lucy looked as if she were having second thoughts but Verity gave her a reassuring smile and a few minutes later, Verity was alone with Josh.

'Would you like a glass of wine?' she asked, suddenly feeling like a sixteen-year-old on a first date and having finished the brandy-laced hot chocolate, she needed a touch more alcohol to steady her nerves. 'I think I'll have one.'

'Thanks,' Josh said, looking equally unsure of himself.

'Sit down then. I'll be back in a minute.'

She was so glad that her bedroom was accessed via the kitchen. She quickly nipped through into the ensuite bathroom and checked her reflection in the mirror. She cleaned her teeth, touched up her mascara and brushed her lips with a smear of lipstick – she didn't want to make it obvious. She dabbed on more perfume and considered changing her jumper for a blouse, but thought better of it. Be casual, she told herself, this is *not* a date. After brushing her hair and adding a touch more lipstick, she took a deep breath and headed back to the kitchen.

'Oh!' She didn't know what to say. Josh was standing in the doorway and he looked as though he had been wondering where she was. Had she been that long?

'I ... I thought I heard my phone ringing,' she lied, feeling her cheeks burning and her heart thumping. 'It's ... it's in my handbag. In the bedroom.'

He creased his dark brows but a smile appeared within seconds. 'And was it?'

'Um. No. I must be hearing things. That's what happens when you get old.'

'How old *are* you, Verity, if you don't mind me asking? I know Lucy's twenty-one because Joanna told me, but you honestly don't look old enough to be her mother.'

She was a little surprised by the question and she grabbed a bottle of wine from the rack whilst she thought of a suitable reply. She was even more surprised when he took the bottle from her and opened it without saying another word. She placed some glasses on the worktop in front of him. He stood so close to her as he poured the wine that she could feel the heat of his body and smell his subtle aftershave. She eased herself slightly away.

'If ...if you're worried about my ability to cope, Josh, please don't be. I know I said that I'm exhausted – and I am – but that's got more to do with skiing again after all these years than it has with working here, I assure you. I won't let you down. At least I'll try not–'

'It's got nothing to do with working here,' Josh interrupted. 'That wasn't why I asked your age. I ... I'm just curious, that's all.'

Verity giggled. 'Phew! I thought for one moment I was being sent packing.'

Josh tilted his head to one side and studied her face. She felt her cheeks getting hotter – her whole body getting hotter.

'I thought you didn't care if you worked here or not?'

'I didn't.'

'But now you do? What made you change your mind?'

She wanted to tell him to stop looking at her like that, but she wasn't sure that she wanted him to stop. She wasn't sure of anything, except perhaps that she wanted to kiss him. Right here, right now. She really must pull herself together.

'Lucy,' she said, forcing herself to look away from him. 'She really wants to do this. She has done for as long as I can remember. I can't let her down.'

'Oh.' He sounded disappointed.

'And in answer to your question – although it's not polite to ask a woman's age – I'm forty. But only just. It was my birthday the week before we came here.'

'Really? Happy belated birthday! So ... you were about nineteen when you had Lucy?'

'I was a child bride,' she joked. For some absurd reason she didn't want to say that she was pregnant when she married Tony.

'Well, you don't look forty,' Josh said.

'Thanks. People often say that Lucy and I look like twins.'

He smirked. 'I wouldn't go quite as far as that, but sisters, yes.'

'Thank *you*!' she said, giving him a playful shove.

He grabbed her hands, their eyes met and she was in his arms with his lips on hers before she knew what was happening.

CHAPTER ELEVEN

The kiss lasted just a matter of seconds but even that was long enough for Verity to know she wanted more. Much, much more. And unless she was mistaken, so did Josh. The look in his eyes told her so. If the five guests who had barrelled through the front door and were now doing a conga line around the kitchen, hadn't returned when they had, who knows what would have happened.

She watched Josh run a hand through his hair, lick his lips as if he were still savouring the taste of her, and screw up his eyes for the briefest of moments. She wondered what he was thinking. That it shouldn't have happened, or that he wished the guests weren't there? She wasn't completely sure herself.

He smiled half-heartedly as he was pulled into the line, just as Verity was seconds later, but they both quickly managed to extricate themselves. They faced one another in silence until the party moved into the sitting room.

'I'm so sorry, Verity, I never should have done that,' he said, his hand in his hair again.

Clearly regret then, she thought. 'It doesn't matter. These things happen.'

'I suppose I should be glad you didn't karate kick me or something.'

She forced a smile. 'Yes. I suppose so.'

Roars of laughter emanated from the sitting room and Josh glanced in that direction.

'Will you be okay with that lot, or would you like me to handle it? They rarely do any damage and if they do, they always pay for it, so don't worry about that.'

Back to business as usual, it seemed.

'I'm sure I'll be fine. Besides, I've got to get used to it. It's not as if you'll always be here, is it?'

It took him a few seconds to reply. 'No,' he said eventually. 'In fact, I think I'm going to be away for a week or so.'

'Oh?'

'Business.'

She could see he was lying. 'Well ... have a safe trip.'

'Thanks. Er ... call me if there's anything important but other than that, Etienne will be able to help you with anything you need, or questions you may have.' He moved towards the door. 'I really am sorry, Verity. It won't happen again.'

He was gone before she could reply.

***

'Mum. It's time to get up.'

Verity opened her eyes with some difficulty. 'Is it really morning already? I feel as if I haven't slept a wink.'

'I don't think you did. Were ... were you dreaming about Dad? You kept calling out, "Don't go!" and you were sobbing at one point. I shouldn't have gone out and left you last night.'

Verity let out a long breath. 'It had nothing to do with you going out last night, darling, and I'm sorry I kept you awake.'

'I ... I thought you were coping a bit too well. You haven't cried since we've been here so I suppose it had to happen. You've been trying to pretend that you're not upset, haven't you?'

Verity pulled herself upright. 'To be honest, darling, I'm not really sure what I've been doing. But don't worry about me. I'll be fine. I'll get showered and go and shovel some snow.'

'I'll do that, Mum. You take it easy this morning. You need to look after yourself.'

Verity almost burst into tears at that. She wondered what Lucy would say if she knew the real reason for her tears because she had a feeling they had absolutely nothing to do with Lucy's father.

'Seriously, Lucy, I'm fine. Although I don't think I'll go skiing today. Why don't you show me how to make that yoghurt cake thing and I can have a go at that instead. Did you have a good time with Etienne?'

She saw the colour creep into Lucy's cheeks and the slow smile appear on her lips.

'Not bad. He said he may stop by later. What about you? Did Josh stay long?'

Verity cleared her throat. 'Er ... not long, no. Some of the guests returned and they were a little ... lively. I think he thought it was time to leave. He said he'll be away for a week or so.'

'Really? That's odd. Etienne said that we should all go out on our day off on Wednesday. He didn't say Josh would be away.'

'Perhaps it was a last-minute decision.'

'I assume he'll be back before Christmas. Can you believe it's only just over two weeks away?'

'To be honest, darling, I haven't even given Christmas a second thought!'

***

Verity still hadn't given it much thought by the time Christmas week actually arrived. She and Lucy dressed the tree and hung a few decorations around the chalet. Etienne helped them hang the coloured lights – of which there were many, both inside and out. Josh, it seemed, was as partial to fairy lights as Verity and Lucy were. But that was the extent of their preparations. She decided she'd better ask Etienne exactly what was expected of them. There had been no sign of Josh since the night of their 'kiss' so she couldn't ask him.

'Only what it says in the info pack,' Etienne said. 'Christmas is always a bit manic out here, but you've handled the last two weeks like real professionals, so I don't think you'll have a problem.'

'I just wondered if we're supposed to organise games or anything. We've wrapped the Christmas gifts for under the tree and the food and drink are sorted but it is Christmas and I wondered about carol singers or something – just to make it a little bit special.'

'I told Mum that just being in a place like this over Christmas is pretty special, but it's always been a big thing at our house and she doesn't want anyone to be disappointed, do you?' Lucy said, hugging her mother.

'I don't think they will be,' Etienne replied. 'We've never had any complaints before. The chalet looks very Christmassy and the snow outside makes all the difference. I'll see if they give any hints of their expectations when I chat to them on the way from the airport, but I'm sure it's all good. You can check with Josh though, if you're worried. He'll be back this morning.'

'This morning? Oh! Um ... Thanks, Etienne.' Verity quickly turned away. She didn't want Etienne or Lucy to see her flushed cheeks.

'Josh is back today? That's good news. We've missed him, haven't we, Mum?'

'Uh huh.'

'Are you okay down there?' Lucy asked.

'Uh huh.' Verity rummaged in the cupboard and grabbed the first thing she could find.

'I hope you're not going to hit me with that,' Etienne said when she straightened up.

She realised she was holding a pan up in the air as if that was exactly what she intended to do. She placed it on the worktop and laughed.

'Sorry. I seem to be having one of those days.'

'Well, we'd better get this lot in the minibus and off to the airport,' he said, referring to the departing guests. 'See you both later with the new batch of party animals.'

'If they're anything like those two guys who went back on the Eurostar this morning,' Lucy said, '*animals* is the right word for them!'

'Not all guests are perfect,' Etienne replied, grinning broadly.

'And some are barely human,' Lucy said.

'Speaking of animals.' Etienne nodded towards the Golden retriever curled up in front of the kitchen hearth. 'You'd better do something with Mistral before Josh sees her, or we'll all be out of work over Christmas!'

***

'That smells good.'

Verity recognised Josh's voice instantly – and the hint of apprehension in his tone. She wondered if he felt as nervous as she did. Telling herself to keep calm and taking two deep breaths, she turned and grinned at him.

'It's chicken casserole.' She hoped he'd guess it was *coq au vin*.

Humour danced in Josh's eyes. 'I love chicken casserole.'

Their eyes met and held.

'Hello, Josh. It's good to see you again,' she said in the lightest tone she could manage.

'Hello, Verity. It's good to see you too.'

'Hey, Josh!' Lucy said, returning from the cellar with several bottles of wine. 'How are you? If I'd known you were here I'd have asked you to go down there.' She nodded towards the cellar door. 'That place really gives me the creeps.'

'Hello, Lucy. I'm sorry about that,' Josh replied, laughing. 'It gives me the creeps too. Send Etienne. He's not afraid of anything.'

'I usually do,' Lucy admitted, 'but he's at the airport and I forgot to ask him before he left.' She headed towards the dining room with the wine. 'We've missed you. Oh. Am I allowed to say that to my boss?'

Josh darted a look at Verity. 'Yes. And I've missed you. It's good to be back.'

'Would you like a coffee?' Verity asked, trying to avoid meeting his eyes.

'Um ... I'd better not. I came here straight from the airport ... just to say hi and let you know I'm back. I'd better get home and see if there're any messages I've missed. Unless you need me for anything.'

'Oh. Um. No.'

Verity hoped she didn't sound too disappointed. She considered broaching the subject of Mistral – who was currently asleep on Lucy's bed – but she didn't feel this was the time for that potentially difficult conversation.

'I'll see you soon then,' Josh said. 'Etienne tells me things have been going well. The chalet looks lovely by the way. Just like a Christmas card. The guests last week must have been very impressed and it's particularly important for the guests this week.'

Verity wanted to shake him. All he seemed interested in was the chalet and his business.

'Things have been going very well, even if I say so myself. You only have to read the guest book comments,' she said.

'We have a guest book?'

'I thought it would be good for us to get feedback. To see if there's anything we're not doing that we should be. Is that a problem? Do you mind?'

Josh shook his head. 'No. It's fine with me if the guests like it.'

'Well, they've all written in it, so I can only assume they do.'

'Great. I look forward to reading it.' He hesitated for a moment. 'Um. I'll be off then.'

'Bye,' Verity said, turning her back on him and pretending to be busy.

Oh well, she thought, hearing him leave a few moments later, at least that's over. She was dreading seeing him again after that kiss but clearly, as far as he was concerned, it was as if it never happened.

CHAPTER TWELVE

'Good morning!' Josh called out from the hallway the following day.

Verity and Lucy stared at one another across the bed they were making.

'That's Josh,' Verity said. 'And Mistral's in the kitchen!'

'Oh shit! We're upstairs, Josh,' Lucy yelled.

'Okay,' Josh yelled back.

'He's not coming up,' Lucy said after a few moments.

They both dashed towards the stairs.

'What the fuck!' they heard Josh say.

'I think he's seen, her,' Lucy said as they ran down the stairs as fast as they could.

Josh spun round at the kitchen door, a look of both astonishment and anger on his face.

'Would someone mind telling me why there is a dog asleep in the kitchen?'

'It's my fault,' Verity said, walking past Josh towards Mistral, who was once again curled up in front of the fire. 'We found her a few days after ... after you left. She was just lying in the snow and she had blood on her head. Peter said she'd probably been hit accidently by a skier or snowboarder and had just run off and collapsed where we found her. He fixed her up and ... and we're looking after her.'

'You're what? Who's Peter?'

'He was a guest. He's a vet and–'

'You asked a guest to tend to a stray dog!'

Verity could feel her hackles rising. 'I didn't *ask*. Although I would have if he hadn't offered. He was skiing with us so we found her together. He was the one who suggested bringing her back here, actually.'

'A dog? In a ski chalet?'

'What's wrong with that? I didn't know dogs were forbidden in ski chalets,' Verity said icily. 'There's nothing in your info pack that says they're not allowed.'

Josh scowled. 'That's because it never occurred to me that anyone in their right mind would bring a dog into my chalet! And what is that awful smell? Is it diseased or something?'

'*She* is not diseased. She's injured!' Verity said, emphasizing the 'she'.

'Then why does *she* smell so awful?'

'She ... she has a bit of a ... stomach problem.'

'Dear God. In my kitchen!'

'It's only wind,' Lucy chimed in. 'That's why Etienne suggested we should call her Mistral actually, because she suffers from strong wind and ...' Her voice trailed off.

Josh's face looked like thunder. 'Etienne knows about this? Etienne allowed it?'

'It's not his fault either,' Verity said. 'It's mine. Completely mine. He said you'd be furious but I didn't believe him. I didn't think anyone would object to helping an injured animal. Am I wrong?'

'I don't object to you helping it ... her. I object to it ... her ... being in my kitchen. There are hygiene regulations for chalets, you know!'

'She's very hygienic. And she's never in here when we're preparing food.'

'Not that it improves things in the slightest – and I almost dread to ask – but where is it ... she ... when you prepare food? Please don't tell me you put her in the sitting room. Please!'

'Of course not. We put her in our bedroom,' Lucy said.

Josh shook his head. 'Well, she'll have to go. I'll take her to the pound. There must be one–'

'You won't!' Verity snapped.

Josh's mouth fell open. 'Excuse me! This is *my* chalet, Verity, and I will not have a dog in *my* chalet! Do I make myself clear?'

'Abundantly,' Verity hissed. 'Then I have no choice but to leave with her. I'll find somewhere and we'll be gone by the end of the day.'

'What the!–' Josh let out a derisive snort. 'You'll be lucky to find accommodation for yourself during Christmas week, let alone you *and* a dog!'

'Well, I'll have to try. Come along, Mistral. We're leaving.'

Mistral got up and sauntered over to Verity, licked her hand and sat down beside her.

'Mum?' Lucy looked uncertain.

Josh raked a hand through his hair and shook his head. 'This is fucking unbelievable!'

'You're who's unbelievable! Making all this fuss over an injured dog. I really had a higher opinion of you than this,' Verity snapped.

His head shot up and his eyes turned a deep dark grey. 'Don't push me, Verity.'

'I have no intention of *pushing* you,' she said, an inappropriate memory flashing through her mind. 'I still remember what happened the last time I *pushed* you, although you seem to have conveniently forgotten it!'

'I have *not* forgotten it, I assure you,' he almost growled.

Mistral barked and got to her feet as if she wasn't sure what to do.

'Don't upset her!'

'Oh forgive me! Perhaps I should just leave and let you get on with it.'

'That would be wonderful, but I don't suppose you'd do that, would you?'

'No. I won't. This is *my* chalet, Verity!'

'So you constantly remind me. Fine. We'll go.'

'I'm ... I'm coming with you,' Lucy said.

They turned and marched towards the bedroom and Mistral followed at their heels.

'Where do you think you're going?' Josh yelled.

'To pack, obviously,' Verity said without a backward glance.

'Fucking hell! Stop!' he demanded.

Verity turned to face him. 'I think you mean, 'Stop *please*, don't you?'

'Verity, I am very close to considering murdering you right now. Be careful what you say. I can only take so much.'

'As can I,' she said. 'From the moment we arrived you have treated me as if you owned me. You walk in and out of here – even coming into our bedroom on our first day, sorry, *your* bedroom – and you never consider that we may be ... well, you never consider us. You think just because you own this chalet, you own us. You even thought you could kiss me and walk away because you wanted to.'

'He kissed you!' Lucy said, her mouth dropping open and her eyes bulging. 'When?'

Both Josh and Verity glanced at Lucy.

'It doesn't matter, darling. Nothing happened.'

'It was a mistake,' Josh snapped.

'Believe me!' Verity snapped back.

Lucy looked from one to the other before disappearing into the bedroom.

'Now look what you've done!' Verity said. 'Are you happy?'

'What *I've* done? You're the one who brought up that unfortunate kiss. Not me.'

Verity sucked in her breath. 'We'll be gone in half an hour.'

She turned away but he grabbed her arm and pulled her back. Mistral barked and growled.

'Stop this! Please.' He let her go and raked his hand through his hair. 'I don't know how this got so out of hand,' he said, calmer now. 'I can't have a dog in my chalet,

Verity. Can't you understand that? There are all sorts of health and safety implications. What if it ... she... bites someone, apart from anything else? You must see that this is impossible.'

Verity calmed down too. 'I .can see that it's ... awkward, but she doesn't bite and where else can she go?'

'She looked as if she was going to bite me just now.'

'That's because she was protecting me. We ... we have become quite close, Mistral and I.' Verity shrugged. 'I can't let her go to a pound. Surely you can see that? Now I really must go to Lucy. She's ... she's clearly upset.'

'She's not the only one,' Josh said. He let out a long, loud sigh. 'This is impossible. Absolutely, bloody impossible! Look, I'm going for a walk. You talk to Lucy and I'll come back in half an hour. We'll ... we'll see what can be done then.'

'What do you mean by "what can be done"?'

'Frankly, Verity, I have absolutely no idea. But clearly I'll have to think of something. Just ... just don't ... go.'

Josh turned on his heel and stormed from the room.

CHAPTER THIRTEEN

'So you can see why I'm annoyed, Etienne,' Josh said, gulping down a very large whisky.

They were sitting beside the fire at Josh's home on the evening of his row with Verity.

Etienne sniggered and shook his head in disbelief. 'Look, Josh, I'm really sorry about the part I played in this. Mistral was already at the chalet when I got there and it was obvious there was no way that Verity or Lucy – or even that vet guy, Peter – were going to let her go to a pound. Not that I actually know where there is one.'

'Neither do I as it happens.'

'Well, what could I say? They told me they'd already asked around, and they were going to put notices up in the bars and tell the information bureau, the police et cetera. We all thought someone would come forward and claim her. She's not a bad looking dog and apart from the cut on her head, she's as fit as a fiddle, so Peter said. No one would have dumped her, I'm sure.'

'She may be as fit as a fiddle but she smells like a bad drain sometimes. I wouldn't blame someone for dumping her.'

'Josh! You know you don't mean that.'

'No, I don't know how or why anyone would dump an animal. She doesn't seem to do very much except sleep though.' He nodded towards the bundle of golden fur curled up on his rug.

Etienne chuckled. 'I still can't believe that Verity got you to agree to look after a dog!'

'Neither can I! But I didn't have much choice, did I? I couldn't allow Mistral to stay in the chalet and unless I did something, both Verity and Lucy would've left. Although they wouldn't have found anywhere to go, so it was a bit of an empty threat. The woman is stubborn enough to do it though and I couldn't have them wandering around looking for somewhere to stay.'

'Besides which, you'd have had a chalet full of guests with the prospect of no one to look after them.'

Josh sighed. 'That's the worst part. Not that I had a chalet full of guests and potentially no one to look after them, but the fact that I didn't even think about that! All I could think about was not letting Verity and Lucy walk the streets. I really should have told her to go, but I just couldn't do it.'

Etienne studied Josh's face. 'So going away didn't help one little bit then?'

Josh sighed and ran a hand through his hair. 'Nope. Not one iota. Although it did mean I could close the deal on that parcel of land I've been negotiating over all summer and start to draw up the plans for the new chalet, so it did me a favour on that score.'

'But ... you still feel the same about Verity?'

Josh smirked. 'More so, if anything. You'd have thought I'd have learnt my lesson from the last time. I said then that I'd never get involved with one of my chalet girls, again. Ever. Yet here I am, even more besotted by this bloody woman now than I was the day I left, and I have no idea why. From the moment I met her, I wasn't sure whether I wanted to kill her or kiss her and I felt that again today. Times by ten!'

'I know how you feel,' Etienne said, looking rather despondent.

'No good news for your love life either then?'

Etienne shook his head. 'No. Every day I tell myself to forget it. There are plenty more skiers on the mountain, as they say, but every day I find I've asked her again!'

'And she's still saying no?'

'Yep. She's still saying no.'

'I keep telling myself that Verity is nothing but trouble. She's in the middle of a marriage break-up, she's lost her job after God knows how many years and she's doing something she wanted to do when she was in her teens. It's a recipe for disaster. I know it is. And yet ...'

'And yet you can't stop thinking about what it would be like to hold her in your arms and show her how you feel.'

Josh threw Etienne a sardonic look. 'Something like that,' he said, grinning. 'The woman certainly drives me crazy. And on top of everything else, I've now got a bloody dog to look after!'

'And a smelly one at that.' Etienne screwed up his face as another fart escaped from Mistral's rear.

***

'Are you sure you're okay about it?' Verity asked Lucy as they prepared for bed.

'Yes, Mum. I've told you one hundred times already. I'm fine. It ... it was just a shock, that's all. Not as much of a shock as finding Dad in bed with Daniella of course, but a shock all the same. It's clear Josh fancies you but I ... I didn't realise you *liked* him.'

'That's the strange part about it. I'm not sure I *do* like him. From the minute we arrived here, it's as if I've become a completely different person. I get drunk. I dance on tables. I behave like a sixteen-year-old with a crush! I ... I keep wondering if this is all just ... some sort of reaction to your father's infidelity. I still love your father, Lucy. But part of me hates him for what he's done. He's leaving me though, so there's nothing I can do to change things. Whether I like it or not, my marriage is over. But as for Josh fancying me, I don't think he does. I ... I think it was just one of those spur of the moment things.'

'I'm not convinced about that. As for you behaving differently, that's a good thing, in my opinion. It's better than sitting around moping and there's nothing wrong with letting your hair down and having a bit of fun. I ... I honestly don't know why I was so surprised but it sort of felt as if you were cheating on Dad! And that's just plain stupid. Dad was the one who cheated, not you, and he made it very clear that he wants out of the marriage. You've got every right to move on and find someone else to love.'

'Hold on, Lucy! I'm not in love with Josh. I ... I just think I'm ...'

'In lust with him?'

Verity met Lucy's eyes. 'Yes. I suppose that's about it. And ... I suppose I feel as if I need some male attention. Rejection does that to you.' She forced a smile. 'But as I said, Josh clearly regretted kissing me, so it won't happen again anyway.'

'I think that's just because you work here. It would be very awkward, wouldn't it, if you started dating and things didn't work out? Perhaps he's got a rule against going out with his staff. He seems to have a rule for everything else,' Lucy joked. 'I can't believe he took Mistral home with him though.'

'And I can't believe he apologised! When I thought about it afterwards, I was the one in the wrong. This is his chalet and it's his business so I should abide by his rules. ... All of them,' Verity added with an impish grin. 'A ski chalet kitchen is obviously not the best place for a dog. I should've known that. We couldn't have just left her though, so I'm not sure what else we could've done. I think he realised that when he went for a walk.'

'And that's why he apologised,' Lucy said, 'because he realised that we weren't doing it to be difficult, we simply had no choice. I hope he remembers to get her dog food. And take her for her walks.'

'I'm sure he will, but we can always remind him. ... So, are you sure you're okay about that kiss?'

'For heaven's sake, Mum! Yes! Now go to sleep. Goodnight.'

***

Verity didn't see Josh until Tuesday and although it had only been one day, she was wondering whether he was regretting taking Mistral – and letting her and Lucy stay. But that was the least of her problems. This was her third attempt at making crème brûlée and it was another abysmal failure.

'Bloody hell!'

'Everything okay?' Josh asked from the kitchen doorway. 'May I come in?'

'What? Oh, it's you.' She was very tempted to tell him to bugger off but she thought better of it. She wished he hadn't witnessed her latest cooking disaster though. 'Yes, of course you can come in. You don't need to ask.'

'I rather got the impression on Saturday that I did.'

'Oh. Yes, I'm sorry about that. I was angry.'

Josh raised his brows. 'Really? I hadn't noticed.'

She thought he'd reverted to sarcasm but when she glanced across at him there was a look of amusement in his eyes and a hint of a smile on his lips.

'Yes. Well, I'm sorry about that too,' she said, dropping the ramekin full of gooey custard into the sink.

'Having problems?'

'I just can't get this thing right. This is my third attempt and ...'

She darted a look in his direction, realising that she shouldn't have admitted that to him. She saw his creased brows and the look of confusion in his eyes.

'Is it crème brûlée? That's notoriously difficult to make really well. Although for a cook as good as you I would have thought it would be a piece of cake ... or should that be, custard?' He grinned at his own joke.

Verity smiled but turned away in case he saw the guilt in her eyes. 'Well, it isn't. How's Mistral?'

'Ah, Mistral. That's what I came to tell you.'

Verity's head shot round. For one dreadful moment, she thought he was going to tell her that he'd taken Mistral to a pound, but he wouldn't do that – would he?

'What?' she said, her focus fixed firmly on Josh's face.

'I've found her owners.'

'You have? That ... that's wonderful.'

'Not exactly. Er. I don't suppose I could ask for a cup of coffee, could I?'

Verity was worried. There was something about his tone.

'Yes, of course. Sit down and I'll make some.'

'How's it going, Mum? Have you cracked it yet?' Lucy asked, strolling in from the hall. 'It's just started snowing really heavily and it's freezing out there. Oh. Hello Josh.'

'Hello Lucy. How are you?'

'Fine thanks. You? And how's Mistral?'

Verity noticed a distinct chill in the air in the kitchen too.

'That's what he's come to tell us, Lucy. He's found Mistral's owners.'

'Really?'

'Yes, but don't get too excited,' Josh said. 'This doesn't have a happy ending.'

'What ... what do you mean?' Lucy asked, clearly upset.

'Is she okay?' Verity added anxiously.

'She's fine. That's not what I meant.' Josh sighed and ran his hand through his hair. 'I made a few phone calls on Sunday and yesterday, I took her with me to Val Thorens because someone told me they thought they knew who may have owned her. It seems Mistral is ... was ... an avalanche dog.'

'An avalanche dog?' Verity asked. 'That's a rescue dog, I assume?'

Josh nodded. 'Her previous owner took her to the ANENA training in Les Deux Alpes. They graduated and were awarded the Maitre Chien d'Avalanche certificate.'

'What's ANENA?' Lucy asked. 'I didn't know Golden retrievers were used as rescue dogs.'

'Translated, it stands for the National Association for the Study of Snow and Avalanches. For several years now, they've run a three-week course at the resort of Les Deux Alpes. Dog teams come from all over France. They cover everything from diet to rescue techniques and much more besides and several breeds of dog are used, including Golden retrievers.'

'So ... why is that a problem? You said that she *was* an avalanche dog. Are you saying that she isn't now? Is that because of her accident?' Verity fired questions at him.

'No. Um. Is that coffee ready, please? I could murder a cup right now.'

'Sorry. Yes.' Verity poured each of them a cup of coffee and waited. She felt that Josh was delaying telling them something, and that could only mean it was something bad.

'I'm sorry to say, Mistral's real owner, her handler, Claude ... is dead.'

'Dead? Was he very old?' Verity asked.

'No, he wasn't. In fact ... he was young. In his thirties. He died in an accident – a skiing accident. An avalanche, ironically.'

'Josh! That's ... Oh how awful. Poor Mistral,' Verity said.

Josh raised his brows.

'And Claude, of course. That's dreadfully sad. When was it? The accident I mean.'

'The first week in December. It was a freak accident. There was so much snow so early this year followed by a bout of mild weather before even more snow. Many places were off limits due to avalanche risk. Claude was just very, very unlucky. He knew the mountains like the back of his hand apparently, but he was guiding some off piste novices – chalet staff as it happens, but that's irrelevant. One of them set off the avalanche by going where Claude had specifically told him not to. It happens unfortunately. Claude and the guy died. The rest of them got out. It was on the news at the time, I seem to remember.'

'Bloody hell!' Lucy exclaimed.

Josh nodded. 'Claude's parents have been looking after Mistral but ... well, they were finding it difficult to cope with her and they have no use for an avalanche dog, especially one that ... seems to have forgotten its job description, shall we say – and that keeps running away.'

'Running away? She hardly moved all the time she was here,' Verity said.

'I know. I think that may have something to do with her being hit on the head though. Perhaps she's lost her memory or something. It happens in humans, so I suppose it can happen in dogs. She was always running away apparently and they think she used to run into the mountains to look for Claude. It was understandably very distressing for them.'

'I'm sure,' Verity said. 'You ... said they had no use for Mistral. And ... that she'd forgotten her job description. What does that mean? Don't they want her? Did ... did they dump her?'

'No.' Josh shook his head. 'They wouldn't do that. Claude loved Mistral – her name is Sabine by the way, but I'm still calling her Mistral. Anyway, they wouldn't abandon her. They were trying to find her a new home but they weren't having much success. After Claude's death, she kept burying things as well as running off, and when a couple of other handlers tested her, she was hopeless. It's as if she's lost her sense of smell. And this was before her accident, remember. A good sense of smell is at the top of the list of requirements for an avalanche dog. Especially an air-scenting trained dog such as Mistral.'

'So what will happen to her? Have you returned her to the family already? I would have liked to see her again. I've grown very fond of her. In fact ...' Verity looked Josh directly in the eye.

'No, Verity. She is not coming back here with you,' Josh said.

'But they don't want her and we can't just leave her,' Lucy pleaded.

'We ... we could arrange for her–' Verity began.

Josh cut her off. 'She has a new home, so don't worry about her. She'll be fine. Although I'm not sure I can say the same for her new owner.'

'So the family found someone? That's good news,' Verity said.

'Do you know who her new owner is?' Lucy asked, clearly still a little worried.

Josh ran his hand through his hair and sighed. 'I am.'

'But ... but ... you don't even like her!' Verity said, astonished.

'Apparently I do. I offered to take her and they agreed. She's at home, curled up in front of my fire as we speak. And no doubt, stinking the place out. Something else that seems to have happened to her after Claude's demise. Wind, apparently, wasn't a major problem before. It may have something to do with her change in diet and they've told me what she should be fed. I'm hoping that will help.'

He shook his head and drank his coffee. He still couldn't believe that he was now the proud owner of a very smelly, ex-avalanche dog.

CHAPTER FOURTEEN

Verity was amazed that Josh had adopted Mistral but she thought it said a great deal about his true character. She'd also thought a lot about her own behaviour towards him and she realised that not many bosses would have tolerated it.

She knew of course, that it would have been an absolute nightmare for him if she and Lucy had walked out – especially during Christmas week. His reputation in the ski holiday business would be severely damaged if his guests were left to fend for themselves. Not that he would have let that happen. She was sure he would have managed to sort something out. His business was very important to him and that was completely understandable. It should be.

And that made her behaviour seem even more appalling. He'd actually been very reasonable … and very kind. She must find a way to thank him.

'I know we've bought Josh a little gift for under the tree,' she said to Lucy, after showing Josh out, 'but I'd like to get him something extra. Just a little 'thank you' gift.'

Lucy nodded. 'I agree. I still can't believe he's adopted Mistral but I'm so pleased. It means we get to see her again. I really liked having her here even if it was against all the rules.'

Verity giggled. 'Before he left, he asked me to remind him to add, 'No dogs allowed' to all his info packs. Just in case any future chalet girls feel tempted to take in a stray!'

Lucy laughed. 'What did you say?'

'I told him he'd better include cats as well. He said it will now forbid 'all and any living thing, other than human'. So I told him about those two guys we had here when he was away and how I wasn't sure if some of the guests would pass the 'human' test.'

'Oh, Mum, honestly! You really do seem to like winding him up, don't you?'

'Do I? I hadn't noticed. Anyway, he just sighed, ran his hand through his hair as he often does, and said he'd clearly have to rethink the whole thing but that if I had any doubt at all in the meantime, perhaps I would ask him first. He was smiling though, so I'm sure he was joking.'

'He's got quite a good sense of humour, hasn't he? When he's not angry, that is. I don't know why Jo said that he was a bit of a miserable git. He doesn't seem at all miserable to me. So, what do you think we should buy him then, for Christmas? We've only got today to get it because it's Christmas Eve tomorrow and I think it's going to get a bit hectic around here.'

***

Christmas Eve wasn't exactly hectic but it was a very full day.

As usual, the guests went skiing after breakfast whilst Verity and Lucy spent the morning baking. They made mince pies and festive-themed cupcakes for afternoon tea and put the finishing touches to the Christmas cake they'd iced the day before by adding handmade marzipan and icing, polar bears, a little mountain, a tiny *Chalet Marianne* and some not-to-scale trees.

Verity was pleased they'd finished their Christmas shopping yesterday because no sooner had they completed their chores and wrapped the last of the presents than Etienne and Josh turned up to take them out to lunch.

Meribel was definitely getting into the Christmas spirit and skiers and boarders alike were dressed as Santa or his elves or donned comical reindeer hats or antlers. Carols were being sung; everyone exchanged Christmas greetings, and locals, resident staff and tourists made merry all day long.

As darkness fell and ski slopes closed, crowds of spectators watched the annual torchlight descent. Father Christmas arrived in his sleigh, bringing screams of joy from delighted children and even from some adults, including Verity and Lucy. The bars were packed from wall to wall and Verity was actually relieved to return to the relative peace of *Chalet Marianne*.

Verity had decided that Christmas Eve should be extra special and, because Lucy's French was perfect, whereas Verity's definitely was *not* – she had arranged for some of the local children to come to the chalet and sing a few carols. She also arranged for Etienne to dress as Santa and instead of handing out the Christmas tree gifts before dinner that evening, Etienne handed them out after tea, which they served later than usual.

Lucy was wearing an elf's hat and was helping Etienne hand out the presents, not just to the guests but to the children as well.

'I can't believe you've done this,' Josh said, standing beside Verity at the sitting room door.

'You don't mind do you? I know I should've asked yesterday but it was all rather last minute and we didn't know until this morning that the kids would definitely come. I asked you as soon as I knew.'

He smiled down at her. 'Don't you mean 'told me'? But I don't mind at all. In fact, I may include it in the info pack. The guests clearly love it.'

'Oh dear,' she said. 'I seem to be rewriting all your rules, don't I?'

His eyes met hers and she saw the look she hadn't seen since the day he'd kissed her.

'More than you could possibly imagine, Verity.'

'This is for you, Josh,' Lucy said, handing him a small present. 'But ... we have got you another gift, haven't we, Mum? To say thank you. You don't get that until tomorrow though. We will see you tomorrow, won't we?'

Josh looked surprised. 'Er. Yes. Yes you'll see me tomorrow. I've got gifts for you, as it happens. But you shouldn't have gone to the trouble of getting me something. Thank you though. I really appreciate it.'

'Don't get too excited,' Verity said. 'We had absolutely no idea what to buy, so we just got you something that we hope you'll like – or at least, will find amusing. We would've asked Etienne but we couldn't reach him, so we had to make do. And this one of course, we bought a while ago ... before you went away, in fact.'

He opened his mouth to speak, closed it, clearly thought for a moment and opened it again.

'Thank you. I'm sure I'll love it, whatever it is. Shall I open this one now?'

Verity and Lucy grinned at him.

'This is just a jokey present, too, so don't take it as anything other than that,' Verity said, 'and remember, we got this *before* you went away.'

Lucy gave her an odd look but her expression changed and she must have realised that Verity meant it was before *that kiss* because she nodded.

Josh opened the gift and his brows drew together before a huge smile appeared on his lips.

'Thank you,' he said, chuckling. 'I'll treasure this. It's a lovely photo of the two of you.'

He shook the photo snow globe and little white grains of snow fluttered down over a picture of Verity and Lucy standing arm in arm outside *Chalet Marianne*.

'You can throw it out when you get home,' Verity said, grinning. 'We just followed your rules in the info pack. All the gifts under the tree have something about *Chalet Marianne* on them – including yours.'

'I'll do no such thing,' he said. 'This is taking pride of place on my mantelpiece. If nothing else, it'll remind me that I need to rewrite that damn info pack!'

He laughed and Verity thought the sound was music to her ears. More so than any of the carols she'd just been listening to.

'And this one's for Mistral,' Lucy said. 'Will you give it to her, please?'

It was clearly a bone and Josh grinned. 'Does this have a picture of the chalet on it too?'

'No,' Lucy said, 'but it did come from the joint of meat we cooked for dinner on Sunday, if that counts.'

***

'You look lovely, Mum!'

'Please try to sound a little less surprised, darling. My ego could do with a boost at the moment. I'm feeling really nervous about tonight.'

Lucy giggled. 'I'm sorry. You always look lovely but tonight, you look especially good. That dress is one of my favourites. Why are you nervous? It's only Etienne, Josh and some of their friends, after all. Or is it the thought of karaoke that terrifies you? I must admit, I didn't realise people still liked karaoke but obviously they do. It was good of them to invite us to the party though so I mustn't complain.'

'I'm not going to be singing so that doesn't bother me. It's … Actually, I'm not sure what it is. I just feel ... strange.'

'Perhaps it's because we would normally be at the Annual Christmas Eve Party at Dad's restaurant tonight, and it feels strange to be here instead.'

'Perhaps,' Verity replied. 'I did think about it a couple of times after Josh invited us to this one. I ... I wonder if your father's still holding it this year. I suppose he will, and Daniella–'

'Let's not think about that. I'm sorry I mentioned it. Let's just go and have fun. I think I heard Josh's car pull up a few minutes ago. They're probably waiting in the kitchen.'

'Actually, I think it may just be because I'm not used to going out at almost eleven o'clock at night!' Verity said as Lucy took her hand and led her from the bedroom. 'I'm usually on my way to bed.'

Etienne wolf-whistled and Josh smiled and ran his hand through his hair when Verity and Lucy walked into the kitchen.

'You look ... lovely!' Josh said, staring at Verity. 'You both look lovely.'

'Thank you,' Verity said. 'But I do wish everyone wouldn't sound so surprised about it.' She saw the confused look on his face and giggled. 'Lucy sounded astonished too.'

'I'm not astonished,' Josh said. 'I'm not even surprised. You always look lovely to me. ... I mean ... you always look very nice. So do you, Lucy. I mean–'

'Stop digging that hole, Josh, as Mum would say. We get what you mean, don't worry.' Lucy grinned at him. 'Let's go and get very merry. It's nearly Christmas Day!'

***

The chalet where the party was being held was almost twice the size of *Chalet Marianne* and, as Verity soon discovered, every room was bulging at the seams with people intent on getting very merry indeed.

'Louis hosts the best Christmas Eve party in Meribel,' Josh said as the four of them made their way to a comparatively quiet corner.

Apart from the karaoke, there were of couple of local bands providing music to dance to – assuming you liked *Bon Jovi* style cover groups or a mixture of Pop slash Soul – which Verity did. There was a huge games room with a pool table; an outdoor, heated swimming pool and a hot tub; several bars throughout the chalet including one outside, and enough food to feed the whole of Meribel.

'He must be very well off,' Verity said, thankful that she had worn her 'little black number' rather than the trousers and blouse she originally intended. Some of the party guests were wearing designer creations whilst others sported jeans and T-shirts but she felt she blended in and that helped her to relax.

'He is,' Josh said.

'Have you known him long?' Verity asked.

Josh nodded. 'About sixteen years in my case, but Etienne's known him all his life,' he said with a grin.

'Let's dance,' Etienne said, grabbing Lucy's hand and finding a space amongst the whirling masses.

Josh smiled at Verity. 'Are you up for that?' he asked, nodding in Etienne and Lucy's direction.

'Not without several drinks inside me, I'm afraid. But don't let me stop you.'

'I'm fine standing here,' he said. 'Er ... would you like ... a toffee vodka, wasn't it?'

Verity tutted. 'Not unless you want me dancing on the tables.'

His eyes narrowed for a split second. 'Not particularly.'

'You prefer women to behave with decorum then, do you?'

'I prefer women not to lie to me and ...' His voice trailed off and he turned his attention towards the dancers.

'You ... you think I've lied to you?'

'No. I wasn't referring to you. Sorry. Forget it. It's in the past.'

She studied his face as he appeared to watch the gyrating bodies, his mouth in a tight hard line and his eyes fixed straight ahead. She thought his mind was somewhere else entirely.

'It clearly isn't. Do you want to talk about it?'

He glanced at her briefly. 'No, Verity. I don't.'

'Josh!' A stunningly beautiful, dark-haired woman sashayed towards him, her arms outstretched and her eyes alight with pleasure. 'You came! And Vérité, yes? Come and dance with me. I want to speak with you.' She waved at Verity in a seemingly friendly gesture, grabbed Josh's arm and pulled him towards the dance area.

'No, Christelle,' Josh said with a smile.

'I want to dance, Joshua!' Christelle pouted, clearly already very merry. 'Dance with me. It's been so long.'

'Don't mind me,' Verity said, smiling outwardly but inwardly seething with irrational jealousy especially as the band were now performing a ballad and that meant a 'slow dance' situation. 'Go and dance with ... your friend. I'll be fine.'

'Are you sure you don't mind?' Josh asked, an odd expression on his face.

'Not in the least,' Verity lied.

'Okay. Just one dance, Christelle.'

Christelle smiled at Josh but as she wrapped her arms around him, the look she gave Verity was the same one Daniella had given her just a few short weeks before. Verity was sure of that.

***

'There you are!' Josh exclaimed, 'I've been searching for you for the last half hour! I was getting worried.'

Verity tried to focus on his face but the room just wouldn't stop spinning – or perhaps she was the one who was spinning? She wasn't completely sure. Either way, she couldn't seem to stop it. She looked down at her feet. At least she wasn't on a table; she had no idea where she was but it definitely wasn't a table.

'Why?'

'Why? Because when I looked back, you'd disappeared. Will you please stand still!'

'Why?'

'What? Because, apart from the fact that you're making me feel dizzy, I'd like to talk to you.'

'Why?'

'Are you ... drunk, Verity?'

'Very possibly. Why?'

'Please stop asking why. And please stop spinning!'

'Why? I'm dancing! You go back and dance with ... Christelle,' Verity said icily.

'Dance with ...? I don't want to dance with Christelle. I want to talk to you. Is ... is that what this is about? Is that

101

why you disappeared? Because I danced with Christelle? You said you didn't mind.'

'Well, I lied. And you don't like that, do you? And it's not the only thing I've lied about. I can't cook! But I didn't lie about that really because you didn't ask. You just assumed. Like you assumed you can kiss me and walk away and you assumed you can go off and dance with the most beautiful woman in the world, and I'll be waiting in the corner for you. Well, I wasn't, was I?'

CHAPTER FIFTEEN

Josh wasn't sure whether he should be pleased or furious. Was Verity really jealous because he'd danced with Christelle? If so, that must mean that she felt something for him and that was definitely good news ... wasn't it? But had she also just said that she couldn't cook? And that she'd lied about it? Memories flashed through his mind. That first evening – Lucy was clearly in charge of the kitchen. And the crème brûlée incident, amongst other little hints.

He shut his eyes tight for a moment as the truth slowly dawned on him and his spirits dropped like a sunken soufflé. She'd lied to him for the last three weeks. She'd turned his world upside down and all that time, she'd been lying. Why hadn't he seen it?

Well, they say that love is blind, and he had clearly been blind. But he wasn't in love. Was he? Wasn't what he felt for her just some crazy, spur of the moment, madness brought on by the sight of her half-naked body on the very first day they'd met? Wasn't this just lust?

Admittedly, he couldn't stop thinking about her. And when he'd kissed her that day he realised he had to get as far away from her as he could. He couldn't get involved with one of his chalet girls. Not again. Look how that had ended last time.

But going away hadn't worked. All he'd done was spend his time wondering what she was doing. What she was wearing. Who she was smiling at. How she was coping.

How she was coping! Hadn't he known that something wasn't quite right? Deep down, hadn't his intuition told him that it wasn't just nerves she was suffering from? And she was right. Technically she hadn't lied. He hadn't asked if she could cook. He hadn't asked her anything, really. He had just assumed. He watched her spinning and his mind spun with her.

'Okay. That's quite enough,' he said, reaching out and grabbing her arm to make her stand still.

'Oh!' she said, coming to an abrupt halt. She glanced at his hand and began to sway. 'Am I still spinning? I feel like I am. Am I?'

'No. The room probably is though. Toffee vodka?'

'Uh? No thanks! Had some!'

'That's what I meant. You've been drinking toffee vodka.'

'I've ... been drinking ... lots of things. I'm getting in the Christmas Spirit! Or maybe the Christmas Spririts have got into me! I've had lots and lots and ...' She promptly threw up over Josh's shoes.

'Dear God,' he sighed. 'This night just keeps getting better and better. Take this. And come with me.'

She lifted her head and took the handkerchief he gave her as he led her out into the cold night air. He took off his leather jacket and wrapped it around her shoulders. With one arm around her waist he made her walk, first in one direction and then the other.

'Breathe!'

'I am breathing!'

'I mean take deep breaths. The air will make you feel better.'

'It isn't,' she said giving him a doubtful look.

'Trust me. It will.'

He'd try and sober her up a bit before taking her back to the chalet. The best place for Verity right now, in his opinion, was home in bed. Why did the woman insist on drinking toffee vodka? One was enough for most people. She'd said she'd had more than toffee vodkas though. She'd clearly been sampling a variety of alcohol – and much of it now appeared to be on his shoes. He stopped and wiped them in the snow as best he could.

Now stationary, Verity leant into him and rested her head against his chest, letting out a little sigh as she did so.

Josh felt a jolt of electricity shoot through him and it took him completely by surprise. How could something as mundane as a sigh have his testosterone levels soaring? His pulse was racing and his mind was already imagining ways to make her sigh like that again; only louder and longer and ...

His phone rang and he ran his free hand through his hair. His other arm was still wrapped around Verity, as was his jacket – and that contained his phone. It was in the inside pocket which was currently just below Verity's left breast. Could he retrieve it without touching her? Just the thought of accidently brushing his fingers against her breast was filling him with sexual desire.

'Verity,' he murmured, easing her away from him and trying to rid his brain of the images it seemed intent on displaying in his mind's eye. 'Verity, I need to get my phone. It's in my jacket. Okay?'

She nodded sleepily, her eyes half closed and her lips slightly apart.

'Verity!' he snapped, more to bring himself to his senses than her. 'My phone!'

Her eyes opened wide and she shook her head. 'What?' she said. She cast her eyes down to the jacket and the ringing phone and as if realisation dawned, she held the jacket open.

She'd clearly done that to let him get to the phone but his brain gave him other ideas. He quickly grabbed the phone and turned his back on her hoping 'out of sight, out of mind' would actually work.

'Etienne!'

'Haven't you found her yet?' Etienne asked, obviously misreading Josh's curt greeting.

'Oh. Yes. Yes I've found her. She was in the workshop leading off the garage.'

'What was she doing in there?'

'Other than spinning, I have no idea. Perhaps she was trying to find her way out or something and got lost.'

'Spinning? Spinning as in ... going around in circles?'

'Yes. And she's not the only one. Listen. She's had rather a bit too much to drink and I think she should go home to bed. I'll take her because I need to take Mistral for a walk so I was leaving soon anyway. You and Lucy stay and have fun. I'll see you tomorrow.'

'Okay. Merry Christmas, Josh!' Etienne said, chuckling loudly,

'Thanks,' Josh said drily. 'The same to you. Oh, and you'd better tell Lucy that her mother may not be up and about very early tomorrow – if her last drunken session is anything to go by.'

He heard a distinct whump behind him as he ended the call. When he looked round, Verity was sprawled on her back in the snow. The look of surprise on her face immediately turned to one of amusement and she moved her arms and legs repeatedly to make a snow angel.

'And now she's soaking wet,' Josh said in an exasperated tone. He ran a hand through his hair and slid his phone into his trouser pocket. 'Yep. This night just keeps getting better and better!'

***

'Don't look at me like that, Mistral,' Josh said some while later as Mistral sat at his feet staring up at him. 'It was the right thing to do! I couldn't take her back to the chalet. What if she woke up and wondered where she was? What if the guests returned and found her sprawled out somewhere? What if she did something embarrassing? Or hurt herself? I had to bring her here. You know I did.'

Mistral smacked her jaws together, yawned, farted and curled up in front of the fire.

'Oh! Thanks, Mistral,' Josh said, wafting his hand in front of his nose. 'If that's your opinion you can keep it to yourself next time.'

'Josh!' Verity was standing in the doorway wrapped in his dressing gown and looking very worried indeed. 'Where am I? What am I doing here? Is ... is this your home?' Her eyes darted to Mistral. 'Did we ...?' Her voice rose by several octaves as she pulled the dressing gown tighter around her.

Josh leapt to his feet. 'No! Nothing happened. Well, nothing like that anyway. Come and sit by the fire. I'll get you a drink.'

She remained where she was. 'I think I've had enough. What do you mean, "nothing like that"? What *did* happen? How did I ... get undressed?'

He smiled in an attempt to put her at her ease. 'Nothing very much. You had a few drinks too many, wandered off and when I eventually found you ... you ... were flat on your back making snow angels and completely soaked. I brought you here because it's much closer to Louis' than the chalet and I needed to get you out of your wet clothes before–'

'*You* undressed me!' She was clearly horrified.

'Well, I did ask Mistral to but–'

'That's not even remotely funny, Josh. How dare you!'

'How dare I? Would you rather have caught pneumonia?'

'Yes!'

He blinked several times. 'Don't be so ridiculous. We're both adults – and it's nothing I haven't seen before.'

'Nothing you ...! You haven't seen *mine* before. My body may not be anything special but it is *mine* and I only show it to people of my choosing. And you're not one of them!'

'Really? You seem to have forgotten the day we met. You showed me quite a lot of it then. That T-shirt didn't leave much to the imagination, believe me.'

'That ...! You are unbelievable. Where are my clothes? I want to go. Right now!'

'Your clothes are still wet. You'll have to go as you are if you want to go.'

He saw her eyes flash and her lips tighten. 'Fine,' she hissed. 'Where are my shoes?'

'They're beside the bed you woke up on. I left them there after I cleaned your vomit from them – and from mine.'

Her expression softened just a fraction and turned to one of remorse. 'I ... I was sick?'

'Violently. Don't worry though. I removed all traces from your things.'

She looked unsure now. 'I suppose I should thank you for that.'

'No need.'

She turned to go but immediately turned back. 'My ... my shoes weren't beside the bed. I ... I looked for them – and my clothes – before coming downstairs.'

It was Josh's turn to be unsure. 'I put them there. I know I did. I'll go and look.'

He walked towards her and she pulled the dressing gown even more tightly around her. He knew he'd probably regret it but he couldn't help himself and he smiled lasciviously.

'You're forgetting,' he said with a pointedly salacious drawl, 'I've already seen everything you have to offer. Oh – and I disagree. Your body is very special – in my opinion at least. I found I couldn't keep my eyes off it!'

She let out a sound between a scream and a gasp as he passed her and headed towards the stairs.

He wondered if he should tell her that he didn't see very much at all when he undressed her. Not because he was being chivalrous but because he didn't want to have to go and take the very cold shower he knew he'd need if he did look. She drove him to distraction with her clothes on; if he saw her without them, he didn't think he'd ever be able to erase that image from his mind.

He walked into the guest bedroom and glanced at the rug. She was right about her shoes. They definitely weren't beside the bed. He went over his movements since returning home with her. He'd brought her straight up to this room, undressed her quickly and covered her with a dressing gown and the duvet. Took her wet clothes and dirty shoes downstairs with him. Rinsed out her clothes and cleaned her shoes. Put her clothes on the radiator and brought her shoes back upstairs.

He scratched his head and looked around the room. Unless he had poltergeists –which he knew he didn't – her shoes must be here. No one else was in the house except ... Mistral! He'd left the kitchen door open for Mistral to go out because he couldn't leave Verity and take Mistral for a walk. Had she come up, taken Verity's shoes and hidden them somewhere? Or worse still, buried them? Her former owners said she did that. Was her memory returning?

He ran back downstairs and found Verity sitting in his chair beside the fire, stroking Mistral. Something seemed to hit him hard in his chest as she turned her eyes to him. She looked so lovely with the firelight reflecting on her soft skin; her cheeks flushed by the warmth from the flames and her large blue eyes filled with anxiety and doubt and ... something else he couldn't quite fathom.

'I hate to tell you this,' he said when he could finally speak, 'but I think Mistral may have buried your shoes.'

CHAPTER SIXTEEN

Verity hadn't meant to laugh. She had no idea why she had but there was something about the whole situation that bordered on the ridiculous. She just couldn't help herself. She'd actually been intending to storm out into the night. Now Josh was telling her that Mistral had buried her shoes!

What was she supposed to do? Go barefoot? Demand to borrow a pair of Josh's? She saw a vision of herself traipsing through the snow in a dressing gown that swamped her, and her feet swimming in Josh's shoes. She couldn't help but burst out laughing.

She'd wanted to stay mad at him. Knowing he'd undressed her and had seen her naked made her want to curl up and die of embarrassment. But as she'd sat by the fire stroking Mistral and waiting for Josh to return, she wondered what she would have done had the roles been reversed.

Would she have left him in wet clothes?

No.

Would she have undressed him?

Yes.

Would she have looked?

Absolutely!

And he'd told her she'd been sick. He'd not only looked after her but also cleaned her things. He deserved some brownie points for that! She'd just behaved like some virginal miss from a Regency romance; he'd behaved like a rake, but that thought brought a wry smile to her lips. She did love a good Regency romance.

Now this! Mistral had buried her shoes. It was just too much.

'Well,' she said, still chuckling, 'if that's the thanks I get for rescuing a dog, perhaps I'll think twice about it in future.' She patted Mistral on the head and Mistral licked her foot in return. 'I don't suppose there's any point in asking you to go and dig them up, is there?'

'Me? Or Mistral?' Josh said, hovering in the doorway.

She smiled at him in spite of herself.

'Does this mean you're no longer mad at me?' he asked, running a hand through his hair. 'Is it safe for me to come in?'

'It's your house,' she replied, playing it cool. 'You must do as you please. You clearly have so far. But I'm still a little cross.'

He sighed and walked towards the fire, sinking into a chair opposite her.

'Can we call a truce if I tell you that I didn't actually look? Well, not much anyway. I had to look a bit because I couldn't do it properly with my eyes closed.'

She raised her eyebrows at him. 'Really? You surprise me.'

He grinned. 'You have no idea how difficult it was. I think I deserve a medal for bravery and self-sacrifice.'

'I'll mention it in dispatches. I believe my mother knows some influential people.'

'You're clearly feeling better. To be honest, I didn't expect to see you until at least eleven tomorrow morning.'

Verity frowned disapprovingly. 'Speaking of tomorrow – well, today now – I'll have to get Lucy to bring me some clothes and shoes or something so that I can go home. I expect most of the guests are still out but I can't turn up dressed like this, just in case.'

Josh shrugged. 'I think you look very fetching. Lucy and Etienne are still at the party but ... I can take you home if you're sure you're okay ... or you can stay here the night and I can take you back later. I can carry you to the door so you won't need shoes and I'm sure no one will see you because the guests usually lie in a bit on Christmas Day.'

'I can't stay here!'

'Why not? Don't look so worried, Verity. You're perfectly safe, if that's what's bothering you. I won't ... try to seduce you.'

'That's a relief,' she said, wondering why she didn't actually sound – or feel relieved.

'I expect so.'

He held her gaze and she had an insane urge to fling herself into his arms. She had to grip the arm of the chair to stop herself from doing so. She took several deep breaths to regain her self-control.

'Don't ... don't you want to get back to the party?' she said, lowering her eyes to the belt of the dressing gown as she twisted one end around her finger. 'And ... Christelle?'

'No.'

'I don't mind.'

He studied her face for a few moments before replying and she had to look away.

'That's what you said about me dancing with her, but apparently you lied.'

'Who told you that?' Her eyes shot back to his.

'You did.'

'Me! When?'

'Shortly before you threw up over my shoes.'

'Oh! I ... I was drunk. I must have been because I can't remember that at all.'

'So you obviously can't remember telling me that you can't cook, either.'

Verity could feel her mouth falling open but she was powerless to stop it. She couldn't remember saying that but she must have. How else would he have known? Unless Etienne had told him. And it was true about him dancing with Christelle so she'd obviously told him that too. Now, she *really* wanted to die of embarrassment.

'I can explain,' she said.

'I was sure you could.'

'Are you really cross?'

'Not yet.'

'Okay.' She took another deep breath. 'You know that I'm married, obviously, and I assume Joanna told you that ... Actually, what *did* Jo tell you?'

He gave a little cough and ran his hand through his hair. 'She told me that you'd found your husband in bed with a waitress from his restaurant, and that you wanted time to consider your future. I was reluctant at first because I thought you might up and leave and go running back to him but she told me later that in fact, he said he's leaving *you*.'

'Humph! Pretty much everything then.'

'Pretty much. She also told me that you'd just lost your job so—'

'I didn't *lose* my job! Well, not exactly. My old boss retired and my new boss – who is a total lech – made a pass at me. I kneed him in the groin and ... long story short ... I left with a rather large sum of money by way of a ... redundancy package. Large in comparison to my normal standards, that is.'

'Really? That I didn't know. It seems you're ... surrounded by lecherous bosses.'

'What? Oh! Because I called you a lech, you mean? Don't worry, you're nothing like Alfie.'

'That's good to know.'

'And I didn't knee you in the groin when you kissed me, did I?'

His eyes narrowed and he furrowed his brows. 'No you didn't, thankfully. Why was that?'

'Um ... It's irrelevant.'

'Not to me.'

'It doesn't matter. Anyway, Lucy wanted to come here and when Jo suggested I take her place, Lucy and my mother persuaded me that it was a good idea. Lucy said she'd do the cooking and I could do all the prepping, and chat with the guests because I'm good at that. We all thought it would work very well – and it has. Hasn't it?'

He nodded. 'I can't argue with that. It has. So far.'

'We thought if I told you I can't cook, you wouldn't want me to come and then Lucy wouldn't have come either. Jo said you were desperate, and that we wouldn't see you very much anyway, so we didn't think you'd ever find out.'

'Jo said that I'm desperate *and* a miserable git. She's clearly a big fan.'

'She meant desperate for staff, not anything else.'

'That's nice. And that's true, I suppose.'

'Having been let down by ... your previous team?'

'No. Having only decided at the last minute to take guests at *Marianne* this year.'

'But you said ...? You told us that one of them moved on to better things and–'

'That was the year before. I didn't open *Marianne* for guests last year. I only opened this year because my regulars wanted me to and my sister, Chloe – Joanna's mother – nagged me until I agreed. Chloe can be very ... persuasive when she sets her mind to it.'

'Why didn't you open last year?'

'I didn't want to. But we're getting off the subject. This is about you and your cooking skills. Or lack of them.'

Verity shook her head. 'That's it. End of story. My ... husband, Tony's a chef, as you know, so he did all the cooking. My mother isn't exactly the domestic goddess type so I never really learnt anything other than the basics, and I married young. Tony told me my cooking was ... abysmal so I just ... stopped cooking. But Lucy clearly takes after him as far as that goes. I sent her on the chalet-hosting course so that she could come here. She's always wanted to do a few seasons as a chalet girl.'

'I heard that you wanted to be one too, when you were young. And by the way, I know it's none of my business but I really don't like the sound of your husband.'

Verity tutted. 'You're right! It is none of your business. Who told you I wanted to be a chalet girl? Oh, I suppose it was Lucy, wasn't it?'

'I apologise. I'll keep my views on your husband to myself in future. And no, it was Etienne, but I suppose we can safely assume that Lucy told him – unless you did.'

Verity shook her head. 'No. It was obviously Lucy. So ... do I still have a job?'

Josh stared at her for several seconds. 'Yes, Verity. You still have a job.'

The fire hissed and crackled and neither of them spoke for some time until Mistral got to her feet, farted and headed towards the open door of the sitting room. They both screwed up their eyes and burst out laughing.

Josh got up and followed Mistral out. 'Excuse me, Verity,' I assume nature calls.'

He returned alone a few minutes later. 'She may be some time. I'll leave her to it.' Resuming his seat opposite, he grinned at her. 'I suppose I should be glad you came. After all, if it weren't for you, I never would have become the ... devoted owner of such a delightful dog.'

'And I'd really like to thank you for that,' she said, grinning back. 'Seriously, if there's anything I can do to repay you, please let me know.'

His eyes held hers and the grin turned to that sensuous smile of his. 'You may regret saying that because I can think of something, as it happens.'

Verity swallowed and fidgeted in the chair. It wasn't just the fire that was making her temperature rise now. 'What is it?' she squeaked, wondering if she sounded like a mouse to his ears too.

He didn't answer immediately and she cast her eyes downwards, unable to meet the look in his.

'Two things, actually.' You can tell me why you didn't ... stop me when I kissed you. And why you minded me dancing with Christelle.'

Verity's head shot up but she quickly looked away again. 'Oh! Um. Well ... the reason I didn't stop you was because it happened so suddenly and ended just as quickly. By the time I realised what was happening, you had

115

stopped. As for you dancing with Christelle, my husband has just left me for a very young and very beautiful, woman. I'm feeling a little ... unattractive at the moment. To go to a party with you and have a very beautiful woman drag you off to dance with her just ... reinforced that feeling, I suppose. I know we weren't on a date or anything and I'm not suggesting you shouldn't have danced with her. I'm just saying that ... well, it's about me, not you.'

'So what you're actually telling me is that it could have been anyone kissing you and it wouldn't have made the slightest difference and that if Etienne had danced with Christelle and left you standing there you would have felt exactly the same?'

'No! I mean, yes! Yes. Exactly.'

'And tonight was just because you feel unattractive?'

'Yes.'

The fire crackled in the silence and as she watched the flickering flames, she could feel his eyes almost burning into her skin. After what seemed like an eternity, he spoke:

'I can do something about that, Verity. If you'll let me.'

She didn't dare look at him. She felt him watching her every move and as she fidgeted in the chair and bit her lower lip, she became excruciatingly aware of the fact that she was naked beneath the dressing gown.

'Please stop looking at me like that,' she said, staring into the fire.

'Like what?'

'That!'

'Er ... how do you know how I'm looking at you? You've been avoiding looking in my direction for the last five minutes – at least.'

'I don't need to look at you to know. I can hear it in your voice. And you've looked at me like that ever since that first day when you wouldn't stop staring at my legs!'

'You have very nice legs. I couldn't help myself. Surely that tells you you're not totally unattractive.'

Her eyes shot to his face at that, but she saw the smile on his lips and the desire in his eyes, and she quickly turned away.

'You're doing this on purpose.'

'Doing what?'

'Making me feel ... uncomfortable.'

'Do you feel ... uncomfortable?'

She couldn't take this any longer. She wanted him so badly right now that it was almost a physical pain. It was madness. The whole thing was madness. She still loved Tony. Not that that mattered. She was history as far as Tony was concerned. But to feel like this, and about a man she hardly knew. It was nothing short of insanity.

'I need to go.' Without looking in his direction, she got to her feet and virtually ran towards the door.

He was by her side in seconds, his hand on her arm. It was not a forceful, restraining grip – more a gentle 'plea' to stay. She could feel the heat of his body; see the rhythmic motion of his chest; hear the rapid breaths. And she knew without seeing his face that he felt the same as she did.

'Verity, I–'

Mistral gave a loud bark and the moment was gone. The thud on the floor was the sound of one of Verity's rather battered shoes dropping from Mistral's jaws.

Both of them stared at Mistral who sat proudly in the hallway, slowly pushing the shoe towards them with one paw.

'Good girl,' Verity said when she gathered her senses. 'Go find the other one. Bring it to me, Mistral. Fetch!'

Mistral cocked her head to one side as if she didn't understand.

'Ask ... ask her in French please, Josh. Her owner was French. Perhaps she'll understand.'

Josh raised his eyebrows and shook his head in doubt but he did as she asked and was clearly astonished when Mistral barked and ran off, returning just a few seconds later with the other shoe.

'Her memory's come back! Don't you think? Oh Josh, that's wonderful!' Verity stared at her wet, slightly chewed shoes, lying on the floor in front of her.

'Wonderful,' Josh repeated although he didn't sound entirely thrilled.

'Thank you, Mistral!' Verity bent down and hugged the panting dog. 'Will you get a taxi for me please?'

'A taxi?'

'Yes.' She smiled up at him. 'I have my shoes. I can go home now.'

CHAPTER SEVENTEEN

Verity wielded the shovel as if her life depended on clearing a path to the chalet door. Snow fell thick and fast and she knew she was fighting a losing battle but she couldn't stop. She needed to keep busy. She'd hardly slept last night and even though today was Christmas Day and breakfast wasn't until nine, she was up at six and prepping vegetables by six-thirty – and that was after only three hours in bed.

'Mum! What are you doing?' Lucy called from the doorway at seven forty-five. 'It's snowing, in case you hadn't noticed. You look like a snowman! Come in and get warm. You'll catch your death of cold!'

'I'll be fine. Just five more minutes then I'm done.'

'Really? I can't see any difference. The snow's already covered where you've dug. Leave it for now. No one's going anywhere for a while. None of them is even up yet. Mum! Leave it.'

Verity finally stopped shovelling. She arched her back and straightened up. Her entire body ached and she shivered from head to foot. Lucy was right. This was a futile exercise.

'Okay. I'll make some coffee and start breakfast instead.'

'I just told you. No one's up so it's too early to start breakfast. And I've just made some coffee. Come in and sit down. Tell me what happened last night.'

Verity's head whipped round and she stared at her daughter. 'Nothing happened last night!'

'Really? Etienne told me that Josh brought you home because you'd had too much to drink. I was going to come back but Etienne said to leave you be. Are you telling me that nothing happened? On Christmas Eve? After a party and alcohol? Seriously? Josh didn't even try and kiss you good night?'

Verity walked into the hall and removed her snow-covered boots and jacket. She shook her head and tutted when she saw the pile of snow on the floor. 'I'd better clear that up.'

'Mum? Answer me. Did nothing really happen?'

Verity sighed. 'Nothing worth talking about. Oh, except that Mistral may be getting her memory back. That's really good news, isn't it? She buried my shoes but she brought them back!'

Lucy looked confused. 'When did you see Mistral? And how did she manage to bury your shoes in the first place? Mum? There's something you're not telling me.'

Verity went into the kitchen and poured herself a cup of coffee. She pulled out a chair and sat at the table resting her elbows on the top and holding the mug to her lips.

'There's really nothing much to tell,' she said eventually, after trying to think of a way to leave out most of the story. 'I was a little drunk and I'm afraid I ... threw up. And not just over me, but over Josh's shoes too.'

'What?' Lucy burst out laughing. 'Sorry. I know that's not really funny. Was he cross?'

Verity shook her head. 'Amazingly, he wasn't. Oh, and I also told him that I can't cook.'

'You did what?'

'Don't worry. He didn't seem very concerned about that either – oddly enough. I explained about Tony and everything and pointed out that it's been working well so far. He agreed and ... he didn't say anything else about it.'

'So ... we're still chalet girls then? He hasn't sent us packing?'

Verity smiled. 'No. He hasn't.'

'But ... how did Mistral get your shoes?'

'Oh! Josh lives very near to Louis so he took me back to his place. Just to get cleaned up. Um, my shoes were messy too so he cleaned them and ... Mistral obviously spotted them. When I went to put them on again, they'd gone. She'd run off with them. Josh told us that her former owners said she had a habit of burying things. Remember? Anyway, a bit later she brought them back. Josh brought me home and that, as they say, was that.'

'So ... not even a peck on the cheek?'

'Nope.' Verity shook her head, wishing more than anything now that Mistral hadn't returned her shoes.

Josh hadn't tried to persuade her to stay. 'You don't need a taxi,' he'd said. 'I'll take you home.' He handed her a coat to wear over the dressing gown and he didn't say another word until he dropped her at the chalet, only saying: 'Goodnight, Verity. Merry Christmas.'

'Merry Christmas, Josh,' she'd replied and just moments after she got out, Josh sped off.

'Mum! Are you listening?'

'Sorry, darling. I was miles away. What did you say?'

'I asked if you were disappointed that Josh didn't try and kiss you.'

'Oh! Of course not, darling. Not in the least. Anyway, what about you? Did you have a good time? I didn't hear you come in.'

Lucy smiled half-heartedly.

'Yeah. Yeah, I had a great time. And you'll never guess what. It turns out that Louis is Etienne's dad! Can you believe it?'

That came as no surprise to Verity. 'Do you know I had a feeling he might be. It was when I asked how long they'd known him. Josh said that Etienne had known Louis all his life and he grinned when he said it – although why he didn't just say that Louis was Etienne's dad is beyond me. Nothing is ever straightforward with that man. Anyway, Etienne told us at the airport that his dad had persuaded him to return to Meribel, remember? I didn't really think about it last night though. I mean, Louis could have just been a long-standing family friend. Well, fancy that.'

'I can't believe it,' Lucy said. 'He's absolutely loaded. Etienne says it doesn't make any difference but it does, doesn't it?'

'Does it?' Verity looked her daughter in the eye. 'Why?'

'Well, Etienne's rich. I'm poor.'

'You're not poor exactly, darling. But why would it matter if you were?'

'Because ... because I can't be with a man as rich as Etienne! Even if he didn't think I was after his money, everyone else would, wouldn't they? That's what lots of chalet girls do, you know. They come out to the Alps to find a rich husband!'

Verity almost choked. 'Find a rich husband! Er ... hold on a minute. I didn't even know you were *dating* Etienne. Are you? Since when?'

'I'm not! But now I can't.'

'Sorry darling, you've lost me. Has he asked you out?'

Lucy nodded. 'Every day. Since the second day we were here. I should have told you about it but ... well, it didn't feel right to, what with Dad and everything. He was ... asking me when you burst in on us in the kitchen that night. You asked me about it, remember?'

Verity frowned. She was feeling a little bemused. This was all news to her. 'Yes. And you said there was nothing going on.'

Lucy shook her head. 'I said Etienne was just being silly. Which he was. He told me that he'd fallen in love with me the minute he saw me at the airport! Can you believe it? What a line! I was sure he was interested in you. He kept asking questions about you on the way here. I told you that, remember?'

Verity nodded. 'I do remember. But I also remember telling you that it was you he was interested in, not me. It was the way he looked at you, darling. And what makes you think the airport thing was a line? People do fall in love at first sight, you know. It happens all the time. Of course he is a ski guide and–'

'Precisely! We all know the reputation ski guides, ski instructors and ski chalet owners have, don't we?'

Verity was surprised Lucy had lumped Josh into that but evidently she had. 'Yes we do. They're not all like that though. That's a generalisation. I don't think Etienne's like that at all. Of course ... we don't really know him that well so ... There's something you're not telling me, isn't there?' She studied her daughter's face. 'Let me get this clear because I'm a bit confused. Etienne's been asking you out every day but you're not going out with him. You've been saying no, is that right?'

Lucy nodded.

'But we haven't seen him every day, so how?'

'By text.'

Verity tutted. 'Not another man who texts everything!'

'He's not like Dad! At least, I don't think he is. He might be. I don't know! No. I'm sure he's not.'

'Um ... You sound rather defensive of a man you're refusing to go out with. And you said that now you know he's rich, you can't go out with him. But if you don't want to anyway, why is that a problem?'

'I do want to! Now I can't!'

'Lucy, please darling, I am utterly confused. I didn't get much sleep and I really need you to explain this to me because I honestly don't understand. If you want to go out with him, go out with him. It doesn't matter whether he's rich or poor if you like him. And as long as *he* doesn't think you're after his money – which I'm sure he doesn't – why does it matter what other people think? What *is* the problem here? Oh! It's not what I said about him being nine years older than you, is it?'

Lucy shook her head.

'Well then, what is it? It's ... not because of *me*, is it? You're not refusing to go out with him because you think I might be upset or something? Oh please, Lucy, don't worry about me!'

'I'm not! It's not you ... exactly. It's Grandma, I suppose. And Dad of course.'

'Grandma! What's Grandma got to do with it? Or your father? Have you been asking their advice because–?'

'No! Grandma is the last person I'd ask advice from. She can't even get her own love life sorted. And Dad never talks about stuff like that. You know that better than anyone. But that's the point.'

'Sorry, *what's* the point?'

'Mum! Grandma's had more relationships than hot dinners and she's always going on about men being nothing but cheats and liars and only interested in sex. I thought it was just her, but both the guys I've been out with were jerks. I used to look at you and Dad and think Grandma was wrong because Dad wasn't a cheat or a liar or anything. Now I think that Grandma may be right.'

Verity was stunned. Lucy didn't sound upset exactly but she did sound very disheartened.

'Now, you listen to me.' She took Lucy's hands in hers and squeezed them tightly. 'Your Grandma is wrong. She's my mother and I love her but she talks a lot of nonsense. She behaves just as badly as the men she berates so don't take any notice of her. She'll never be truly happy with anyone until she decides what she really wants from life.'

'It's getting a bit late for that, isn't it? She's nearly seventy!'

Verity grinned. 'It's never too late, darling. As for your father, I'm as surprised as you are about that, but we have been married for a long time, and people drift apart. I wish he'd told me how he felt but he didn't. If you're saying that you won't go out with Etienne because you're frightened he'll hurt you, I understand completely. But life is about taking risks, Lucy – especially where love is concerned.'

'You've changed your tune. You told me to be careful with Etienne because he was older, was a ski guide and lived in a ski resort. Now you're saying, take a chance!'

Verity shrugged. 'I'm not really sure what I'm saying but yes, I think so. If you like him, take a chance.'

'But he lied. He didn't tell me he was rich.'

'Did you ask him if he was?'

'Of course not!'

'Well then, he didn't lie. He just didn't tell you. That's not the same thing as lying, exactly. I didn't tell Josh I couldn't cook, but I didn't say I could, so I didn't really lie. Perhaps Etienne wanted to get to know you first. Perhaps he wanted to make sure you weren't out here ... "to find a rich husband". There's nothing wrong with that and if he's been asking you out every day, he's clearly very keen.'

Lucy let out a long breath and fiddled with her coffee mug. 'I suppose.' She looked Verity directly in the eye. 'The thing is, Mum, I just thought Etienne was trying it on. You know – new chalet girl – new challenge and all that. I said no initially because I thought he was too old for me. But I really do like him and I ... I was going to say yes if he asked me out again, last night.'

Verity waited for her to continue but she didn't. 'So are you saying that he didn't ask you out last night? Or that he did, but when you found out he was rich, you said no ... again because of Grandma and your father? And that was because you think he lied to you, and you don't want to get hurt? I'm sorry, darling, but I'm utterly confused.'

'I'm utterly confused too, Mum! I just wanted to come out here to have fun. That's all. I'm only twenty-one and there's a whole world out there waiting to be explored. I know both you and Grandma married young but I don't want to. Not for years yet. I'm not ready to get serious about someone ... especially someone who didn't bother to mention he's rich!'

'Whoa! Hold on, darling! Aren't you rushing ahead a bit? You haven't even said yes to a date yet.'

'Precisely! And now there's an even bigger problem. We were both rather drunk last night and ... well, it was

Christmas Eve and people do silly things on Christmas Eve, don't they?'

'Lucy. Please. What's the problem?'

Lucy took a gulp of coffee and glanced at her mother over the rim of the mug.

'Etienne didn't just ask me out again last night. He ... he asked me to marry him. And I've got a dreadful feeling I said yes!'

CHAPTER EIGHTEEN

Verity thought that nothing could ever surprise her as much as finding her husband in bed with one of his waitresses, but Lucy telling her about Etienne's proposal had equalled that – or at least come very close. She couldn't speak for several seconds and by the time she could, it was too late. Josh arrived, bearing Christmas presents.

'Merry Christmas! May I come in? I apologise for being here so early but ... er ... Am I interrupting something?'

Lucy jumped to her feet. 'Not at all, Josh. Merry Christmas to you, too. Would you like a coffee and a mince pie?'

'No thanks. I've already had breakfast. I just wanted to drop your presents in. I've got to head over to Val Thorens. There's been a bit of a– Is everything all right, Verity?'

'What?' Verity turned to face him and saw the look of concern in his eyes. 'Oh, yes. Everything's fine. I was miles away, sorry. I ... didn't get much sleep last night, that's all. Um. Merry Christmas.'

'You and me both,' he said, holding her gaze. 'Merry Christmas.'

'You said you're going to Val Thorens,' Lucy said. 'Is Etienne going with you?'

Josh glanced at her. 'No. I'll be seeing him later though. We're having Christmas dinner with Louis this evening. Actually ... when you finish here tonight, why don't you both drop by? Louis has a sort of open house after dinner. Not quite a party like last night but several close friends come for drinks and it often goes on until the early hours. I'll mention it to him but I know he won't mind and–'

'No!' Lucy shrieked. 'I mean ... it'll probably be a late night here because we've got the full Christmas dinner and

... Mum has organised games, of course. I'm shattered from last night so I'd like a relatively early night, to be honest.'

'Um ... I would too, if you don't mind,' Verity said. She could hardly leave her daughter on Christmas Day and it seemed clear that Lucy wanted to avoid Etienne for a while after the events of last night.

'Oh.' Josh sounded disappointed. 'Of course. Er ... games, Verity? That sounds fun.'

'Don't worry. They're harmless. Just a couple of games like 'pass the parcel' – or in this case – present – and a 'guess which Christmas character I am' kind of thing. It's just something silly to keep the guests entertained between courses that's all, and after a few drinks, I'm sure everyone will get into the spirit of it.'

'I'm sure they will. I'm almost tempted to come here for dinner instead of going to Louis',' he said with just a hint of a smile. 'Right. I'd better go.' He placed the presents on the worktop but he made no move to leave. 'If ... you change your minds about tonight, just call me.'

Verity nodded. 'We will. We've got your present somewhere. Hold on, I'll get it.' She dashed into the sitting room and returned a few seconds later. 'Remember, like the photo snow globe, this is really just a jokey present because we had no idea what to get you.'

'Thanks, and I love the photo snow globe.'

'I'll walk you to the door,' Verity said. It seemed Josh still didn't want to go and for once, she wished he would. She really wanted to talk to Lucy about Etienne and his proposal.

'Don't you want us to open these now?' Lucy asked, nodding towards the presents.

'No,' Josh said, grinning. 'I'd rather not be around when you do. Er ... may I pop in later though, if I get back from Val Thorens in time?'

'Of course!' Verity grinned back. 'We're always happy to see you.'

'Hmm. That's not the way I remember it.' He laughed as he left the kitchen.

'I'll give you back your dressing gown another time if that's okay,' Verity said as they headed to the door. 'I've only told Lucy a bit about last night and if she sees me giving you a dressing gown, she'll have all sorts of thoughts racing through her head.'

He stopped on the threshold and looked down at her. 'I'm still having several of my own.'

She felt the colour rush to her cheeks and she couldn't meet his eyes.

'Yes, well, we should just be grateful that Mistral returned my shoes when she did.'

'You may be grateful but I'm definitely not. I've given her a stern talking to this morning, I assure you.'

Verity lowered her head even further. There was humour in Josh's voice but she could feel the chemistry between them bubbling just beneath the surface.

'In French I hope,' she joked, trying to keep the conversation light. 'She didn't seem to understand English.'

'Actually, I've written an information pack for her. She's at home reading it as we speak.'

Verity chuckled and finally looked up. 'You should've brought her with you.'

'To my ski chalet!' Josh said in mock horror. 'I was going to but I'm heading straight to one of my chalets in Val Thorens. I think it's best if she stays where she is. I've asked Etienne to pop in and check on her.'

'You've spoken to Etienne? Did ... did he say anything about last night?' She hoped she didn't sound as anxious as she felt.

'Don't worry,' he said with a smile. 'I just told him that I brought you home. He doesn't know I took you back to my place first or that I wanted to have my wicked way with you.'

'That wasn't what I ... mean, thanks. Um. Did he say if he had a good time?'

Josh gave her an odd look. 'Yes. He said he had a very good time. He'll tell me later I expect. Is there something I don't know?'

'What makes you say that?'

'Your tone for one thing and the fact that I thought I'd walked in on an awkward situation this morning between you and Lucy. Is everything all right?'

Verity smiled and tried to act casually. 'Everything's fine. Lucy just had a bit too much to drink and she couldn't remember much about last night, that's all. Like mother, like daughter.'

Josh smirked but he didn't seem convinced. 'I hope you'd tell me if there's a problem. I've known Etienne for years and he's a really nice guy but I think you'd have to be blind not to realise that he's very keen on Lucy. I know he's been asking her out because he told me, and he also told me that she's been saying no. If it's upsetting her or anything, then all she has to do is say so and he'll stop. Honestly. He will. He ... he is crazy about her but the last thing he'd want is for her to feel ... under pressure or anything.'

'Oh! I didn't realise you'd been discussing it! Anyway, it's not that exactly. She likes him ... rather a lot I think but ... this business with me and her father has upset her and she ... she's just feeling a little unsure, that's all. She doesn't want to rush into anything.'

Josh visibly relaxed. 'I can understand that. And so will Etienne. If that's what's worrying her all she has to do is tell him. I promise you. There's really nothing to be concerned about.'

'Thanks, Josh,' she said as he turned towards his car. He clearly hadn't heard what happened last night then, she thought.

'Verity?' He glanced back at her with a rather serious expression on his face. 'The same goes for me, you know. I know I kissed you and I shouldn't have, and last night ... well, I think we both know what I wanted to do last night but I would never ....' He ran a hand through his hair and

130

sighed. 'Let's just say that you don't have anything to worry about as far as I'm concerned either. And if you want me to leave you alone, you only have to say so and I will. I'd hate you to think that because you work here, I think I can–'

'I don't, Josh! I know I said that you behave as if you own me but I didn't mean it ... not like that anyway. I know you'd never try to ... take advantage of me. And I would never do anything I didn't want to, you can be sure of that.'

'That's good.' He smiled a little warily. 'This is a rather serious conversation to be having on Christmas morning, isn't it? But whilst we're on the subject – do you? Want me to leave you alone, I mean?'

The question took her completely by surprise. 'I ... I ... My husband has just left me, Josh and my life has completely changed. I have no idea what I want at the moment.'

She saw his expression harden just a fraction and the warmth in his eyes seemed to cool slightly.

He nodded. 'I understand.' He smiled briefly and walked to his car. 'Just tell me if you do. Merry Christmas, Verity. I hope you and Lucy have a really good day.'

A moment later, he was gone.

***

Verity returned to the kitchen where Lucy was shaking her present from Josh.

'It doesn't make a noise,' Lucy said, 'and neither does yours. I've tested it. That was a lengthy goodbye, wasn't it? We should've got some mistletoe and put it over the front door. You could have insisted he kiss you then. Or ... did he anyway?'

Verity tutted. 'No, he didn't. I was trying to find out if Etienne had told him anything about last night. Josh has spoken to him this morning but he clearly doesn't know about the proposal, so either Etienne can't remember that he proposed, or he realises it was all a bit sudden and he's having second thoughts.'

'Oh, I'm not sure whether to be pleased or offended,' Lucy said, grinning with evident relief. 'I've been thinking about it and I've decided the best thing to do is phone him and tell him I can't remember a thing about last night. I can say that I just want to have fun, or something like that. That way, if he just said it because he was drunk, he's off the hook but if he said it because he meant it, then he'll realise that it's not the right time and he won't mention it again ... I hope.'

Verity nodded in agreement. 'That's a good idea. And I'd do it soon if I were you.'

'I'll do it as soon as we've opened these presents.' Lucy tore at the wrapping paper on hers. 'Oh look! These are the ski gloves I told Etienne I was going to buy out of the money I get from Grandma. He must have told Josh. Wow! They're *really* expensive, Mum.' She broke the tag holding them together and slipped them on, twisting her hands to admire them properly.

Verity opened her present and burst out laughing. She held up a white T-shirt – not unlike the one she'd been wearing the first day she and Josh had met – but this one had a cartoon illustration on the front with several lines of writing underneath. The image was of a rather buxom and dishevelled chalet girl wearing a tight-fitting low cut top. She was on her knees, cleaning the floor with one hand and stirring a bowl on a table with the other, whilst pots boiled over on a stove in the background. The inscription read:

This chalet girl believes:
1. My boss is always right.
2. It is wrong to argue with my boss.
3. I should obey my boss in all things.
4. I am very lucky to be a chalet girl.
5. My boss is the best!

'The cheeky devil! He'll pay for this,' she said, still laughing as she turned it around to show Lucy.

Lucy laughed too. 'Great minds think alike! He obviously got it from the same place we got the one for him. The girl evens looks a bit like you, Mum!'

Verity twisted it back so that she could see the picture again. 'Very funny! Her hair's the same colour as mine but the resemblance ends there. Unfortunately. How odd though that we bought him a jokey T-shirt too!'

'Great minds think alike! I know we got the one that said: "*World's Best Boss – In My Opinion*" and had that smug cartoony face, but what did we have printed on ours? I can't remember. *Chalet Girls Do It My Way!* Was that it?'

Verity nodded. 'Yes. I was feeling a bit nervous about it to be honest because it suddenly occurred to me that the sentence had ... sexual connotations and he might take it the wrong way, but having seen this, I think it'll be okay.'

Lucy grinned mischievously. 'I thought that was how you meant him to take it! What else did he get you?'

Verity opened one of the two other presents, which had been wrapped inside the one containing the T-shirt. She laughed again. 'I am definitely going to kill him! Where did he get this from though? It must be a book he had at home, I suppose.'

'*The Chalet Girls' Cook Book*!' Lucy said. 'Oh. Because you told him last night that you couldn't cook. Yeah. It looks several years old so perhaps he got it when he first started his chalet business, to see what sort of meals his staff should cook. What's the third one?'

Verity unwrapped the smallest of the three presents and gasped when she lifted the lid of a beautiful gift box. Inside was a delicate, silver bracelet of interlinked cut-out hearts with a small, silver filigree charm in the shape of a snowflake dangling from the clasp.

'Wow!' Lucy said, taking the box from her mother to get a closer look. 'This is gorgeous! Are you ... crying?' She gave Verity a half-smiling, half-questioning look.

Verity wiped away the stray tear trickling down her cheek. 'No! It's just that it's so beautiful and ... well, quite a surprise after the other two gifts. It's far too much though. I can't accept it.'

'What? Why on earth not?'

'It's jewellery, darling and it's too ... personal. It's something you buy for ... Well, it's inappropriate, that's all.'

'Bullshit!' Lucy said. 'I'd accept it if he'd given it to me.'

'Oh you would, would you? Weren't you the one who was so worried about what people might think if you went out with Etienne, now that you know he's rich?'

Lucy frowned. 'Yes. But what's that got to do with you accepting a bracelet from Josh?'

'People may get the wrong impression.'

'Who? Only you, me and Josh ... and possibly Etienne, will know who bought it for you so I don't follow that argument at all. Unless you mean that if you accept it, Josh may be the one getting the wrong impression – but I still don't get that. It's just a bracelet, and although it is gorgeous, it's hardly diamonds or anything. It's just a Christmas present, Mum! And to put it in perspective, these gloves probably cost about the same – if not more – and I've got no intention of giving them back!'

'But all we bought him was that T-shirt and a rather garish scarf! I thought he'd just buy us a little token present but he's spent much, much more on us.'

'It's not a competition, Mum. It doesn't matter who spent what. Oh, I think I can hear stirrings from upstairs. The guests are getting up. We'd better start breakfast.'

'I'll do that. You phone Etienne. Even I can manage to make Buck's Fizz and a Full English Breakfast.'

CHAPTER NINETEEN

Verity couldn't believe how quickly the day was going. Breakfast, which usually started at eight and was over by nine, began later today and she and Lucy were still clearing up at ten. Beds had to be made and all the other chores done, despite it being Christmas Day, and the evening meal took longer to prepare because turkey and all the trimmings was an even bigger pain when you were cooking for sixteen other people, besides yourselves. Especially when three of those people were vegetarians and that meant also making a nut roast.

On a 'normal' day, the guests were eager to get to the slopes after breakfast but these guests – a group of sixteen family and friends – had brought their own Christmas presents on holiday with them and wanted to open them first. They finally headed out at around twelve-thirty, leaving their own mountain behind, in the form of discarded wrapping paper. Verity didn't mind that, but she was soon cursing them over the hundreds of tiny pieces of Christmas confetti that was embedded in the rug, sofas and cushions.

She and Lucy finally took half an hour to relax over a sandwich and a glass of champagne at around three o'clock.

'So what did Etienne say?' Verity asked. This was the first chance they had had to talk since before breakfast.

'Not much actually.' Lucy emptied her glass in just a couple of gulps. 'God, I needed that! Who'd believe it's Christmas Day?'

'Whoever invented that Christmas confetti needs bashing over the head with a cold turkey. The bloody stuff is everywhere! Anyway, Etienne?'

'Oh. I told him that I was very drunk and I couldn't remember anything at all about last night and that I hoped I hadn't done anything I might regret. He hesitated for a bit and then he said, "Nope. Nothing at all – although I can't remember much myself so that's no guarantee." That was it. I told him that Josh had dropped in and might pop by later but that we would be busy all day here and we are both planning on having an early night.'

'So basically, you told him you don't want to see him today then?' Verity said, grinning.

Lucy shrugged. 'Sort of. But then I remembered that we'd got him a silly T-shirt too, and he said he's got us both a little something. He asked if he could drop by when the pistes close because he's out with guests all day. I had to say yes, didn't I?'

'Of course you did. So that means he'll be here around afternoon teatime.'

Lucy's phone rang and she glanced at the screen. 'It's Dad. He left me a message earlier. Do ... you mind if I take this?'

'Of course not, darling. I'll go and get mine. I expect your Grandma has left several messages too.' Verity headed for the bedroom. That was one conversation she didn't want to overhear.

She was right about her mother. Laura had left her six messages. She dialled her number and took a deep breath.

'Merry Christmas, darling,' Laura said. 'I've been calling you all morning. You weren't joking when you told me that your boss is a slave-driver. Or have you and Lucy been out having fun? I've left her a couple of messages too.'

'Merry Christmas, Mum. I wasn't serious about the slave-driver bit but we have been working virtually nonstop until now. We started later this morning and there's loads to prepare for Christmas dinner this evening. Have you had a good day so far?'

'Not particularly. Bertie bought me a new vacuum cleaner thingy. One of those lightweight rechargeable jobs. What an absolute idiot the man is! No one in their right mind would buy me a domestic appliance – especially not for Christmas! He's definitely got to go. I've decided to tell him about that little dalliance I mentioned to you. That should set the ball rolling. What about you, dear? Have you heard from you-know-who?'

'Mum! If you mean, Tony, no. But he's speaking to Lucy right now as it happens. And you can't tell your husband on Christmas Day that you had a fling with your dance instructor. That's really unkind.'

'Darling, the man bought me a vacuum cleaner! Do I really need to say more? *That's* unkind! We clearly have nothing in common. Telling him will probably be a blessing.'

'What did you buy him?'

'An annual membership of the Golf Club.'

'But ... I didn't think Bertie played golf?'

'He doesn't. I bought him lessons too. And I had to pull some strings to get him in, let me tell you. Not that he seemed to appreciate it any more than I appreciated the vacuum thing. You see. Nothing in common. Even the sex is boring. Anyway, I don't want to talk about him. I want to hear all your news. I'll call Lucy again later but if I don't get to speak to her, tell her I transferred her Christmas money online into her bank account the day before yesterday. And yours – into our 'secret' account of course, as usual.'

Verity sighed deeply. 'Thanks for that, Mum but you really shouldn't keep putting money into that account for me, especially now that I've got the money from my former employers. I don't need it, and Tony won't try to cheat me financially, I'm sure ... if it comes to that.'

'If it comes to that? The man has left you for some young strumpet. Of course, it'll come to that! He wants to sell the house and he'll want a divorce. And if he doesn't, then you certainly should! I do hope you're not deceiving yourself into thinking that you may get back together. And as for the account, I told you the day I opened it that I'd be putting money in it every year on your birthday and at Christmas because all women need to have a separate nest egg just in case. And I'll keep making deposits until you and Tony are divorced!'

'Thanks! I wondered when we were going to have the 'I told you so' conversation. And no, I'm not deceiving myself that we'll get back together. I think his texts made his intentions clear but it is early days yet and ... anything could happen. I just–'

'You are! You're actually holding out some hope that he'll dump the strumpet and come grovelling back to you! Oh darling, please don't do this–'

'That's enough, Mum! I don't want to have this conversation, especially not on Christmas Day. I know you mean well but it was bad enough that you opened that account for me in the first place – and made me promise to keep it a secret from Tony, let alone telling me about it on my wedding day! And yes, you were right. He is leaving me as you said he would all those years ago, but we have been married for twenty-one years so I think we both deserve some credit!'

'Fine. And I'm not going to say, "I told you so", darling. I'll even admit that it lasted a lot longer than I thought it would, but you've always known I've never really liked Tony, so there's no point in either of us pretending otherwise. The money is there and it's yours. I won't say another word about it.'

'Fine. Thank you.'

'So, have you met any nice men in Meribel?'

Verity hesitated for a second too long, partly because she was amazed by her mother's thought process.

'You have!' Laura said with genuine excitement in her voice. 'Ooh! Tell me all about him. What's he like in bed? There's nothing quite as exciting as that first time with someone new and–'

'Mother! We're not all sex mad you know! I haven't slept with him yet ... I mean ... there isn't anyone. There are several very attractive men out here – it's that sort of place. You'd love it. But I'm not seeing anyone. And as much as you dislike the fact, I'm still a little in love with my husband!'

'Well, of course you are. You're the loyal type, I know that. But you must face facts darling, and you're not getting any younger. You should be out there having fun and–'

'And jumping into bed with the first man who asks me – is that what you mean by having *fun*? Surely that's just having sex!'

'Well yes. If he's good looking. And sex *is* fun, darling. Or have you forgotten that? But ... what did you mean, I'd love it out there? Are there several available men in my age group?'

Verity tutted. 'As you consider any man between the ages of thirty and seventy in *your age group*, yes, there are hundreds of them.'

'That's interesting. Although I'm not a great lover of snow, as you may recall. It's pretty to look at when you're snuggled up in a chalet with some gorgeous hunk but it's not so pleasant by the time he starts to get on your nerves and you have to battle arctic conditions just so that you can get to the nearest bar to give yourself a five-minute break from him!'

Verity tutted again. 'Are you referring to husband number two or husband number four in that statement?'

Laura didn't answer immediately and Verity wondered if, by some miracle, she'd actually said something that had made her mother stop and think about her ways. She should have known better though.

'Both of them actually, darling, now that I think about it. Anyway, despite your protestations, there clearly *is* someone you're keen on. I know you better than you think. No! Don't try to fool me. It won't work. I know you never take my advice and that's probably just as well but I'm saying this because I love you more than anything in the world, my darling. Don't give Tony another moment's

139

thought. If he does ever want to come back, you can think about him then. In the meantime, enjoy yourself! Let your hair down for once and see what the world has to offer you. Just take a chance. You may be pleasantly surprised.'

***

A few minutes later, Verity marched into the kitchen, grabbed the champagne bottle and filled her glass to the brim.

'How I have managed to get to forty without murdering my mother is beyond me!' She tipped back her head and emptied the contents of the glass in several gulps.

'That bad? Was she giving you another lecture about Dad?'

Verity slumped onto a chair and let out a long breath of frustration. 'She's always lecturing me about your dad. I'm not sure what she'll do if we actually get divorced. Perhaps she'll still lecture me on spending so many years of my life with him. What's the matter? You look ... upset.'

Lucy fiddled with the stem of her glass. 'I'm fine.'

'No, you're not. Is it Etienne? Oh! Is it something your father said?'

Lucy bit her lip. 'It's nothing.'

'Lucy, please. If something is bothering you, tell me. Please don't feel you need to keep things from me. If you've got something to say, say it.'

'I miss Dad!' Lucy blurted out. 'I know I shouldn't, but I do. It's ... it's just because it's Christmas Day, I think. I miss us as a family. I even miss Grandma!'

Verity reached across, hugged her daughter tightly, and tried to stop the threatening tears from falling. She blinked several times but even she could tell her voice was full of emotion when she finally spoke.

'Of course you do, darling. And you have every right to. I miss him too and yes, I also miss my mum. Even though she's just spent the last ten minutes or so driving me insane. Christmas just doesn't feel the same this year. Not that it could, of course. We're in a ski chalet hundreds of miles from home, and we've spent most of the day working. But ... it doesn't feel like Christmas. It just feels like an ordinary day.'

Lucy sniffed and wiped the tears from her eyes. 'Exactly. Apart from the presents Josh gave us, it's been horrid. I think being here, surrounded by snow and log fires and all the Christmas lights and stuff, and watching all our guests with their friends and family opening their presents, just made it worse. It all looks so Christmassy. So perfect. And it sort of brings it home that it isn't.'

Verity had to agree with that.

'I know we were going to save our presents for each other until tonight,' she said, 'but why don't we open them now? We could both do with a bit of cheering up before we have to get afternoon tea ready.'

***

Having stuffed themselves at afternoon tea with mince pies, Christmas cake, vin chaud and brandy-laced hot chocolate, most of the guests went to lie down, leaving only a few remaining in the sitting room 'playing' with their presents. There was no sign of Etienne or Josh and both Verity and Lucy began to wonder whether they would see them now as it was six in the evening and they all had Christmas dinners to either cook or attend.

When Lucy's phone rang just a few minutes after six, they both thought it was Etienne; but it was Joanna.

'Hi Jo! Merry Christmas,' Lucy said, having cheered up considerably, possibly because she hadn't had to face Etienne yet but more likely because she was thrilled to bits with the new snowboard Verity had bought her.

Verity wandered into their bedroom to give Lucy some privacy.

'Hi babe! Same to you, with snowballs on!' Jo said. 'How's your day been so far? I bet you've been lazing by the fire drinking champagne and stuffing your face with mince pies.'

'How did you guess?' Lucy said, laughing. 'If only! We've been slogging our guts out and we've got the whole Christmas dinner thing to go yet. Mind you, it's all under control – at the moment. I haven't heard from you for a few days. Still screwing Rich, the builder?'

Jo chortled. 'As often as possible, babe. Which reminds me, is your Mum there? Wish her a Merry Christmas for me will you? And say I've forgiven her for telling Uncle Josh I called him a miserable git. Thanks for the heads-up on that by the way. Not that he's even mentioned it, but anyway, you should see the present he bought me! And Mum says he's cheered up a bit, lately. We both reckon it's because he's got the hots for your mum. Tell her, if she screws him I'll be her friend forever. He could do with the sex. It's been ages since he's had any – according to Mum.'

'Jo! Yuk. Does he discuss his sex life with his sister? I'm not sure I'd like that if I screwed him. Not that I ever would, of course but ... Eew! That's gross! Has he actually told your mum he fancies my mum, then? It's obvious he does and I told you about *that kiss* but nothing's happened since then, so Mum says.'

'Not in so many words, and he doesn't exactly discuss it with her but you know what my mum's like. She could wheedle out secrets from a secret agent.'

'And she tells you?'

'Don't be stupid! My mum's not as cool as yours. She tells Dad. I just eavesdrop. I heard her say that she was really surprised because she didn't think he'd even take a second look at another chalet girl after what happened with the last one and–'

'What do you mean, "what happened with the last one"? Tell me what you know. And make it quick because I can see Etienne and Josh's cars pulling up so I'll have to go in a second.'

'Oh! Well the quick version is Uncle Josh was screwing her. She got serious. He dumped her. She went mad and smashed up *Chalet Marianne*.'

'What?'

'You said you wanted the quick version. It's a long story.'

'Bloody hell! Okay, I'll call you back later for the full version. I need details.'

'I'm out bonking Rich tonight, babe, so it'll have to be tomorrow.'

'Sod it! All right. Call me the minute you get up. Oh, hold on. Just tell me one thing. I know he's your uncle and everything but ... does he sleep with many of his chalet girls?'

'No idea. But I do know she wasn't the first. Why? Oh, you're worried your mum might get hurt again. Maybe a quick screw would do her good.'

'Maybe. But I don't think Mum is the 'quick screw' type. I've got to go. Call me tomorrow with the full story.'

'Okay. And I want to hear the latest on the Etienne saga. It's about time you said yes and had a bit of rampant sex yourself. I know he's thirty but it's not that old and men hit their sexual prime around that age, don't they? Hot sex with a hunky ski guide. I'm almost jealous. Get to it, girl. Love you!'

Lucy rang off and dashed into the bedroom to check her make-up, almost bumping into Verity in the doorway.

'They're here!' Lucy said a little breathlessly.

'I know. I heard the cars. Are you okay?'

Lucy nodded. 'Fine. I'll be back in a mo.'

Seconds later, Josh and Etienne strolled into the kitchen.

'What a coincidence that we arrived at the same time,' Etienne said.

'Yes, isn't it? Merry Christmas, Etienne.' Verity had the distinct impression they had planned it. Safety in numbers, she assumed.

'Sorry it's so late but we're not staying long. I just wanted to say thank you for this lovely scarf,' Josh said, pointing to the scarf around his neck. 'And for this equally lovely T-shirt.' He undid his jacket and lifted his sweater to

143

reveal what he was wearing. 'I'm a little disappointed to see you're not wearing yours.' He grinned mischievously.

Verity grinned back. 'I'm saving mine for later. Thank you so much for the wonderful presents but you shouldn't have done it and ... well, I need to have a little chat with you sometime, please.'

Josh frowned. 'That sounds ominous. You haven't found another dog you want me to adopt have you because I'm not sure I could manage a second one?'

Verity giggled. 'No. No dogs. And it's nothing serious. How did it go in Val Thorens? All okay, I hope.'

'Yep. Disaster averted. One of the bathroom taps wouldn't turn off, that's all, but it's virtually impossible to get a plumber in Val Thorens on Christmas Day so I had to go and fix it before it got any worse.'

'Oh. You're a plumber too? How useful.'

'I'm no plumber, but when you own several chalets you have to become a bit of a Jack of all trades. I do employ a handyman but he's away for Christmas.'

'Josh is very good with his hands, I believe,' Etienne said, grinning broadly and winking at Verity. 'Hello Lucy. Have you had a good day?'

'Not bad thanks, but exhausting,' she said, collapsing dramatically for effect onto one of the kitchen chairs.

'Er ... perhaps now would be a good time for that little chat, Verity,' Josh said, nodding his head towards the dining room.

'Um. Yes. You don't mind do you, darling?' She squeezed Lucy's hand.

Lucy shook her head. 'No. Not at all. I'd like a little chat with Etienne, as it happens.'

Verity was surprised by the eager look on Lucy's face and wondered for just a second whether her daughter had suddenly changed her mind about Etienne's proposal. He was an incredibly good-looking man and this evening, for some reason, he looked even more handsome than usual.

144

'What did you want to have a chat about?' Josh said, closing the dining room door behind them.

'Your presents. I loved the T-shirt and the book was very amusing. Do you want that back by the way?'

Josh raised his eyebrows. 'Your need is greater than mine, I believe. You can keep it. There's even a recipe for crème brûlée, if I remember correctly,' he said with a cheeky grin.

'Thanks. But I'll leave that dish to Lucy. The thing is, Josh ... the bracelet is gorgeous and I do love it but ... I can't accept such a personal gift, or such an expensive one.'

'Well I wish you would. I didn't think a bracelet was that personal. I think perfume or bath products are more personal than that and I did think about buying you those, but I didn't know what you like so I didn't. I was getting Joanna a present in the jeweller's and when I saw that bracelet, I just thought of you. I don't know why. I suppose it's the snowflake charm and the fact that the little hearts are the same shape as the ones in the balcony balustrades here. It ... just seemed appropriate. As for it being expensive – it wasn't – and besides, you and Lucy have been great, and I wanted to get you both something nice. You can change the bracelet if you don't like it.'

'No! I do like it. Very much but ...' Verity couldn't think of anything else to say.

'That's settled then. I'm very pleased you like it. But I must insist that you wear the T-shirt the next time I see you,' he said with a grin. He nodded his head towards the kitchen. 'I think Etienne is giving Lucy the same speech that I gave you. The "I'll leave you alone if you want me to" one, so I think we may need to give them a while.'

'Oh!' Verity wasn't sure how Lucy would react to that. 'We'd better stay here then.'

He grinned at her again. 'Yes. What shall we do to keep ourselves occupied? I can show you a few other things I can do with my hands besides mend taps, if you like.' His eyes were almost dancing with delight.

145

Verity gave a little gasp but quickly replied: 'You could make yourself useful and throw some more logs on the fire.'

He cocked his head to one side. 'I thought that's what I was doing,' he said, his grin widening even further.

'Are you ready, Josh?' Etienne said, opening the dining room door, a broad smile on his face. 'Louis is expecting us at seven. Sorry we have to rush, Verity. I've left your present with Lucy and I'll see you both later tonight.'

Josh gave Verity a look as if to say, "That was quick". 'Yes, I'm ready. Er …will we see you later, Verity? I thought you both wanted an early night?'

'So did I.'

'Apparently not,' Etienne said. 'Lucy wants to ask me something and I'm in a bit of a rush now so she's coming to the house when you finish here. She said you'd both be coming.'

'Well then, I suppose we shall. Will Louis mind, Etienne?'

'Not in the least. He's cool about that sort of stuff. Did I mention that he's my dad, by the way? I can't remember. I just assume everyone knows but I forget that because I call him Louis, some people may not realise I'm his son.'

Verity wondered for a second if this was a test to see if Lucy had told her.

'No, you didn't. But it did occur to me last night when Josh said you'd known Louis all your life. You told us at the airport that your father lived in Meribel and I could see the resemblance. I meant to ask Lucy if she knew but it completely slipped my mind.'

Etienne smiled. 'She didn't, but she does now. I thought I'd told her last night but she can't remember – and nor can I. Not that it's a big deal. Anyway, see you later.'

Josh grinned at her. 'You don't have to wear the T-shirt tonight. I'll let you off the hook on that.'

Etienne was already heading towards the door and Josh followed him. He turned suddenly, ran a hand through his hair and smiled seductively, his blue-grey eyes still twinkling in the glow from the fire.

'I feel it's only fair to warn you, Verity. If you wear anything like that black dress you wore yesterday, I may start thinking of some pretence to try to get you back to my place – unless you tell me to leave you alone. Mistral should have read the info pack by now, so she won't be returning your shoes or any other discarded item for that matter.'

He winked and a frisson of excitement shot through her. He left before she could think of a retort and she had a very definite feeling that somehow, the dynamics of the entire situation had just changed.

'Why the change of mind?' she asked as she sauntered back into the kitchen.

'He was in a rush and I didn't get a chance to say much more than I'd said on the phone. That's why I'd like to go tonight. I want to make it clear that I don't intend to settle down for a very long time. I'd like to be his girlfriend and I don't need to tell you that I'd *really* like to get him into bed, but marriage – no way!'

'I'm not sure that's the sort of thing a mother wants to hear,' Verity said with a chuckle.

'It's in the unwritten *Chalet Girl Rules* book, Mum. A chalet girl's gotta have fun.'

Lucy winked at her and Verity found herself wondering what she had brought with her that was anything like that black dress.

CHAPTER TWENTY

'What are you doing, Mum?'

Verity was standing in the bedroom in just her underwear and rummaging through the pile of clothes on her bed for the umpteenth time.

'I don't know what to wear! I wore the black dress last night and the other few I brought are boring. Other than those, it's trousers and tops and I ... I want to look nice as it's Christmas Day.'

'You want to look nice for Josh, don't you mean? What about the new navy blue dress then? I know you brought it with you because I insisted that you did.'

Lucy stuck her head in Verity's wardrobe and brought out the dress in question. It was a last-minute purchase on that fateful shopping day and Lucy had persuaded Verity to buy it for her fortieth birthday party. After finding Tony in bed with Daniella, she hadn't had any reason to wear it.

'I couldn't possibly wear that!' Verity said, grabbing the dress and hastily slipping it on.'

'Bloody hell, Mum! It looks even better on you tonight than it did in the shop.'

There was a full-length mirror on the inside of the open door of the wardrobe and Verity twisted back and forth in front of it.

'Are you sure it's not too much?'

'It's perfect, Mum. And you look sensational. The only thing that worries me is that Etienne may decide he'd rather have you instead of me!'

'That'll never happen. He's crazy about you. I told you earlier, even Josh knows that.

I do love this dress but ... isn't it a bit revealing?'

'As I told you in the store, you've got it, so flaunt it. You always wear 'safe' things. That black dress is the only thing that looks sexy. Even that comes down to your knees and the skirt is loose fitting. This ... well, this one oozes sex in every thread. Trust me. And let's put your hair up. It'll show off your shoulders.'

By the time Lucy had finished, Verity was stunned by her reflection.

'Wow! Even I'd find me attractive,' she said.

'Mum.' Lucy looked troubled. 'I ... think there's something I should tell you. I wasn't going to until I knew the details and I had to ring off before Jo could tell me. She's out with Rich tonight so I can't find out and when I asked Etienne, he said it's a long story – which is one of the reasons I wanted to go to Louis' this evening. I'm hoping he'll tell me tonight. And I don't want to spoil things for you but–'

'Lucy. Just tell me.'

Lucy looked her in the eye. 'You know we've been joking about the last chalet girls who worked here? Well, I think something pretty serious happened between Josh and one of them. Romantically, I mean.'

'Oh? What makes you think that?' Verity felt herself tense.

'As I said, I don't know the details. And I'm not saying he did anything wrong. There's nothing wrong with a holiday romance, or in this case, a romance for the season. And he was the one who ultimately 'suffered' and that's why Jo's mum was surprised that he "would even take a second look at another chalet girl after what happened with the last one". I don't really get it.'

'That makes two of us. Sorry darling, I'm not following you at all. Was Jo's mum talking about me when she said "another chalet girl"? And ... are you saying that he had a fling with the last one? I thought you said it was something serious. I'm confused.'

'I said something serious happened. And it did. All Jo told me was that Josh slept with her – the chalet girl not Jo, obviously – and that she got serious. Josh dumped her and the girl went berserk and wrecked this chalet.'

'What! I ... I don't understand.'

'Neither do I really. It's obvious Josh fancies you – even to Jo's mum which is why she's so surprised.'

'Hold on. Jo's mum thinks that Josh is interested in me? Has ... he told her he is? Oh, I suppose you've told Jo about that kiss, haven't you, and she's told her mum?'

'Yes, I told Jo, but I don't know if she told her mum. They don't talk like we do. And I don't think Josh has said anything. She's just convinced he likes you. But after the last one, she's surprised.'

'I'm still confused. Why?'

'Mum! I've just told you. Josh slept with the last chalet girl and then dumped her. She was so upset that she smashed this place up. Jo's mum thinks it's strange that he would risk getting involved with another chalet girl after that but she's convinced he likes you. We're all convinced he likes you. And you like him. And if you both want to ... have a bit of fun together. Well, there's nothing wrong with that and it might do you good. Only, I'm not sure if this is something he does with all his chalet girls. And I don't want you to get hurt.'

'Something he does with all his chalet girls!' Verity dropped down onto her bed. 'Oh, I see,' she said, feeling like a helium balloon with all the air sucked out. 'But just because he slept with one, it doesn't mean ... Oh! Are you saying there were others before her?'

Lucy sat beside Verity and wrapped an arm around her. 'I'm only telling you because ... well, after Dad, I don't want you to get hurt again and I do think Josh really likes you so as long as you both go into it with your eyes open then it's fine, isn't it? But yes. Jo did say that this last girl wasn't the first chalet girl he'd slept with. She knows of five.'

'Five! Oh shit! Trust me to fall for a bloody serial chalet girl dater!'

'I'm really sorry, Mum. I wasn't sure whether to tell you or not. The week we spent at Grandma's was horrid and I was very worried about you. Since we've been here, you've been happy! I ... I think he's good for you but ... I just thought you should know, that's all. Are you very upset?' Was I wrong to tell you?'

'I'm ... a little hurt, yes. And surprised, to be honest. I didn't think he was that sort of man. But then I didn't think your father was the sort of man to do what he did, so what do I know?' She smiled half-heartedly at Lucy. 'I'm glad you told me. At least now I won't do anything tonight that I might live to regret.'

'Do you want to stay home? Or shall we just go and have a good time, and I'll see if I can get all the details out of Etienne. Or you could just ask Josh. He'll tell you anything you want to know when he sees you in that dress! Although he might not tell you the truth.'

Verity stood up and caught her reflection in the mirror. She really did look pretty good, she thought. She was sure Josh would like what he saw. The deep navy colour of the strapless, satin crepe, fitted dressed really suited her. It somehow made her blue eyes even bluer and her blonde hair, more blonde. The little notch in the bodice showed just the right amount of cleavage, and having her hair up made her neck appear longer and emphasized her shoulders.

'Let's go and have some fun,' Verity said, taking a deep breath. 'I may show Josh just what he's missing. And I may even teach him a little lesson.'

CHAPTER TWENTY-ONE

Josh couldn't speak when he saw Verity and her dress. Neither could Etienne, for that matter, although as Lucy had dressed up too, Etienne's attention quickly turned to her and he let out the longest, loudest wolf whistle she had ever heard.

'Shit, Lucy,' he said. 'You and your mum make all the other women here look like uglies. I thought you both looked pretty hot last night but now ....' He whistled again. 'They look incredible, don't they, Josh?'

Josh still couldn't speak and neither could he close his mouth, it seemed or stop his eyes from travelling up and down Verity's body. He tried to pull himself together but all his blood vessels felt as if they were moving in accompaniment to some rap song and his heart was thumping to the same beat as were his pulse and his lungs. His legs felt weak and he blinked several times but all he could see was Verity; everything else appeared to be out of focus. He wondered if he were having some sort of a transient ischaemic attack: a TIA or mini stroke as they're known but he lifted his arm and ran his hand through his hair to make sure that wasn't the case.

'Perhaps I should have worn the T-shirt after all,' Verity quipped.

He could see she was blushing furiously under his intense scrutiny but she smiled up at him and met his eyes – when he could stop them from frantically scanning her body.

'I thought that *was* a T-shirt,' he finally managed to say. 'I don't think there's enough of it to count as a dress!'

He realised too late that it sounded as if he were chastising her when in fact, he should be thanking her. It had been a very long time since he'd feasted his eyes on anyone quite as stunningly beautiful as Verity. And even longer since he'd seen anyone who had made him feel like this. She oozed sex appeal; and that's exactly what was appealing to every inch of him right now.

'Oh! Don't ... don't you like it?' she asked, lowering her head towards the exposed flesh of her décolletage and her bare shoulders.

He could see she was disappointed.

'You are joking?' he said. 'A man would have to be dead not to like it. You look breathtaking. You certainly took my breath away. I thought I was having a heart attack!'

She brightened visibly. 'And I'm wearing the bracelet.' She held out her arm and wrist towards him.

He could smell her perfume and his head swam. The caveman instinct was alive and well: he could attest to that beyond any doubt because all he could think of right now was dragging Verity back to his chalet and spending the next few days showing her just how much he liked her dress. Or more precisely, how much he liked what was inside it.

'So I see,' he said, running his hand through his hair.

She cocked her head to one side. 'You do that a lot you know. Run your hand through your hair.'

He was surprised. 'Do I? I hadn't noticed. Sorry.'

'No! Don't be sorry. I like it. To tell you the truth, I ... I've been wondering what it would feel like.'

He was finding it difficult to swallow. 'What! What *what* would feel like?'

She reached up and her hand hovered just in front of his temple. He sucked in a breath and found he couldn't let it out.

'Your hair,' she said in a far more sultry tone than she usually used. 'It looks very soft and lustrous but I wonder if it'll be rough ... to the touch. May I?'

He almost choked but before he could answer, she brushed his temple with her hand and slowly slid it in his hair. Using the tips of her red-painted nails followed by the soft pads of her fingers, she traced a path along one side of his head and round and down to the nape of his neck.

He felt as if he were a puppet that had been shut away in a box, suddenly brought to life by her teasing fingers as she gathered up each nerve and made every inch of his body respond to her touch. Sex messages flew to his groin and his brain struggled to retain control.

'Verity,' he said on a sigh.

'Sorry.' She quickly pulled her hand away.

It was as if she had released him from a spell and he glanced around, noticed that Etienne and Lucy were nowhere in sight but that one or two other people were looking in his direction. He coughed lightly and smiled at them before grabbing Verity, a little roughly he realised, and almost dragging her into Louis' study nearby. He closed the door behind them and leant firmly against it.

She spun around and he saw fear in her incredibly blue eyes.

'Would you mind telling me what's going on?' he asked. 'I may be wrong but it felt very much like you were seducing me out there, but by the look on your face now, it's clear you don't intend to follow through.'

'I ... I wasn't trying to seduce you!' she said, looking like a rabbit caught in the headlights. 'I just wondered what your hair felt like, that's all – and you do do that a lot, you know. Run your hands through it, I mean.'

'So you said. And believe me, Verity, you weren't *trying* to seduce me. You had me. Hook line and sinker. So I'll ask again. What's going on?'

'I just wanted to be ... friendly ... and to thank you for the bracelet, that's all – and for taking Mistral, and all the other nice things you've done for me since I've been here.'

He studied her face. She was lying, he could tell. 'Yeah, right. I'm such a great guy. Are you going to tell me the truth or are we playing some sort of game? Ah! Is this another of your Christmas party games? Let's drive Josh mad with sexual desire and then walk away and leave him frustrated? Or was this to repay me for that kiss – and for flirting with you earlier. I'm not quite sure what I've done to deserve that. But fair's fair.'

He pushed himself away from the door and took a step towards her. She backed away. This could be fun, he thought. He took several more steps and she matched each one with a retreating step until she had retreated right up against Louis' massive oak desk.

She turned and glanced at it and her eyes shot to his face.

'Dead end,' he said, grinning at her. 'Now, I've been wondering what it would feel like to run my hands through your hair but I don't want to spoil it, so ... perhaps I could run my hands somewhere else instead.'

He slid one arm around her waist and pulled her towards him. He could feel that he'd actually lifted her off the ground and he held her firmly against his body.

'Josh!' she squealed. 'Please! Put me down.'

'Certainly.'

He lifted her onto the desk and as she was forced to sit, her already short dress crept further up her legs until almost her entire thigh was exposed. She struggled to get down but he blocked her way.

'This isn't funny,' she said. 'I'll scream.'

'Scream all you like. This room is soundproofed. The chalet's original owner was a rock musician and this was one of the studios.'

She looked terrified. He thought he should stop but something about her egged him on.

'So,' he said, tracing a line along her shoulder with his forefinger and moving down her arm and back up again. 'What shall I ... run my hands over?' He let his eyes linger on her breasts.

She straightened her back but leant away from him at the same time, as far as his restraining arm around her waist would let her.

'Nothing!' she hissed. 'I mean it, Josh. Stop this. Stop this now. Oh!'

He felt her shudder as his fingers brushed her leg and he ran his hand up her thigh. His hand tightened on her waist and he moved his body closer to her.

'Josh, please!'

'Tell me what's going on then!' he said, looking directly into her troubled eyes. 'I was beginning to hope that you were interested in me but even I couldn't have wished for the sudden increase in ... enthusiasm you showed tonight. Tell me the truth, Verity.' He pulled her back towards him and moved his lips to just a fraction away from her ear, whispering into it. 'Is this some sort of game you're playing because I'm deadly serious. I know we hardly know each other but I want you more than you can possibly imagine and it's taking every ounce of self restraint not to kiss you – amongst other things – right now.'

He heard her gasp and suddenly, unexpectedly, she raised her hands to his chest and pushed him with all her strength. He stumbled back just a fraction but it was enough to allow her to slip from the desk and dash around behind it.

'Surely you have rules about not getting involved with your chalet girls, don't you? You have rules for everything else,' she hissed.

He couldn't understand where this venom had come from because venom it definitely was.

'I'm sorry. I ... I didn't mean to upset you. I was teasing you. Just like you were teasing me just now. Although I don't think you quite appreciate what you did to me out there. I wanted to ... well, we both know what I wanted to do – and I've never felt like that about anyone. Then you go all coy and play the innocent. Why? What have I done to deserve this? Was it because of earlier? I didn't think you minded.'

'Well, I do. It seems to me that you think you can just do whatever you like where your chalet girls are concerned. I was just giving you a taste of your own medicine.'

He felt as if she'd hit him in the chest and winded him.

'I'm sorry. Truly I am. I really thought you were beginning to like me.'

'Don't you mean that you thought I might soon be another notch on your bedpost? Sorry to disappoint you.'

He couldn't understand what was happening. 'Verity, I'm lost. I thought we were friends and ... well to be honest yes, I did think that ... something might happen between us. But I can assure you there are no notches on my bedpost – or anywhere else for that matter and I don't know why you would think there are.'

'Really? Are you telling me I'm the first chalet girl that you've ... tried to get into bed?'

'What? I don't understand. I ...' A thought suddenly occurred to him. 'Has someone told you something?'

'Very little actually but I'm not, am I? The first I mean?'

He let out a deep sigh. 'I'd rather not have this conversation right now, but I'll be perfectly honest. No, you wouldn't be the first chalet girl I've slept with – or wanted to in your case – but I don't see what being a chalet girl has to do with it.'

'How many?'

'What? Why does it matter? They're in the past. The only person I'm interested in is you. Surely you can see that?'

'They? So there was definitely more than one?'

She gave him a look of contempt and he felt his backbone stiffen. Was she the type of woman who judged a man on the number of women he'd slept with? If so, he was possibly fighting a losing battle – although there hadn't been that many.

'There have been a few,' he said honestly. 'Look, Verity, I'm forty-two years-old and I'm no saint. I've slept with a few women.' He did what even he was beginning to realise was a habit, and ran his hand through his hair. 'Some have meant more to me than others but I really like you. I know you're feeling vulnerable at the moment and it's probably far too soon for you to even think about getting involved with anyone else after your husband but I ... I think we could be good for one another.'

'I bet you do. But I'm not so sure that you would be good for me.'

She met his eyes and he saw determination there. And possibly a hint of disappointment.

He nodded. 'I'm sorry you feel like that. Perhaps we just need time. I can give you that.'

Her eyes flashed and she tilted her chin up. 'You told me that if I wanted you to leave me alone I only had to say so. Did you mean it?'

He ran a hand through his hair again. 'Y …yes. I meant it. Although it'll be very difficult I'll admit. Especially now.'

'Then please leave me alone. Starting from right this second.'

If she had slapped his face she couldn't have stung him more. He swallowed what felt like a lump of poisoned ice and yet his chest burned. He felt as if some ghostly apparition had just sucked the breath out of him. He took a final look in her direction but the vision of her fried his brain and he turned and left the room without saying another word.

CHAPTER TWENTY-TWO

Verity collapsed onto Louis' chair. Her breath came in short sharp gasps. She was having palpitations. She thought her heart had broken when she found Tony with Daniella, and it felt as if the same thing had just happened with Josh. She wanted him so badly but she couldn't have him. One lying, cheating bastard was enough. She wasn't going to fall head over heels in love with someone who had sex with every chalet girl who crossed his threshold.

'There you are, Mum!' Lucy's voice brought Verity back from her depressing thoughts.

'You won't believe it, Lucy! Josh just showed me his true colours after I flirted with him, by dragging me in here and ... and ... trying to seduce me! And he admitted that he sleeps with all his chalets girls. I'm just surprised he picked me and not you! He probably thought I'd be gagging for it and I'd be an easy lay and–'

'What? You're right, I don't believe it!' Lucy interrupted.

'But he admitted it!'

'What did he say exactly? Because I've just asked Etienne about it and I think I've made a big mistake.'

'A ... mistake? Well. I asked if I was the first chalet girl he's tried to get into bed and he said there've been a few. That clearly means several! You were right about that.'

Lucy frowned. 'I told Etienne what Jo had said and that I was concerned. I explained that I thought Josh liked you and I didn't want you to get hurt. Etienne says that since Josh opened his first chalet here more than sixteen years ago Josh has only dated about eleven women – he counted them just now – and eleven women really isn't a lot. Most of the men I know date that amount in one year!'

'It seems like a lot to me, darling. But then I've only slept with one man, and that's your father. I'm beginning to feel I've missed out! But isn't that almost one chalet girl for every season – give or take a few years. He did say that his staff usually came back so perhaps there were some ... repeat performances.'

'No. Because Etienne says only five of them were chalet girls as far as he recalls and only one of those actually worked for Josh. The other four were just out here working and Josh met them in the usual way. Bars, parties, the ski slopes. The other women were nothing to do with the chalet business, although one did work for the tourist office and that lasted a couple of years apparently. I don't think dating five chalet girls out of eleven women in sixteen years, makes him a serial chalet girl dater. Especially as he does live in a ski resort.'

'Surely Etienne was still living in Kent with his mum sixteen years ago? Josh could have dated more than Etienne knows.'

'No. He moved out here to live with his dad when he was thirteen. His mum remarried and Etienne wanted to come and live with Louis, so he did. Louis owned a couple of chalets in those days and Josh bought one from him the following year. That's how they all met and they became good friends from the word go.'

'How odd! A fourteen-year-old, his father and however old Josh was at the time. I'm guessing around the mid-twenties.'

'Etienne told me just after we got here that he and Josh are more like brothers than friends. He said they've got a lot in common and they just gelled from day one. Oh ... and I don't know all the details about the girl who worked for Josh – the last girl – because Etienne says it's a long story and one that really Josh should tell us if he wants to, not Etienne. He did say the same as Jo did though. That Josh ended the relationship and the girl went berserk and wrecked the chalet. So anyway ... that's a relief, isn't it?

And I'm sorry that I made a mistake and gave you the wrong idea about Josh.'

Verity nodded. 'Yes that's– Oh shit! If this is all true then I've just realised I behaved appallingly to Josh tonight! And ... I told him to leave me alone! I've got to find him and explain.'

***

Verity summoned all her courage and rang the doorbell at Josh's home. She'd searched for him at Louis' until someone finally told Etienne that they'd seen him storm out sometime before. Just after she'd told him to leave her alone, Verity realised.

She wasn't sure at first whether she should be doing this, but her mother's words rang in her ears. "Let your hair down for once and see what the world has to offer you. Just take a chance. You may be pleasantly surprised", and hadn't she been telling Lucy to take a chance on Etienne?

When she'd got her coat and walked the few hundred metres to Josh's door, not only was she convinced that this was the right thing to do, she realised she wanted him more than she'd wanted anything in a very, very long time. And whatever the truth was about the last chalet girl, did it really matter? She *wanted* Josh. The only problem was, would he still want her?

She knew he was still up because the lights were on but it was past midnight and she didn't know how he would react when he opened the door – assuming he did open the door. What if he looked out and saw it was her and just left her standing there? She probably deserved it, she thought.

'Oh! It's you! What are you doing here? Has something happened? Are you all right?' She saw him look behind her. 'Are you alone?'

'Yes,' she said with a friendly smile.

'Is that wise? I might try to force myself on you.' He gave her an icy stare.

She shook her head. 'No, you won't, Josh. You know it and so do I now. May I come in?'

He hesitated for a moment. 'Seriously, Verity? Are you sure? I really don't think you should. You told me to leave you alone and I will. But I've just had a few drinks and as much as I would despise myself for it, I'm not sure *I* trust myself. Unless this is an emergency, couldn't we do this tomorrow?'

'No, Josh, we couldn't. If I don't do this now, I may live to regret it.'

His face hardened further. 'Don't tell me you've come to hand in your notice. I'll leave you alone, Verity. I can promise you that. You don't have to leave. I'll stay out of your way from now on.'

'That's what worries me. I don't want you to stay out of my way. Or to leave me alone. Quite the opposite in fact.'

He blinked several times and his mouth fell open but he seemed to quickly recover himself.

'If this is a repeat performance of your little seduction scene, I think I'll pass, thanks. I couldn't take that again. Seriously, why are you here? If you're worried that *I* might ask *you* to leave, don't be. The job is yours for as long as you want it.'

'That's not why I'm here. I'm here because I owe you an apology ... and an explanation.'

He studied her face. 'You owe me nothing. I'd be interested to know why you did what you did but really ... not now. Not tonight.'

'Yes, Josh.' She held his gaze and moved towards him. 'Tonight.'

'Shit, Verity!' He ran a hand through his hair. 'Don't you realise that I'm absolutely fucking crazy about you? Sorry! No pun intended. Every time I'm near you I just want to take you in my arms and kiss you – and a lot more than that, believe me. Unless you want to spend the next few hours trying to fight me off, I suggest you go. Please! Go!'

She shook her head. 'And I rather like you. I've just tried to convince myself that I don't. And ... *you* might be the one fighting *me* off, not the other way around.'

Josh visibly gulped. 'What? This isn't funny. I don't like being lied to and–'

'Josh! It's absolutely freezing out here and as you know, I'm only wearing this skimpy dress beneath my coat.' She undid her coat and opened it to remind him what she was wearing. 'Couldn't I come in and discuss this in the warmth?'

His eyes travelled up and down the length of her body and despite the cold night air, she suddenly felt very warm indeed.

He ran a hand through his hair again and Verity glanced at it and smiled. He smirked when he realised what he was doing.

'What about everything you said at Louis'. You didn't seem so keen on me touching you then? What's suddenly changed your mind?'

'If you let me come in, I'll tell you. Let's just say that I made a mistake – a big mistake.'

'Are you sure you're not making another? This is your last chance to go home. I warned you before what might happen if I got you back here. And I'm serious when I say that if you come in, I probably won't be able to keep my hands off you. Do you really want to risk that?'

'I don't see that as a risk. And I'm not sure that I'll be able to keep my hands off you, either.'

She could see the conflict in his eyes and his expression told her that he wanted to believe her but he just wasn't sure he could.

'You ... you really want to do this?'

She nodded. 'I really want to do this.'

He reached out for her and pulled her inside, closing the door behind them but he let her go immediately.

'Let me just get this straight,' he said, 'because I'm not sure I believe this is happening. What exactly is it we're going to be doing?'

She looked up into his eyes. 'I'm going to be apologising and telling you why I did what I did earlier and you're going to be listening.'

'Is ... is that all? You told me to leave you alone earlier and now you've just told me that you rather like me and ... you don't want me to leave you alone. Do you really mean that?'

'I really mean that.'

'But ... apologising, explaining and listening. Is that it? Because that isn't what I just heard you say so I may have misunderstood and it may just be wishful thinking on my part.'

She turned away from him and walked towards the sitting room door. 'Well, I'm hoping we're going to be doing some kissing in between the apologising, explaining and listening.'

She eased her coat from her shoulders and glanced back at him seductively as it fell to the floor.

'Shit!' He stood his ground as though he were too scared to move. '*Please* don't look at me like that!'

She continued towards the sitting room.

'Verity!'

She turned and looked him full in the face, tilting her head to one side and smiling at him as provocatively as she knew how.

'Yes, Josh.'

She saw him tug at his shirt collar although the top button was open; it clearly wasn't the shirt that was troubling him.

'I ... I don't think I'm making myself clear,' he said, running his hand through his hair. 'So let me be blunt. The kitchen is that way.' He pointed along the hall. 'If you just want to apologise and explain, you can do that in there

He kissed her throat and shoulders, her décolletage and collarbone. When his mouth replaced his hand, she moaned his name, tugging at his shirt so that she could feel his bare flesh against hers.

'Oh, Josh!' she said. 'Please! I want you so badly that it hurts. It actually hurts!'

He smiled longingly up at her. 'I know exactly what you mean. But I think we're forgetting who's the boss here.' He laughed throatily and his eyes were alight with desire.

Verity sucked in a breath as he kissed her stomach and, summoning every ounce of her strength, she pushed him onto his back.

'I am,' she said with a smile, 'and you'd better get used to it.'

He quickly sat upright, a broad grin on his face. 'Perhaps we should compromise.' He looked her directly in the eye and, putting his hands either side of her waist, he lifted her onto his lap.

'Compromise is good,' she said, wrapping her legs around him as he kissed her again.

Verity didn't get a chance to apologise. Every time she began, Josh kissed her or caressed her and she forgot everything other than his touch and the immense pleasure he gave her, time and time again. She had never experienced sex like this. She'd always thought sex with Tony had been good, but this was heart-stopping, even earth-shattering. And neither of them seemed to want it to end.

'I really have got to go,' she said at seven the next morning after several earlier attempts to leave – and very little sleep. 'I've got to help Lucy with breakfast and I've got to have a shower first. Josh! No! Stop it! Oh! ... No. I mean it. I *must* go.'

He popped his head from beneath the covers and grinned. 'Spoilsport!' Okay, let's compromise ... again. You have a shower here with me and I'll take you back to the chalet. I'll even help with breakfast. I think you'll have to agree that's fair.'

She laughed as she jumped out of bed and pulled him into the shower.

CHAPTER TWENTY-THREE

Verity and Josh didn't arrive back at *Chalet Marianne* until five minutes to eight and Verity had to quickly change whilst Josh started breakfast. There was no sign of Lucy until five minutes later when she and Etienne arrived, looking flushed and just as sleep deprived but as equally happy as Verity and Josh.

They all grinned at each other.

'Well,' Etienne said, 'it looks as though we all had a very happy Christmas night and that we all finally got what we wanted.'

'I know I didn't get much sleep,' Josh said, 'and now I'm slaving over a hot stove. And Verity says *I'm* the slave-driver!'

Verity hit him with a tea towel. 'Less of the cheek, skivvy! Get on with your chores.'

'I've got to go soon,' Etienne said. 'I promised to show the new guy, Francois some of the off piste areas because with all this sun and the recent heavy falls, it's really important that he knows where it's safe and where to avoid. There're quite a few areas cordoned off as high risk and there'll be more, I'm sure. We're heading out with the piste bashers before the lifts open.'

'It looks like it's going to be a glorious day,' Lucy said. 'I may see if I can hit the slopes later. Fancy that, Mum?'

'Sorry, darling but I think I may be spending my free time in my bed. Josh isn't the only one who is sleep deprived and I'm not as young as you. I can't take the pace.'

Josh pulled her into his arms and whispered in her ear. 'Come and spend your free time in my bed instead.'

She smiled and pushed him away. 'I need sleep!'

'I can sleep!'

'Get a room, will you,' Lucy said shaking her head and grinning at both Verity and Josh. 'I'll just get changed and then I'll come and help.'

'Lucy,' Etienne said, 'if you do go out today, go early rather than later. There's another weather front coming in, and it should be hitting us this evening but the reports are off sometimes so it may arrive early. And stay on the main pistes, okay? And wear the helmets I bought you both.'

'Yes sir,' she said, 'and I still think that was *so* romantic. What girl doesn't want a ski helmet for Christmas?' But she smiled and kissed him on the lips. 'It was a good thing that helmet wasn't the only thing you bought me though, otherwise you'd have had to wait until Valentine's Day to get me into bed!'

'If I remember correctly it was *you* who got *me* into bed last night! Oops. Sorry, Verity, I don't suppose you wanted to hear that.'

'Don't mind me,' Verity replied, laughing.

'Like mother, like daughter,' Josh whispered into Verity's ear and kissed it.

Lucy giggled. 'And I'll probably be doing the same thing tonight. Catch you later, Etienne. Have a good day.' She skipped through into the hallway towards the bedroom.

Etienne watched her go and smiled lovingly. 'I can't believe how much she means to me,' he said almost to himself. 'Right. I'm sorry you two but I've got to love you and leave you. Don't do anything I wouldn't do.'

Josh pulled Verity into his arms when Etienne had gone. 'And I can't believe how much you mean to me,' he said, kissing her so deeply that she forgot everything.

She even forgot that she had just lit the stove and put a pan of oil on it. It was purely the smell of burning fat and the whoosh of flames that alerted her to the fact that she was just about to set the kitchen on fire.

'Oh my God!' she yelled, searching frantically for something to extinguish the flames.

Josh pulled her away, immediately turned off the stove and grabbed the metal lid of the frying pan to cover the rising flames. He glanced at Verity but kept the frying pan in focus.

'Are you okay?'

She nodded. 'I ... I didn't know what to do! I'm so sorry, Josh. If you hadn't been here ...' her voice trailed off.

'If I hadn't been here, it wouldn't have happened. I was kissing you so it was my fault. Don't worry about it. The lid will put the fire out. Fires can't survive without oxygen. And when I'm sure it's out and the pan has cooled, I'll take it outside in the snow just to be sure it doesn't start up again. If it should ever happen again though and I'm not around, turn the heat off and cover the pan, if you can do so safely, with something metal – never glass or material. If you're not sure, there's a fire extinguisher on the wall just there. They do contaminate kitchens but I'd rather that than you take a risk so just use it.'

'God! What's happened?' Lucy asked, dashing in from the hallway. 'I can smell burning.'

'I nearly burnt the place down!' Verity exclaimed.

'No, you didn't,' Josh said, putting his arm around her and pulling her to him. 'Lucy, I was just telling Verity that if there's a fire, don't ever try to be a hero. If the flames are higher than a couple of inches or it looks like it may get out of control, just get out and call the emergency services on 112. I mean it. There's an alarm – which would have gone off just a couple of seconds later. All the guests would be able to hear that because it's loud enough to raise the dead.'

'So it was just the pan then?' Lucy asked.

Josh nodded. 'Yep. No harm done. I'll take it outside now.

Verity shook her head and smiled wanly. 'I've got a dreadful feeling it's going to be one of those days.'

'Nonsense,' Lucy said, smiling brightly. 'It's a glorious day and it's just going to get better and better despite what Etienne says about the weather.'

But Verity saw the look in her daughter's eyes which, for some reason, seemed to reflect her own feelings.

***

Josh stayed to help Verity and Lucy with their chores before going home to take Mistral for her walk. He had only told Etienne and no one else that he was taking Mistral to different parts of the mountains each day so that she could get a feel for the terrain. She may no longer be a rescue dog but that didn't mean she shouldn't be able to find her way around. He'd never owned a dog before so he had no idea how such things worked.

'I'm still not sure I follow your logic,' Etienne said when he bumped into Josh in Meribel Village and they stopped for a quick beer. 'If she's going to go in search of Claude, she'll remember that she needs to head in the direction of Val Thorens.'

Josh shrugged. 'Possibly, but it certainly isn't doing her any harm to get to know her new territory. I've also bought a GPS tracking collar so if she does wander off, at least I'll know where she's gone.'

Etienne shook his head and laughed. 'So anyway, how did it go with Verity? Obviously very well by the look of the pair of you this morning.'

Josh beamed at him. 'Unbelievably well! Although for a minute there, when we were at Louis', I thought I'd lost all hope. She was acting really strangely and I still don't know why. She was going to tell me but ... we got sidetracked.'

'Ah. I think I may be able to help you with that. Lucy kept asking me if you had a thing for chalet girls. Don't look at me like that. Jo told her that you'd been out with a few and Verity and Lucy got it into their heads that you saw it as your life's work to get every chalet girl who works for you, into bed. I know that's crazy but that's women for you.'

'So ... you told them it isn't? My life's work, I mean.'

'Yep. I told Lucy, not Verity, but Lucy went off to find her later and tell her. You'd left by then, I think. Why did you leave?'

'Verity and I had a bit of a misunderstanding.'

'Hmm. Not for the first time. Anyway, I told Lucy that you'd only slept with about eleven women and only a few of those were chalet girls and even that was pure coincidence.'

'Thanks. It's nice to know that everyone's discussing my sex life! Did you tell her about ...' His voice trailed off.

'Marianne?'

Josh nodded.

'Only in passing. I said that the only girl you'd been out who was a chalet girl *and* worked for you, was the last one and that when you ended it, she went berserk and smashed up the chalet. I told her that if she wanted details, she'd have to ask you – and I really don't think she'll do that.'

Josh sighed with relief. 'That's good because I don't think I come out of that story smelling of roses exactly.'

'Bullshit! It wasn't your fault. None of it was your fault. You just did what you felt was right at the time. Nothing more, nothing less. Don't keep beating yourself up about it and forget it now. You've got Verity. You can be happy at last.'

'Can I?' Josh said, running a hand through his hair. 'Her husband of more than twenty years has just left her for another woman. I think she likes me but am I just the 'rebound' guy? And does she still love her husband? What does she want out of this? And can I give it to her? I'm absolutely besotted with her – you know that but you also know that marriage and commitment isn't my thing. What if that's what she wants?'

'Er ... that's an awful lot of questions and I don't have the answers to any of them. You'll have to wait and see, I guess. And let's not forget. Marriage may not be your thing but commitment is. You committed to Marianne when you thought you had to.'

Josh smirked. 'And look what good that did me. But, I'd never do that again. Love shouldn't be an uphill struggle. Unless I'm one hundred per cent convinced that I want to spend the rest of my life with someone, I'm not going down that path again.'

'Yeah, but at least Verity doesn't seem to be the type who would wreck a chalet because you dumped her.'

Josh let out a heartfelt laugh. 'You should have stayed a little longer this morning. She almost burnt the place down – and that was when I was kissing her. Although to be honest, that was my fault, not hers.'

Josh's phone rang. It was his sister Chloe. He listened to her for fifteen minutes, wanting to suggest he'd call her later but he was unable to get a word in edgeways. When he rang off, he saw he had a message from Verity.

'Hi Josh. I just wanted to tell you that I'm going skiing with Lucy for an hour. She really wants to go and for some absurd reason, I don't want her to go on her own. I'll catch up with you later, if that's okay? I would very much like to continue our conversation of last night. Bye.'

He called her straight back but she didn't pick up and it went to voicemail.

'Hi gorgeous, I'd like that too but I don't think we actually had a conversation, did we? I'm assuming you mean more rampant sex. I'll go home and get some rest in that case. Come round whenever you want to, or call me and I'll come and get you. Looking forward to it already. Bye for now.'

When he rang off, the strangest feeling came over him – as if someone had just walked over his grave.

He simply smiled at Etienne. 'She's going skiing with Lucy for an hour or so.'

'I'm glad about that. I'm sorry you'll miss out on an hour's ... rampant sex and I know this is silly, but I had a strange feeling this morning when Lucy said she wanted to hit the slopes. It was as if someone was running an ice cube down the length of my spine.'

'Shit, Etienne! I just had something similar happen to me a few seconds ago!'

'I suppose that's what falling madly in love with someone does to you,' Etienne said. 'You start worrying about the silliest things.'

Josh wasn't sure what worried him the most – the eerie feeling he and Etienne had both had – or the thought that he might actually have fallen madly in love. That was until he remembered Verity's message about not wanting Lucy to ski alone for some absurd reason.

'Etienne! Phone Lucy, will you? Find out where they are and tell them not to go anywhere without either you or me, and preferably both of us.' He redialled Verity's number, got the message service again and left a message: 'Verity, it's me again. Etienne and I want to ski with you so don't go anywhere without us. Call one of us as soon as you get this message.'

'I'm getting Lucy's voicemail too,' Etienne said. 'I've left her a similar message. What's up, Josh?'

Josh shook his head. 'It's probably nothing, but all three of us can't be wrong.'

'I don't know why it is but there seem to be certain places on these mountains where my phone just can't get a signal!' Verity said. 'I called Josh and left a message, then gave Mum a quick call. Josh called me back and left a lovely message but then I got another one and as soon as I went to pick it up, the damn thing lost signal! That was more than fifteen minutes ago and it's still showing as out of service area! I hope he doesn't think I'm ignoring him.'

'Why on earth would he think that? Isn't it usually the guy who doesn't return the calls after a night of sex, not the other way around?' Lucy giggled. 'Don't worry about it. You can pick it up later. I don't suppose it's anything urgent. My phone's dead too. I checked a minute or so ago. Besides, we'll only be an hour and then we can both go and ... have some après ski with two very hot guys.'

'*Hot* is the word, Lucy! I'm not sure you really want to hear this from your mother – I know it makes me cringe sometimes when I hear it from mine – but last night, the sex was unbelievable!'

Lucy beamed at her. 'It's so good to see you like this, Mum. You look ... ecstatic. Tired, but happier than I've seen you for a long time.'

'Thanks, I think. Oh look, isn't that Mathieu whatshisname?'

'Mathieu Deschamps,' Lucy said. 'Yes, it is. Shall we stop and say hello?'

'I don't know. Both Josh and Etienne asked us to stay away from him, didn't they?'

'Oh Mum! You're not going to start doing everything Josh tells you to, are you? Besides, if we do talk to him, perhaps we can find out why Josh and Etienne don't like him. I don't know about you but I'd quite like to know. Hello, Mathieu!' Lucy waved at him.

'Lucy! Verity! Bonjour! Did you 'ave a good Christmas?'

His English wasn't as good as Etienne's, Verity thought, but then it wouldn't be, would it?

'Brilliant! And you?' Lucy asked.

'Mais oui! You will join me?' He pointed to the empty chairs at his table and raised his arm to call the waiter over.

'Just for a quick coffee,' Verity said, sitting down. 'Etienne says there's a weather front coming in and we want to do a bit more skiing before it hits. We've only been out for about twenty minutes.'

'Ah yes. Always careful is Etienne.'

'There's nothing wrong with being careful, Mathieu,' Verity said, feeling a little irritated with the man already.

'But careful is not fun.'

'Oh, I don't know about that,' Lucy said, grinning broadly. 'Last night Etienne was a lot of fun!'

Mathieu frowned momentarily. 'Ah!' he said, smiling at her as if he had just realised what she meant. 'You and Etienne are ... together?'

'Yes. Do you know him very well?' Lucy asked. She leant forward conspiratorially. 'Any secrets I should know?'

His eyes narrowed for a split second. 'Etienne? Non. But Josh! Ah, yes.'

Verity sat bolt upright as she and Lucy exchanged surprised glances. 'Josh? Really? He ... he doesn't seem the type.'

'Ah, yes! And women ... women fall for men like Josh.'

Verity didn't feel comfortable talking about Josh like this but something made her want to hear what Mathieu had to say.

'Well, he is very charming,' Verity said, 'and incredibly handsome. I may have even fallen for him myself.'

Mathieu sat bolt upright now. 'Non, Cherie! I ... can tell you of Marianne, and you ... you will no more fall for Josh.'

'Marianne? You mean the chalet where we work?' Lucy asked, looking both confused and concerned.

'Mais non! Marianne ... Josh's amour. A beautiful woman before Josh ...' He let his voice trail off dramatically.

Every fibre of Verity's being screamed at her to get up and leave – not to ask – to ignore this man whom neither Josh or Etienne liked. Hadn't Etienne told Lucy last night that Josh was just your average guy where women were concerned? Admittedly, he'd said that Josh had dumped the last girl and that she'd gone berserk, but why was that? And was that even what really happened? Etienne loved Josh like a brother; of course, he'd take Josh's side. But would he lie? She saw Lucy looking at her as if to say, 'Do you want to ask?'

'Before Josh ...?' Verity found herself asking. She very quickly wished she hadn't.

***

'Do you believe it, Mum?' Lucy asked as they stood at the top of the piste Mathieu had suggested they take.

'I ... don't know what to believe. Why would he lie about something so awful?'

'But Etienne said–'

'Etienne idolises Josh. Of course, he wouldn't say anything against him. But ... Josh just doesn't seem ... I don't know. All I want to do is get home and find out.'

'You're going to ask Josh?'

'Yes. I need to hear his side of this dreadful story. I need to know.'

'But what makes you so sure he'll tell you the truth? I'm not suggesting he won't and I think Mathieu must have made a mistake, or worse still, is lying for his own reasons because as I said, I don't believe a word of it. But ... well, if any of it is true, even the slightest little bit, do you honestly think Josh would admit it?'

Verity looked Lucy in the eye. 'I ... think he will. Don't ask me why, but I do. Which way did Mathieu say we should go?'

'Left, then through the trees and out between the blue and the black runs. But ... Etienne said we shouldn't go off piste without a guide.'

'You were the one who said earlier that we shouldn't do what Etienne or Josh tells us, Lucy. Mathieu assured us it was safe.'

'Yes, but Mathieu also assured us that his story about Josh was true and for the life of me, I don't see Josh as the type of man who would ever hit a woman, and definitely not a woman who was pregnant with his child. I know looks can be deceiving but I don't believe it. Neither do I think he'd wreck his own chalet after she miscarried so that he could blame her and threaten to press charges unless she left Meribel. I'm sorry, Mum, but it's nonsense. I'm sure it is. I just don't believe a word of it.'

'I don't believe it either. But then I would never have believed your father would have an affair – or leave me for an eighteen-year-old girl. People aren't always who we think they are – or who we want them to be. I have to ask. I just have to be sure. And then I have to know why Mathieu hates Josh so much that he would make up a story like that. Come on, the sooner we get down, the sooner we'll know the truth and this weather is getting worse. They'll start shutting lifts before long by the look of that sky.'

The weather front Etienne had mentioned was clearly moving in. The sun was obscured by heavy snow clouds and what, just minutes earlier had been a gloriously sunny day, was rapidly turning into a dark, forbidding yellowy-grey sky as the wind began to bring whirling snowflakes. It was just a light flurry at first but getting thicker and faster by the minute and a grey fog-like mist was gradually creeping up the mountain, forming blind pockets where it was impossible to see for more than a metre in any direction.

As Verity skied behind Lucy and her board, all she could see was Josh's face and his incredible blue-grey eyes and she wanted more than anything for Mathieu's story to be a pack of lies.

'Do you have any idea where we are?' Lucy said, stopping at what seemed to be a large area of unmarked piste. 'Because I don't. We should have seen the trees Mathieu told us about by now. Mind you, in this weather it's getting harder to see by the minute.'

Verity shook her head. 'No, darling. And I really wish I'd listened to you now. I'm so sorry! I can't see the top of this piste and it looks like there're huge rocks over there. We must be off piste somewhere but God knows where.'

'It's okay, Mum. We'll find our way home. I wish I could get a signal on my phone but it's still showing as no service.'

'Mine's completely dead now. I forgot to charge it up yesterday. It was such a mad day.'

'Great. Oh well, onwards and upwards,' Lucy quipped.

'I'm rather hoping it's downhill all the way,' Verity replied, moving away from Lucy slightly to continue down the mountain. 'Oh! Did you hear that 'whoomp' sound? Was that thunder? Can you–?'

'Mum! Quick! Get–'

Verity felt as if she had been hit by a ski-bus, and the last thing she saw was her daughter reaching out for her as the cloud of snow took Lucy too.

***

'I'm getting very worried now,' Josh said as he, Etienne and Mistral were still sitting in the bar where they'd been for over an hour waiting for either Verity or Lucy to call. 'They're still not answering their phones and this weather is getting worse.'

'Me too,' Etienne said, anxiously redialling Lucy's number and getting her voicemail again. 'There's Francois. He was going up on his own for a while whilst I had a beer with you. Francois! Have you seen Verity or Lucy, the beautiful blonde girls who work at Josh's chalet?'

Francois, who was a French-Canadian, shook his head but came over to them. 'No. But there aren't many people left on the slopes and they're starting to close lifts now.'

'Shit,' Josh said.

None of the twenty or so other people they asked had any news of Verity and Lucy.

'You are looking for Verity and Lucy?' Mathieu Deschamps approached them with a concerned look on his face.

'Yes,' Etienne said, none too warmly. 'Have you seen them?'

'Mais oui! Some time ago.'

'Where?' Josh asked, grabbing Mathieu by his arm. 'I know we're not the best of friends, Mathieu but this is serious. They aren't answering their phones. Where did you see them and when?'

Mathieu glanced at Josh's hand on his arm but he didn't try to remove it. Before he had a chance to answer, a man yelled in the distance, 'There's been an avalanche! We saw two people caught in it!'

'Please, God! No!' Josh exclaimed, letting go of Mathieu and racing towards the man, terrified that the victims could be Verity and Lucy. He spotted a member of the Ski Patrol team. 'Jean-Paul!' he called out.

Jean-Paul nodded. He was on his radio co-ordinating with search and rescue. Josh heard him say that the first response team had been scrambled and other members of the Ski Patrol in the area were already near the scene.

'We need to be involved in the search,' Etienne said. 'We think it may be our girlfriends.'

Mathieu was beside him. 'I will come too,' he said, and in less than two minutes, they were heading towards the avalanche zone.

Josh was going mad with worry but a glimmer of hope shone through as they reached the avalanche track. It had clearly been a Sluff avalanche, and few people died in Sluffs, especially if you were at the top near the point of release. Those with knowledge of the mountains sometimes started Sluffs on purpose, to release the loose snow and make it safer for others.

But even small, loose snow avalanches could kill, and as they started small and spread downhill collecting more snow on the way, they held the power to destroy buildings and sweep people over cliffs, or slam them into rocks or trees or ...

No! Josh told himself. They would be safe. They had to be safe. There was a chance.

Time was of the essence. Everyone in the mountains knew there was a fifteen-minute window to find someone alive. The odds reduced dramatically after that and most were found dead after thirty, although there were exceptions. A few extremely lucky ones survived for several hours. But they were all people who were trapped where there was a pocket of air.

Most people caught in avalanches were encased by concrete-like compacted snow, rendering them incapable of moving so much as their fingers, and those who survived the fall, mainly died from internal injuries or asphyxiation. But Sluffs rarely killed, he reminded himself. People often walked away unharmed. Miracles happened and Josh prayed for two such miracles as they raced across the undulating terrain to help the small search team.

They found Lucy within minutes, just a few inches below the surface; apart from a few bruises, shock, and panic for her mother, she was unharmed. She refused to leave until Verity was found and nothing would make her do so. She even joined in the search, as many rescued avalanche victims do. Etienne's prayers had been answered; Josh continued to hope his would be too.

The minutes ticked away and after fifteen, Josh became frantic. The avalanche dogs still hadn't arrived and when Josh heard they had been deployed elsewhere at a second, larger avalanche, he felt as if the gods were conspiring against them. Two avalanches in one day sometimes happened but the Ski Patrollers in Meribel were always so aware of risk areas that they were rarely caught by surprise. But this was an exceptional year for avalanches and there had already been several across the Alps, some of which had claimed lives.

Mistral who had bounded off into the distance just seconds after they arrived, raced back, sat beside Josh and barked, pawing at his leg. He pushed her away. That's what she did when she wanted to play but this was no time for play. The irony of the situation wasn't lost on him though. Mistral's handler, Claude had been taken by an avalanche. Now Verity? No! He wouldn't give up hope. He wouldn't. But Mistral was no help. She hadn't even found Lucy and Lucy was an easy find.

After thirty minutes, he thought he'd lost his mind. The chance of finding Verity alive was now remote. He knew it, the search and rescue team knew it, as did Etienne and Mathieu. For one brief moment, there was hope: Lucy found her mother's sunglasses and search efforts concentrated on the surrounding area but as Lucy let out a heart-rending scream of Verity's name and crumpled to the ground despite Etienne's best efforts to keep her upright, it was obvious that Lucy knew it too. But still she probed around her. Like Josh, she wouldn't give up hope and their efforts became more frantic, if that were possible.

Even Mistral's manic behaviour increased. She charged back and forth and barked at Josh. She pawed at him and tore off into the distance far beyond the search area, the avalanche track or the run-out zone, and raced back. Again, she sat beside Josh as he probed the snow before barking and racing off again.

He wished he'd left her at the bar. He was about to shout at her to stop when a sudden thought occurred to him. A crazy thought, he knew. But was it possible? He yelled to Jean-Paul who shook his head but radioed the handler of an avalanche dog and this time when Mistral came and sat, barked, pawed and dashed away, Josh and the others followed.

CHAPTER TWENTY-FIVE

Verity opened her eyes and saw blindingly white walls. She could feel someone holding her hand so she knew she wasn't alone. Then she remembered where she was.

'You still here, darling?' she said, squeezing Lucy's hand.

Lucy smiled and nodded. 'Yep. You're not getting rid of me until we've had a proper conversation and I'm sure you're all right. The doctors said we needn't worry and all your tests were good ... but still ...'

'What about you? Are you okay?'

'You've already asked me that. The last time you woke up. Don't you remember? I'm virtually unscathed. Just a couple of bruises but other than that, nothing. I've been checked over by the doctors and I'm fine. I'll tell them you're awake again. Do you remember what happened? Are you feeling okay?'

Verity smiled at her daughter. 'I'm fine. Just tired. I remember most of it. I remember getting hit by what felt like a bus and being tossed around like clothes in a dryer. Then being spat out as if I'd been in one of those snow cannons and landing in what felt like a duvet. I ... I remember hanging upside down like a bat in a cold, dark cave and my legs and hips felt encased in concrete but the top half of me was free, and I could breathe.

Lucy grinned. 'I think I get the picture and you're clearly feeling better. You were so lucky, Mum. I was found within minutes but you ... we all thought you ... Well, it took over thirty minutes to find you and the chances of survival aren't–'

'Oh, Lucy! I'm so sorry to have put you through that.'

'It wasn't your fault!'

'It was. If I hadn't been so upset over ... Well, if I hadn't insisted on going off piste and refused Mathieu's offer to go with us, we wouldn't have got lost and we wouldn't have been caught in an avalanche! Oh! What's the time? Where's my watch? Who's going to cook dinner at the chalet?'

Lucy burst out laughing. 'Only you would worry about that after almost being killed! Josh has it all under control. He's really calm and controlled now although he still keeps asking the doctors every half hour if they're sure you're okay. He was like a man possessed when we were searching for you and–'

'Josh was there? And ... and he's here?'

Lucy nodded. 'Yes. We all were. You saw us all when Josh, Etienne and Mathieu got you out of the gully you'd fallen into, after Mistral led us to you.'

'Mathieu was there? And Mistral led you to me? I'm sorry, Lucy, but I seem to have forgotten the part between hanging upside down and waking up just now. Would you please tell me what happened?'

'Yes. But I'll get the doctors first.'

'No, really I'm fine. I'd just like to know what happened.'

'Okay. But I'm telling the nurse at least.' She was gone just a matter of minutes. 'The nurse says the doctors will check on you again in a few minutes so I'll be quick. We were searching for you. Mistral was racing around but as she hadn't found me – and I was right near the surface – everyone assumed she wanted to play and besides, Josh isn't a handler and he hadn't given her the search commands. But she was actually behaving as Claude had trained her to – as an avalanche dog. She'd found you but you were nowhere near the avalanche track so we weren't looking there. You'd been swept down and over to the flank of the avalanche then spat out over the edge of a steep rocky outcrop into a gully below. That's where you were hanging upside down. One ski had come off but the other one was holding you there.'

'Gosh! That sounds rather dramatic.'

'It was, Mum! And all the way here Josh was cursing himself for not realising what Mistral was doing. He was so relieved when they got you out and no one could believe it because you actually said hello. But when they were getting you onto the stretcher you passed out and we were all terrified again. You came to in the ambulance and the doctors here told us that your scans showed no signs of injuries but after all their tests you fell asleep. It really was a miracle though and we all thought you'd have at least one broken bone if nothing else.'

'I'm obviously unbreakable,' Verity said with a little laugh. 'You ... you said Josh was here? Has he gone?'

Lucy shook her head. 'No. He won't leave until he's absolutely sure you're okay but he's gone to make a call about the guests.'

'Oh yes the guests! So who *is* cooking dinner?'

Lucy laughed again. 'Christelle. I'm not sure if you've met her. She's a friend of Josh's and she's–'

'I know who Christelle is. Can ... she cook?'

'Extremely well, apparently. She used to be a chalet girl. And she used to work for Josh. Oh! And we've been on the news. Well, Mistral has anyway. She's even had her photo taken! And I phoned Grandma and she's coming out and–'

'She's what? Why?'

'Because she's worried about you and she's your mother! Josh said she can stay at his house.'

'Josh said what? Dear God! I fall into a gully and pandemonium ensues.' Verity took a deep breath. 'Oh well, I should be very thankful, shouldn't I? Things could have been a lot worse.'

'You're awake!' It was Josh's voice and the relief was evident. 'How are you feeling? Do the doctors know?'

'I've told the nurse,' Lucy said.

Verity smiled warily up at him. She could remember what Mathieu had told her and although she didn't believe a word of it, there was still a lingering doubt.

'I'm fine, thanks, and I hear I have you and Mistral – amongst others – to thank for saving my life.'

Josh ran a hand through his hair and shook his head. 'I don't know how I could've been so stupid. I should've seen that she was trying to tell me something, much earlier than I did. If anything had happened to you because of my delay, I'd never have–'

'It didn't,' Verity interrupted. 'And how could you have known? Even I know that search and rescue dogs normally work from specific commands. I think this just goes to show what an incredible dog Mistral is. Does this mean that she's got her memory back, do you think?'

'It would seem so. Just as well I got her that GPS tracking collar. At least I'll know where she is if she runs off.'

'Perhaps she won't run off,' Lucy added. 'She found Mum so maybe she'll be okay. Perhaps she was just searching for Claude because she felt lost without him.'

'There's some sense in that reasoning,' Josh said. 'I can't believe I'm saying this but I'd hate to lose her now.'

'Especially now she's famous,' Verity said, grinning at him.

'Yes. There is that. I'm thinking ... dog food commercials, pet insurance ...' He beamed down at her. 'Seriously, Verity. Are you sure you're okay?'

'I'm fine. I'm sorry about not being able to cook dinner tonight though.'

He grinned. 'As you can't cook, I'm not sure that's a huge problem. But don't worry, it's in capable hands.'

'Yes. So I hear. What a good thing Christelle was able to step in.'

Josh nodded. 'I'd intended to tell the guests they could eat out but as the weather's still pretty grim, this is a much better option than having them traipse around to restaurants.

And ... I don't think I mentioned it but she once worked for me.'

'Yes, I've heard.'

'The doctors are coming,' Lucy said.

***

Verity slept fitfully. She was impatient to leave. The doctors had given her the all clear and, providing all was well the following day, she would be discharged.

There were so many things on her mind and she wanted to know, more than anything else, the true story regarding Josh and Marianne.

And that gave her other thoughts. She'd been hoping to have a repeat performance of Christmas night with Josh but instead, here she was, twisting and turning in a hospital bed several kilometres away from him.

Now her mother was coming to stay ... at Josh's house! That would certainly put a dampener on any plans either of them might have about embarking on a passionate sex fest. Her single bed at the chalet was totally inadequate even though Lucy would possibly be spending most of her nights with Etienne for the foreseeable future. Not that she could think about spending any nights with Josh until she knew the truth about him and the last chalet girl.

To say that she was glad to be told at eleven o'clock the following day that she could go, was an understatement.

***

'You're staying at my house,' Josh informed her when he and Lucy came to pick her up. 'I've discussed it with Lucy and you're all staying there. You, Lucy and your mother.'

'Oh, you have, have you? Don't you think you should discuss it with me?' Verity said.

Josh frowned. 'No. It makes sense. And it'll only be until you're fully recovered. It's just in case there are any after effects.'

'Like what?'

'I don't know, and I'm sure there won't be. But just in case. You need to rest.'

'I need to work.'

'Don't be ridiculous!' Josh frowned again. 'You won't be working for at least a week, possibly longer. And it's easier for me to look after you at my house. Now don't argue. Your mother will be there anyway, so as I said, it just makes perfect sense.'

'You make it sound so ... romantic.'

Josh's eyes narrowed for a split second and his jaw clenched. 'What's romance got to do with it?'

'Nothing, clearly.'

'I'm sorry. I didn't mean it like that. I just ... I just meant that it's more practical this way – and more comfortable for you, I would imagine. Besides, Mistral wants to look after you too.'

Verity smiled and acquiesced. At least this way she'd get to spend some time with him, even if it wasn't quite in the way she'd imagined.

***

'I can't believe I had to hear it on the news!' Tony Lawton shouted down the phone at Verity's mother, Laura. 'They should never have gone out there! If they hadn't, this would never have happened!'

'Oh do shut up, Tony!' Laura snapped. 'I'm really not in the mood for your histrionics today and there's simply no point in stating the obvious. But I will just say this. If you hadn't screwed your little waitress, Verity would be at home with you instead of lying in a hospital bed in Moutiers!'

'Trust you to blame me. I made a mistake, that's all. It happens. And you're in no position to lecture me on this subject. Where are we now? Husband number five? Or is it six? I lose count. Shit. Even your own daughter loses count. I'm obviously going through my mid-life crisis and when a stunning young woman showed an interest in me, I let myself be led astray. And I foolishly confused sex with love. That's it.'

'Save me the explanations and excuses, Tony. I'm just not interested. I've got a plane to catch because I'm going to see my daughter. I can give her a message if you like but I'd be surprised if she's interested either.'

'No need to trouble yourself, Laura. I can tell her myself. You're not the only one who's got a plane to catch. I'm going to see my wife too. This has made me realise how much I still love her. You'd better get used to having me around for many years to come because I'm going to be bringing Verity home where she belongs.'

For the first time in more years than she could remember, Laura Tennent was speechless, and Tony Lawton ended the call.

**

'Okay,' Lucy said, sitting beside her mother on the king size bed in one of Josh's guest bedrooms with Mistral sprawled out on the other side of the bed. 'I still don't know every little detail but I do know the important bits and nothing Mathieu told us, was true. But it is the version he was told by Marianne, apparently, so he can say he wasn't really lying, even though he was.'

'Who's Marianne, again?' Verity asked, snuggling under the duvet and stroking Mistral's tummy with one hand.

'The last chalet girl. The one Josh had a relationship with when she worked for him.'

'Oh yes. Sorry, I'm still a bit tired after two nights without much sleep and a near death experience, so you'll have to bear with me. And he didn't name the chalet after her, did he? It was already called that, wasn't it? You'd have to be madly in love with someone to name one of your properties after them, wouldn't you?'

'Er ... shall we do this later, Mum? You're rambling.'

'No, no! Sorry. Go ahead. I want to hear this.'

Right. Christelle told me the story this morning at the chalet when she came to help with breakfast and the chores. She's really nice. I'm very glad she fell for Louis and not Etienne.'

Verity blinked several times. 'What? Did you say Christelle told you? And she's fallen for Louis? Well, that's not true because I can tell you now, she fancies Josh! You should have seen the look she–'

'Mum! She doesn't. She's absolutely crazy about Louis. I've seen it with my own eyes and you should hear the way she talks about him. She's besotted. They've been living together for over a year now. She is friends with Josh though, and she does feel guilty about everything that happened between him and Marianne because she thinks she could have prevented it if she'd said something earlier.'

'Are you sure about that because it all sounds very odd?'

'Life is bloody odd. I'm just realising that. 'But yes, I'm sure. Christelle and Marianne were friends and they'd previously worked as chalet girls. Marianne's father is also a friend of Louis' and Louis introduced the girls to Josh. Marianne knew Josh was looking for chalet girls and she asked Josh if they could work at *Chalet Marianne* because it had her name. He said yes. With me so far?'

Verity nodded. 'Just about.'

'Right. So this was in the early summer and all that time, Marianne came on to Josh. Eventually, he went out with her but he made it clear that he didn't see it as a long-term relationship. They dated for the rest of the season and then, during the last week she told him she was pregnant.'

'So it is true then?'

'It's not. She lied. But I'll get to that. Josh said he'd support her and the child and he'd be fully involved – because he's that sort of guy. He also suggested they continue seeing one another to see if there was any chance of a future together. Christelle says that Marianne was livid because she really thought Josh would marry her immediately. Remember I told you myself, that some girls come to find rich husbands. Marianne was one of them.'

'Bloody hell! So she planned it and she lied in the hope he'd marry her. But that was stupid. He could've easily divorced her when he discovered she wasn't pregnant. And besides, that's very old-fashioned thinking.'

Lucy shook her head. 'I know. But Christelle says Josh probably would have married Marianne if he'd loved her, but he didn't. He doesn't believe in loveless marriages. Christelle says she found out later that Marianne was going to say she miscarried and she hoped Josh would stay with her once they were married. When he said he wouldn't marry her, her plans went up the creek. Then one night he found her drunk and dancing on the tables in one of the bars in Meribel. She told him it was because she loved him so much and he'd hurt her. He felt so guilty that he foolishly suggested they live together to see how they got on. She moved in the next day.'

'Oh! Is that why he was so cross when he found out I'd got drunk and was dancing on the tables? It ... brought back unhappy memories or something? Is that what Etienne meant?'

Lucy frowned. 'I suppose so. Anyway, Christelle was dating Louis and she found out that Marianne had started sleeping with Mathieu Deschamps. She confronted her and that's when Marianne told her what she had planned. Christelle says she didn't know and she genuinely believed Marianne was pregnant. She told Louis and Louis told Josh. There was a big scene between Marianne and Josh and he asked her to leave. She refused. I think her dad and Louis eventually got her out and she's living with her mother in Australia now, thank God, but she went to *Chalet Marianne* and virtually wrecked the place. That's why Josh didn't open the chalet last year. It was being repaired. There's more to the story apparently but that's all that matters, I think.'

'That's unbelievable!'

'I know! Oh, and the reason Mathieu and Josh don't get on is because Mathieu actually *did* hit a woman he went out with and Josh saw him do it. Apparently, Josh was furious and he flattened Mathieu with one punch even though he says he shouldn't have. Mathieu's never forgotten it. That's probably why Mathieu slept with Marianne. To get even with Josh – or so he thought. And that's why he lied to us.'

'But ... Mathieu helped with my search and rescue, you said.'

'They all band together in a crisis and it's all very civilised. Again, Louis is a friend of Mathieu's father so they're all very polite. I'm beginning to think this place is like an English village in one of my favourite murder mystery novels! All chocolate boxy and friendly on the outside but ridden with intrigue, lust and rivalry beneath the surface.'

'So ... so Josh did nothing wrong?'

'I think he did everything right, although he was pretty stupid to ask a woman he didn't really love to move in with him.'

'I suppose he was trying to do the decent thing. Oh! No wonder he went all serious at the hospital earlier when I made that crack about how romantic it would be having me stay at his place. He must have heard warning sirens!'

Lucy laughed. 'The poor guy's probably terrified you'll wreck the chalet when he says it's time for you to leave.'

'It's a bit late for him to start worrying about that. I've already tried to burn it down.' Verity started giggling.

'I'm amazed he left us here alone while he went to the airport to pick up Grandma,' Lucy said. 'I'll go and make some tea – and I'll be extra careful now, just in case.'

CHAPTER TWENTY-SIX

'Mum! Mum, wake up.' It was Lucy's voice and she sounded worried.

Verity forced herself awake. 'What is it, darling? What's the matter?'

'It's Dad!'

'Dad? What do you mean, "Dad"?' She saw Lucy had her phone in her hand. 'Oh, he's on the phone you mean? Tell him I'll talk to him later.'

'No, Mum! He's not on the phone. That was Josh. Dad was at the airport too. He came through with Grandma! Can you believe that?'

'What? I must be dreaming. Am I dreaming? This can't be true. Tony can't be here – and certainly not with Mum! This is dreadful!'

'And it gets worse.'

'How could it possibly get worse?' Verity said, pushing Mistral off her legs so that she could sit up.

'Josh is bringing Dad back here. Dad's really upset and he wants to see us so Josh said he could, but only if it's okay with you. If not, he'll take him to Etienne and Louis' chalet. He's already asked if that's okay with them.'

'Josh has done what!' Verity shrieked, making the sleeping Mistral jump.

Lucy nodded. 'I'm beginning to think the man's a fool. No wonder Marianne thought he'd marry her. He's a pushover. Mind you,' she said with a chuckle, 'He'll soon realise his mistake. We both know what it'll be like in Josh's car right now with Dad and Grandma together in such a confined space.'

Verity shook her head. 'I'll be surprised if they all make it out alive. If I weren't so cross with Josh, I'd almost pity him. But I can't see your father, Lucy. I really can't.

Obviously, you'll want to but please just tell him I'm asleep or something when he arrives. I'm sorry to ask you to lie but I really can't face him today. It'll be bad enough dealing with Mum.'

***

Josh was beginning to wish he hadn't offered Tony accommodation. He'd already realised he shouldn't have offered him a lift. But Tony and Laura came through Arrivals side by side so he assumed they got along. And Laura introduced him: 'This is Tony, Verity's ... husband', so how could he know they'd been arguing?

He should've known by their expressions but he'd said the words and couldn't take them back. And they had both agreed albeit grudgingly, he realised, and more for convenience and   to save face than by choice. He'd known it would be awkward but he hadn't expected this.

Between the shouting and the insults, he quickly discovered that Tony and Laura clearly didn't like one another very much. He was just thankful for the prolonged bouts of silent sulking – from Tony. Laura hardly stopped talking from the moment she threw her arms around him at the airport when he introduced himself.

'Your trouble is, Tony,' Laura said when they were on their way to Meribel, 'you didn't appreciate just how lucky you were to have Verity. You don't recognise a good thing even when it's right under your nose!'

'And your trouble is, Laura, you stick your nose where it doesn't belong. Constantly. Marriages get stale after twenty odd years – but you wouldn't know that because you never stay married longer than five minutes.'

'But this isn't about me and my marriages, is it? It's about you and yours. And despite what you may think, it may not be as easy as you expect to persuade Verity to go back to you. Oh! ... What happened, Josh? Why did you swerve?'

Josh ran a hand through his hair and cursed his luck. That had come as a very nasty shock.

'Ice,' he said. 'Sorry. So I know this is none of my business, Tony, but you're not just here to see that they're safe and well. You're ... you're here to ask Verity to go back to you?'

Tony gave him an odd look. 'Yes. I know that'll affect you and I'm sorry for that but I'm sure chalet girls are ten a penny. And Verity can't even cook!'

'Whose fault is that?' Laura asked. 'Perhaps if you'd shared some of your knowledge with her instead of criticising every dish she made, she'd be able to.'

'If I may just butt in here,' Josh said. 'Chalet girl's aren't ten a penny, Tony, especially not chalet girls like Verity. She's very special. And Lucy of course. They're both excellent chalet girls.'

'Hmm. I suppose she's good with people and Lucy probably does all the cooking anyway. She takes after me, thank God. But Verity shouldn't be here anyway. A chalet girl at her age! What was she thinking?'

'She was thinking she wanted to get as far away from her lying, cheating husband as she possibly could,' Laura said. 'And to relive the youth you took from her.'

'The youth I took from her! It takes two to get pregnant you know. She wanted to keep the baby so it was her decision.'

'Good heavens, Josh! Is it safe on these roads? Was that more ice?'

'Yes. Sorry, Laura. I'll be more careful.' So Verity was pregnant when Tony married her? That was news to him.

'At least I did the decent thing and married her,' Tony said. 'Not all men would have done that.'

'Did the ...! Don't you dare act as if you were doing her a favour! You were overjoyed when she fell pregnant. You were worried she'd go off and leave you. You knew she wanted to travel. Wanted to work in the Alps. You knew the last thing she wanted was to settle down and get married. She told you that repeatedly until she fell pregnant. But you didn't want her to go. I do blame myself for that. I

197

should have made sure she understood that contraception isn't always foolproof.'

'Are you suggesting that I got her pregnant on purpose? Why? She was on the pill. I wanted to start my own restaurant. A wife and child weren't in my career plan at that stage.'

'And didn't we know it? I have never seen my daughter so unhappy, so concerned as she was when she thought she had ruined your life! Until she found you screwing your little strumpet of a waitress that is! She was very unhappy about that. And Verity didn't trap you into marrying her. She made it perfectly clear you were free to do what you wanted and she'd never hold it against you. She even told you she'd happily bring up the baby on her own, so don't you dare suggest she 'forced' you to marry her because she most definitely did not!'

'I didn't say she did but I couldn't let her bring up my child without me, could I? My mother–'

'Yes, that's the truth of it, isn't it? You were just content to know that Verity wasn't going anywhere, anytime soon. It was your mother who said you had to marry her, wasn't it?'

Laura twisted in the seat to look at Tony and as Josh glanced at her, he saw that if Laura's eyes could shoot arrows, Tony would be pinned to his seat, looking like a hedgehog.

Tony glowered back. 'Italians are big on family! There's nothing wrong with that! We're all disappointed that Verity and I only had one child. I wanted a large family.'

'Don't you dare suggest that Verity has let you down in some way on that score! You said it yourself. It takes two to get pregnant. Perhaps you should have spent less time at your restaurant and more time with your wife. Mind you, I'm glad you didn't. At least Verity was able to have a career of her own.'

'A career she no longer has, if my information is correct. And if you're suggesting that we rarely had sex then you're mistaken!'

Josh was getting more uncomfortable by the minute. 'Again,' he said, 'this is none of my business but is it possible for the two of you to perhaps agree to disagree, and change the subject?'

'I do apologise, Josh,' Laura said, patting his knee. 'We shouldn't be involving you in our family squabbles. You've probably realised that Tony and I ... don't exactly get along. And I'm afraid I'll never forgive him for cheating on my daughter, even if Verity *is* foolish enough to do so, and takes him back.'

'Which she won't if you have your way, will she? You'll do everything you can to poison her against me. I know you, Laura. And I made a little discovery whilst looking for my passport yesterday. Verity kept it safe with her papers and guess what I found? A bank statement with her name and yours on it – and it contained several thousand pounds! And when I dug deeper, I found a whole stack of statements dating back many years.'

Laura glanced at Josh and smiled apologetically. 'I may as well tell you then, Tony. I opened that account the day my daughter married you because unlike her, I didn't trust you one little bit and I wanted her to have a nest egg of her own to fall back on when you left her for some little tart – which I always knew you would.'

'Our wedding day!'

'Yes, Tony, your wedding day. I made her swear to keep it a secret – which she really didn't want to do. We had a blazing row about it and she told me in no uncertain terms that she believed marriage was for life.'

'Hmm. Unlike her mother!'

'Yes, unfortunately. I'd have loved her to have left you years ago, but she never listens to me. I know that Verity believes this is the first time you've cheated on her, but I don't. I think you've shown several of your young waitresses how to lay a lot more than a table! I even think you screwed one of the bridesmaids at your wedding – but I've never been able to prove it and Verity wouldn't hear a word against you – and yes, I said several words against you, and I still do now. I just wish she'd listen. Unfortunately, my daughter is loyal to her core.'

'Hmm! Well, she certainly doesn't get that from you either, does she?'

'Surprisingly enough, she does. But I'm only loyal to those I truly love – and they are few and far between. Needless to say, Tony, you're not one of them.'

'And neither are any of your husbands!' Tony sank into the seat and sulked in silence.

Josh's head was spinning – not just because of the slanging match. He'd felt as if he were at the helm of a bobsled, not a car, as every new piece of information about Verity was revealed. One piece threw him against the wall with a thud of disappointment; the next revelation sent him speeding ahead with the thrill of discovering he was right about her. Tony's belief that she'd got pregnant to trap him, contradicted by Laura saying she did quite the opposite. Believing she would do anything to get married before discovering she had planned to travel and explore the world. But there was still one major problem: her husband wanted her back, and her mother had said that Verity believed marriage was for life.

So, he wondered rather grimly, where does that leave you, Josh Calder?

***

Josh soon discovered where that left him: very firmly out in the cold.

'At least Lucy's pleased to see me,' Tony told him as they walked to Louis' nearby chalet. I knew she would be, of course. She's been texting me almost every day telling me how much she misses me; how much she misses us, together as a family. That's just one of the things that has made me see sense over this whole business. It's breaking her heart to see Verity and me apart.'

'Really?' Josh didn't think Lucy seemed heartbroken, but perhaps she was just very good at hiding her true feelings – a bit like he could be sometimes.

'Oh yes. We were always so close, the three of us. Laura is a problem though and always has been. Between you and me, I think one of the reasons she hates me is because she's jealous.'

'Jealous?' Josh couldn't see that but then he didn't know her. 'Of what?'

'Of the fact that Verity and I have been married for so long ... and because I'm with Verity in the first place. She had a bit of a thing for me, you know, but of course I wasn't interested.'

'She did?' Josh *really* couldn't imagine that.

'Yes. She likes young men. One of her husbands was younger than I am! Much younger. It didn't last, of course. None of her marriages do. I think that's one of the reasons Verity will definitely come back to me – apart from the fact that she still loves me, of course. She doesn't want to end up like her mother. She hates the way Laura behaves.'

That Josh *did* believe. He remembered what she'd said about losing count of her mother's husbands and how Laura was like a moth, constantly attracted to a brighter flame. Whether Verity still loved her husband, he had no idea and he wondered whether he should have asked her that before he'd spent that incredible night with her. Not that that mattered; he'd have wanted her anyway.

'Does ... does she still love you, do you think?' He cursed himself for asking.

Tony nodded. 'Without a doubt. I know I shouldn't be saying this but my mother has a saying, "In every relationship there is one who loves, and one who is loved," which means that one of them loves the other more than they love them.

'Yes. I get that. And you think that Verity is the one who loves, and you're the one who is loved?'

'Without question. I'm not saying I don't love her because I do. Very much. More than I realised in fact. But I am saying that throughout our marriage, Verity has always been the one willing to ... compromise. I'm Italian, and although I was born and bred in England, I've got the Latin temperament. I'm ... fiery and passionate and ... a deep thinker. Verity will lose her temper very briefly and then she'll do everything she can to smooth the waters. I suppose that's why our marriage has lasted all these years. It's all about compromise.'

Josh had never wanted to hit a man – with the exception of Mathieu – as much as he wanted to hit Tony right now.

'Yes, but I thought both people had to compromise to make a happy marriage, not just one.'

Tony shrugged. 'All I know is this works for me ... for us, I mean. And Verity will come back, not just because she loves me, but because Lucy wants her to and because no way on this planet does she want to end up like her mother, divorced and going from man to man like some old harlot.' Tony had no idea how close he was getting to Josh flattening him.

'I think that's a bit much,' Josh said through gritted teeth.

Tony shrugged again. 'You don't know Laura. You wait and see. She'll be chasing some young guy within a few days, I can promise you that.'

'But Laura seems to think you do quite a bit of chasing young women, yourself. Is she wrong?'

Tony nudged Josh's arm. 'What's a man to do? You should see some of the girls who've worked for me.' He let out a long, loud whistle. 'You'd have to be a monk to ignore some of them – and even a monk would struggle. But I do love my wife and I'd never thought of leaving her ... until Daniella. Wow! That girl is – was – special.'

'And she isn't ... special now?'

Tony frowned. 'She is. But sometimes we have to give up things we want for things we need.'

'And by that, I'm assuming you mean you need Verity?'

'More than I thought possible. Much, much more, in fact. When I heard about the avalanche and realised I could have lost her, it hit me like a truck. I want her back. And I'm here to prove it.'

'Yes. You are.' Josh wondered if there was any chance of another avalanche – one that would sweep Tony to a quick, but preferably painful, death.

And he wondered if he had any right to interfere. He'd told Verity he wouldn't when he'd criticised Tony several days before. But that was before they'd slept together. Did spending the most incredible night of his life with her give him the right? Did thinking that he wanted to pummel her husband into the ground for his arrogance and contempt give him the right? Did the thought that he would be miserable if he could never see her again give him the right? Or the fact that on the mountain, during the search, he'd have willing given his life in place of hers?

Tony clearly didn't love her the way she deserved to be loved: Did that give him the right? Or the fact that there had obviously been other women in Tony's life? Did any of it give him the right?

And what would he say? That she should stay with him instead? They'd spent one night together: one wonderful, sensational, passionate night. But did that mean they had a future? Did that mean anything other than they were good together in bed? And that they wanted one another physically?

Yes, he'd have traded his life for hers on that mountain, but everyone makes deals with either their gods or their devils in that sort of situation. It didn't mean they'd live happily ever after. And yes, he was crazy about her, but was it love? Was it real, long-term, everlasting love? Because he'd never make the mistake of asking someone else to share his life unless it was. Not again – not after the last time. He may not have learnt much from his relationship with Marianne but he had learnt *that*.

And then there was Lucy? She wanted her family back together. Did he have the right to do anything he could to prevent that from happening? Or should he just stay out of it and let whatever was going to happen, happen? Wasn't that the best for all concerned?

He had absolutely no idea, but he had a very definite feeling that the next few days were going to be the most difficult days of his life.

CHAPTER TWENTY-SEVEN

'So tell me all about Josh then,' Laura said sitting on the edge of Verity's bed. 'We've talked about the accident. We've talked about the chalet. We've talked about Christmas. We've even talked about the weather. You've refused to talk about Tony. So, don't you think it's time we talked about Josh?'

'Josh! Why? I mean, there's nothing to tell.'

'Uh huh. I can see by the flush of your cheeks and the look in your eye that there most definitely is. And rather a lot unless I'm very much mistaken.'

'There isn't, Mother. Really, there isn't.'

'Oh good! In that case you don't mind if I flirt with him a little, do you? I've thrown Bertie out and I'm on the lookout for a replacement. Josh would do rather nicely from what I've seen and heard so far.'

'Mother! Don't you dare!'

'Why not? If you're not interested then why shouldn't I be? He's handsome, wealthy, very friendly, kind, considerate, very fit and I suspect he'd be pretty good in bed. What's not to like? And there's the added bonus that he's single. Why, the man is every woman's dream. I'm surprised you haven't grabbed him with both hands, ripped his clothes off and shown him what you're made of. But then I think we both know that you have. Or that you want to if you haven't, don't we?'

Verity tutted. 'All right! I admit it. So you just keep your hands off him, okay?'

Laura raised her hands in the air in a gesture of surrender. 'Hands very definitely off, darling. So, what was he like then? In bed I mean?'

Verity blushed and grinned despite herself. 'Pretty bloody amazing! I ... I've never had sex like it. And I don't just mean the act itself. I mean everything about it. The way I felt, the things I wanted, the way he looked at me.' She gasped and threw her head back against the pillows. 'It makes me get excited just thinking about it.'

'Oh, darling, I'm so pleased for you! It's about time you had some fun and some real romance in your life.'

Verity lifted her head. 'Well, I'm not sure about the romance part. He says he's crazy about me but I think that may just be lust, you know. I get the distinct impression that marriage and all that stuff definitely isn't on his agenda. He's got a great life here and he had a very bad relationship just over a year and a half ago and ... Well, I think it's put him off getting seriously involved with anyone for a while.'

'I see,' Laura said. 'But you know, darling, none of us can control love, whether we want to or not. It's either there or it isn't but if it is then we should grab it and not let it go until we have to – or until it leaves.'

Verity nodded. 'But that's the other thing, Mum. I've only been with Tony until now and ... and I do still love him. I think this may just be some sort of rebound thing on my part. Tony left me for a beautiful young woman and I just need to feel wanted. Sexy. Attractive. I just need attention. And Josh is giving me that. It was strange because from day one, I was attracted to him, even though we were actually having a disagreement at the time. And it was just a sexual thing. From the word go, all I could think about was what it would feel like to have his hands on my body. Is ... is that weird?'

'No, darling, that's not weird at all. And a powerful physical attraction like that doesn't just mean it's all about sex. It can mean that you've found a kindred spirit – the love of your life, perhaps. That's how I felt about ...' She stopped and met Verity's eyes. 'About Noah.'

'Noah? Who's Noah. I've never heard you mention him before.'

Laura shook her head. 'I've never told you about him. I'm not sure why. Possibly because it still hurts me to this day to think about it, but I felt like that once. A very long time ago. From the moment we set eyes on one another, we both felt it. It was an animal attraction and it was so intense that all we could think about was how much we wanted one another.'

'When was this? You didn't marry him?'

'No, I didn't. I–'

'Mum?' Lucy poked her head around the door. 'Josh is back and he'd like a word with you, when you've got a moment he says.'

Verity glanced at her mother. 'Tell him–'

'No, no,' Laura said, getting to her feet. 'It was a very long journey – especially the part from the airport to here. I very nearly killed your father, Lucy dear. But anyway, I'd like to have a little lie down so why don't you talk to Josh and we'll catch up later? It's waited this long. It can wait another few hours.'

She leant forward and kissed Verity on the head.

'What can wait?' Lucy asked.

'I'll tell you both about it,' Laura said, wrapping her arm around Lucy and leading her out. 'But not just now.'

***

'Hello, Josh,' Verity said, smiling up at him as he entered the bedroom. 'So ... now you've met my mother and ...' She lowered her head. 'And my husband. What do you think of them?'

'Your mother seems lovely. Do all the women in your family take some sort of youth potion? She doesn't look old enough to be your mum, and you look more like Lucy's sister than her mother, as I think I've said before.'

'Yes, but not her twin sister, I seem to recall.' She raised her head again and grinned.

Josh smiled and pointed towards the edge of the bed. 'May I?' Verity nodded and he sat down. 'Your husband ...

207

I'm trying very hard *not* to think about. I'm sure I don't have to explain why.'

The look in his eyes made Verity's entire body feel like whipped cream. She shook her head. 'This is very awkward, isn't it? What possessed you to offer him accommodation? He's staying at Louis', I assume?'

Josh nodded and shrugged. 'Yes, he is. He and Laura came through arrivals together and I didn't know they disliked one another so intensely. I'd offered before I realised the true situation and it seemed a little churlish to then tell Tony he'd have to find alternative transport and somewhere else to stay.'

'I don't envy you that journey.'

'It was the longest of my life, and one I'd rather not repeat. Even if they both go back on the same day and the same flight, I'll do a shuttle service. There's no way they're getting in the same car with me ever again.' He grinned at her before adding: 'Are they always like that? You must have felt as if you were living in a constant battle zone if so.'

'They weren't that bad. Mum's never liked him and they would both have a little dig at one another if given the chance but when we were all together as a family, they both behaved with a sort of polite disdain. Did ... did Tony say when he would be going back?' She met his eyes.

'No. Did Laura tell you why he's here?'

He took her hand in his and rubbed her fingers with his thumb; a charge of electricity shot through her. She could tell by the look in his eyes that he felt it too.

'I rarely discuss Tony with my mother. As you've discovered, it's like lighting a touch paper on a very large firework and forgetting to step back. It always blows up in my face. She did start to talk about him but I shut the door on the subject and astonishingly, for once, she let it be. But he's here to see for himself that Lucy is safe ... and to check on me, I think. He ... he may have left me for another woman but we were married – are married, and we have been for over twenty years, so he clearly still has some feelings for me, even if it is only mild concern.'

'And you? Do you still have feelings for him? I know it's none of my business but ... the other night was ... well, I'd just like to know where I stand, that's all.'

Verity held his eyes and tried to read his thoughts but all she could see was passion and longing – possibly even a hint of sadness.

'I'd be lying if I said I didn't. I had absolutely no idea that my marriage was in trouble. This was all a complete shock to me. Perhaps it shouldn't have been. Perhaps I've been a fool, but until I found him in bed with ... Well, I thought we were going to be celebrating my birthday together and I even thought we were going away somewhere special. It was a bolt from the blue and I think I'm partly still in shock. I'm not sure how I feel and that's the truth. But ... I do still love him in a way and part of me always will. We've been married for a long time, Josh and we have a child together.'

'I understand.' Josh let go of her hand as if it had burnt him.

'No, Josh, you don't,' she said, reaching out and grabbing it again. 'I do still love him but if I loved him as much as I thought I did, I would never have slept with you. I know he'd left me and I know I'm stupid but I thought I'd remain faithful to him for ... years.' She let out a little laugh. 'Instead, I met you and from the moment we met – and I do mean the *moment* ... in my bedroom ... sorry, your bedroom,' she teased, 'I wanted you in a way I've never wanted anyone before. And ... I still do.' She smiled provocatively at him and pulled his hand towards her. 'How do you feel, Josh?'

'I ...'

He wrapped his arms around her and kissed her, tenderly at first but with a growing passion before suddenly releasing her from his arms. He took both her hands in his and looked her directly in the eye.

'I have to tell you something, Verity, even though I'd really rather not, but I can't ignore it and hope it'll go away because it won't. More to the point, *he* won't. Tony isn't here just to see Lucy and to check for himself that you're both okay. He's here to ask you to take him back.'

Verity felt as if she'd been hit by a ski-bus for a second time in as many days.

'What? Did ... *he* tell you that? When?'

Josh let go of her hands and ran a hand through his hair. He stood up and paced beside the bed. 'He told me – us – on the way from the airport.'

'My mother knows?'

He nodded.

Verity screwed up her eyes. So that's what she wanted to talk about just now, she thought. I should have let her tell me.

'He ... he seems pretty sure you'll take him back. Will you?' Josh asked. 'I'm sorry. Forget I asked that. You need time to think and it shouldn't be me telling you this, it should be him but ... I know it's none of my business and I know I have no right to say this but ... he doesn't deserve you, Verity. He really doesn't.'

He turned on his heel and marched from the room and Verity was left thinking that her life had seemed so much simpler when she was hanging upside down in that gully. All she'd thought about then, was how much she loved Lucy, and how much she wanted to live to see her, and Josh, her mother and Mistral again. She hadn't even given Tony a moment's thought.

***

'Hello, Verity. You're looking much better than I expected,' Tony said as he came into her room and plonked himself on the bed. 'It must have been a dreadful ordeal and I'm so glad you're safe and well.'

'Thank you,' she said, watching him through anxious eyes. 'It's ... good of you to come all this way to see Lucy and me. I know Lucy's really pleased to see you.'

He smiled at her and she saw the man she'd fallen in love with all those years ago. He was still very handsome, although now that she looked at him, he wasn't quite as good looking as Josh but he still had those chiselled features that always attracted her. The same strong facial features that she'd noticed about Josh when she'd first seen him. But the resemblance ended there.

Tony had always reminded her a little of Michelangelo's *David*: loose curls; aquiline nose; deep set eyes; firm jaw and a face that looked as if the artist himself had sculpted it. His hair was still the light brown of his English father, although he used chemicals now to hide the grey and his eyes were his father's blue but he had his mother's olive skin.

'I hope you're pleased to see me too,' he said, reaching out for her hand.

She pushed her hands under the covers. 'It's certainly better than the last time I saw you.'

'Ah, yes. That.'

'Yes, Tony. That!'

'I've missed you, Verity. There's no easy way to say this, so I'll just come out and say it. I've been a fool, an absolute fool and it wasn't until I realised that I could have lost you forever that I came to my senses. Christmas wasn't the same without you and it brought it home to me that perhaps I'd made a mistake. I missed the way that you decorate the house; I missed the silly joke presents you hang on the tree; I missed our Christmas party; I even missed your mother making barbed remarks about the way I cook the turkey – and I never thought I'd hear myself say that. But when I heard on the news – yes, that's how I heard that my wife had nearly died as well as my child – it hit me with such force that I knew I had to come and beg your forgiveness.'

Verity couldn't believe her ears. 'So ... what are you saying, Tony? Are you telling me it's over with Daniella?'

'Yes. It's over. I told her I was coming out to see you to find out if there is any way we can rebuild our relationship.'

'Rebuild our relationship? Are you saying you want to try again? Are you saying you want me back?' So Josh was right.

'Yes. That's exactly what I'm saying. You still love me, don't you? Can you forgive this one lapse in my loyalty to you? Because it's only ever happened once – and it won't happen again.'

'Well, this is all a bit sudden. The last thing I heard from you was that you wanted to sell the house – and that was via text. When I telephoned you to say that I was coming out here, you just said we needed to talk things through. You sounded pretty certain then that our marriage was over.'

'I'm an idiot. What can I say? I think I'm going through a mid-life crisis. A beautiful, young woman starting paying me attention and I lost my head.'

'*You* seemed to be paying *her* quite a lot of attention the last time I saw you. How could you do that, Tony? And in our house? How long had it been going on? Had you been taking her there on a regular basis?'

He shook his head. 'No, darling, I hadn't. I know you won't believe this but that was the one and only time we'd been to the house. It ... well, it was usually at the restaurant.'

'Eew! I'm sure the Environmental Health Department would have something to say about that.'

'And it had only been a few times.'

'A few times? After more than twenty years of marriage, you screw a young girl a few times and decide you want to leave your wife? Well, you really must have been in love!'

'No. It was never love. I thought it was but really it was just ... lust. And there's a big difference, my darling, believe me. I realise that now.'

'So you thought you'd turn up here, tell me you've changed your mind and I'd go running back with you and all would be forgiven? Is that it?'

'Not exactly, no. I realise it might take time for you to forgive me and forget–'

'I don't think I could ever forget. That image is emblazoned on my mind.'

'Forgive, then. It's what Lucy and I want more than anything in the world.'

'Lucy? What do you mean, it's what Lucy wants? She hasn't said that to me.'

He smiled lovingly at her and she felt herself beginning to slip. 'But she has said it to me, darling – every single day since she came here. Either via text or the phone, saying how much she's missed me. Missed us as a family, and Christmas was particularly bad for her. I told her that if even we ... did part, she'd still see me every day, but you know our daughter. She wants us to be a family. I for one would like to give that back to her. Wouldn't you?'

Verity was speechless. This was news to her, except the part about Christmas Day. That part Verity knew was true and Lucy had admitted that to her. Was it all true? Was what Tony telling her, the truth? Was it breaking Lucy's heart to see them apart? She'd do anything not to cause her daughter pain. Anything at all.

'Lucy hasn't told me that,' she murmured.

'She probably didn't want to hurt you. Let's ask her now? Together? She'll tell you it's the truth. I'll get her.'

He got up from the bed and went to look for Lucy, leaving Verity feeling as if that bloody ski-bus was following her around and hitting her on purpose. She almost wished it would just finish the job.

CHAPTER TWENTY-EIGHT

Tony returned ten minutes later, his arm around Lucy and a broad smile on his face. Lucy looked a little anxious and her eyes darted from her father to Verity and back again.

'Dad says you're getting back together! Is that true?'

Verity almost choked but she managed to stop herself, for Lucy's sake. Lucy didn't look quite as thrilled as Tony had made out but she did look as though such news would please her. She also looked as if she had serious doubts about the truth of the statement.

'Well, it's a bit too soon to say that but ... would it make you happy if we did?' Verity asked almost wishing Lucy would say, "No, I'd hate the idea. Don't give it another thought."

'Of course it would,' Lucy said, smiling. 'But only if it's really what you both want.' Again, her eyes darted from Verity to Tony.

'It's definitely what I want,' Tony said. 'To be a family once again. To do the things we used to do. I can't believe I nearly threw it all away and for what? Sex with someone I hardly knew! How stupid is that! I won't make that mistake again. We'll bring back the excitement in our lives. We'll do things together. It'll be perfect – just perfect.'

'Is ... this really what you want, Mum?' Lucy still looked very doubtful even though she was smiling.

'I wonder, Tony, would you give Lucy and me some time to talk?'

He hesitated and bit his lower lip – just like Lucy did when she was anxious, Verity thought – but he smiled.

'Of course. I'll tell you what, I'll go and see if I can find a nice restaurant and if you're feeling up to it later, darling, we can go out for dinner – just the three of us.'

'No!' Verity said rather abruptly. 'I mean, I'm not feeling up to going out this evening, Tony. I'm sure you can see that?'

'Of course. What am I thinking? I'm just so happy, so excited. I feel like this is a whole new start for us. For all of us. I'll leave you two and come back later.' He kissed Verity on the cheek, gave Lucy a hug and left the room.

'Is this truly what you want, Mum? What about Josh? I thought ...' Her voice trailed off and she fiddled with the top of Verity's duvet.

Verity cleared her throat. 'I ... haven't actually said yes, yet, darling. There are still a few things we need to talk through but is this what *you* want?'

'Me? It doesn't matter about me. It's you two I want to be happy.'

'But you miss your father, don't you? Tell me the truth, darling.'

Lucy nodded. 'Yes, of course I do. But I don't want the two of you to get back together just for me. I'm a big girl now and once the season's over here, I'll probably go travelling with Jo, or I'll maybe go to Australia for the summer or ... Well, what I'm saying is, I won't be around much, so it doesn't matter what I want.'

'Of course it does. Your father tells me that you've been talking or texting every day.'

Lucy shrugged. 'We have. I didn't tell you because I didn't want you to be upset or ... feel I'd betrayed you or something.'

'Betrayed me? Why would I feel that? He's your father, darling and I've told you, you have every right to miss him and love him and talk to him every day, every hour, every second, if that's what makes you happy. Please don't ever think I'd mind about that.'

Lucy nodded. 'Okay. And Josh?'

Verity couldn't answer immediately; she simply stroked her daughter's hair and hugged her instead.

'Josh is a wonderful man and what we had was very special but ... it was just one night and I've only known him for a few weeks. I've known and loved your father for most of my life. You can't throw everything away for just one night.'

'Dad did.'

'Yes, but he says he made a mistake and now he wants to put that right.'

'You don't think Josh was a mistake, do you? You ... seemed so happy with him, Mum. Are you really sure this is what you want?'

Verity shook her head and tried to stop the tears from falling. 'I'm not really sure of anything right now except that Josh definitely wasn't a mistake. But we must face reality, darling. Josh has his life and I have mine. We're from totally different planets as far as lifestyle goes.'

'What does that mean? You said it didn't matter that Etienne is rich and I'm not. Why should it matter about Josh being rich?'

'It doesn't and that's not what I meant. Look at our home compared to his. Look at the way we live compared to him. We ... we're an ordinary family from suburbia. Josh is a carefree bachelor who lives in a ski resort and owns several ski chalets. He has no ties and he clearly likes it that way. The only woman he came close to settling down with had to trick him into it. I like having a family. I like being married. Well, I did. I don't want to flit from one man to another like Grandma does. I want stability.'

'And Dad offers you stability?'

'Yes.'

'Even though just a few weeks ago he said he was leaving? What if he does it again?'

'We'll have to cross that bridge if we come to it, won't we?'

'So ... so that's it then? You're going back with Dad.'

'I ... I think so. But not right away. I'll stay on at the chalet until ... Well, perhaps Jo will be able to come out

216

soon. You said her ankle isn't quite as bad as she first thought and that it's healing well. Perhaps she'll be able to join you in a couple of weeks. I'll ... go home then. You'd like to have Jo here, wouldn't you?'

Lucy nodded. 'Yeah, I suppose so. But ... I don't know. Somehow this just doesn't feel right.'

Verity felt exactly the same way.

***

'You're doing what?' Laura said when Verity told her later that day that she and Tony were thinking of trying again. 'I'm calling the doctors because you clearly hit your head in that avalanche. Are you mad?'

'Perhaps. But it makes sense – and it's what we all want – Lucy, Tony and I. We want to be a family again. I know you don't agree and I know you don't like it but if I decide to do this, I really hope you'll respect my decision and support me.'

Laura shook her head in disbelief. 'And what about Josh?'

'Why does everyone keep asking me about Josh! I've only known the man for a few weeks and it's not as if it was going anywhere!'

'A few weeks when you've been really happy, according to Lucy. Well, most of the time anyway, when you weren't assuming he was a serial chalet girl dater or a woman-beater. Yes, Lucy told me about it. And you said yourself that you've never had sex like it.'

'But sex isn't everything, Mother. I don't want–'

'You don't want what? To be like me? I know you hate my lifestyle, but it is *my* life and I'll live it the way I see fit. And I'll tell you that story I was going to tell you earlier. Move over and let me sit. Where's Lucy? She should hear this too. Lucy?' Laura yelled.

Lucy ran along the hall. 'Yes?'

'Come and sit with us. I'm telling you both an important story. It's about Noah.'

'Noah? Has everyone gone mad today? Why are you telling us biblical stories, Grandma? And I haven't got time for this anyway. I've got to get to the chalet and help Christelle prepare dinner.'

'Biblical stories? Oh! Noah! Not that Noah, darling. This isn't a story about a flood. It's about me and how I lost the love of my life by making the wrong decision. Very much like your mother is about to do unless we stop her.'

'Oh God! You're going on about Dad again, aren't you? I think I'd rather hear about Noah and the flood.'

'Lucy, darling, do sit down. Christelle and the chalet can wait. This is important. And it's not about your dad. Well, not directly, anyway.'

'Five minutes, Grandma, then I've got to go.'

'It'll only take three. Now sit down. And no interruptions.' Laura began: 'I was married to your father, Verity. We'd been married a few years – you were four at the time. He was away on business. He was always travelling. Not that you'd remember that, you were too young. Anyway, I needed the sitting room decorated and – to cut a long story short – I hired someone via an advert in the local paper. His name was Noah and he was the same age as me. He was handsome and he had the most amazing eyes I've ever seen. To this day in fact.'

'Don't tell me,' Verity said. 'You had an affair.'

'I told you, darling, no interruptions. But yes, I had an affair. My first – but not just any affair. From the minute we saw one another it was as if we were two halves come together as one. That sounds corny but it's true. For four weeks we were never apart. But then my husband returned and Noah gave me a choice. Leave and go away with him, or stay with my husband.'

'So you left and that was how it all began,' Verity said.

'So I stayed – and I never saw Noah again. He emigrated to Canada shortly after. That's where he wanted me to go with him. It broke my heart then. It still breaks my heart today. I was miserable and I made my husband miserable too. Noah was the love of my life but I didn't realise it until he'd gone. I've been looking for that same feeling I shared with him, ever since. As I'm now divorcing husband number five, you'll realise I haven't found it. Oh, and the sitting room never did get decorated.'

She shook her head and laughed but even Verity could see the sadness in her mother's eyes. 'Why didn't you tell me this before?'

'It wasn't relevant.'

'Why didn't you go with Noah, Grandma?'

'It was because of me, wasn't it?' Verity interrupted. 'Didn't he want you to take your child?'

'Oh, Noah was more than happy to be a father to you. I couldn't do it to your real father though. Canada is miles away from England and your father loved you very much. I couldn't do that to him. I was also worried that if I had, he would somehow have managed to get custody of you and take you from me and I couldn't bear that. He had all the right contacts and he was a person to be reckoned with.'

'Mum! So you gave up the love of your life ... for me?'

'Oh, don't make it sound so dramatic, darling. I'd do it again if I had to and I don't regret that. What I regret is closing the door so firmly on Noah. I had no idea where he'd gone and no way of finding him. And I should have taken the chance. I should have gone with him but I was too scared of leaving my home, my life, my security, for something unknown. For someone unknown, really.'

'Bloody hell, Grandma! That's ... really sad.'

'Yes, it is. And I don't want either of you to make the same mistake I did.'

'But ... when I followed my heart and married Tony, you were dead set against it. Why?'

'Because Tony never looked at you the way Noah looked at me. And I don't care what you say, that man is *not* the love of your life. I'm absolutely convinced of that!'

***

'Have you seen, Josh, Mum?' Verity asked Laura the next morning.

'Very briefly, darling. He was just going out when I came down at seven. He took Mistral with him and he said he'd probably be out all day because he was off to Val Thorens and then to some building plot or something. Although how one can have a building plot in several feet of snow is really quite beyond me.'

'Oh!' Verity slumped onto a kitchen chair. 'I was hoping to talk to him but I didn't hear him come home last night and I overslept this morning. Did he say anything to you ... about me or about Tony?'

'Not a word. And I didn't say anything to him. He seemed in a bit of a mood to be honest, darling. Do you think Tony has said something about the two of you getting back together?'

'That's what's worrying me. I'm not sure that Josh will ultimately care that much either way but I'd still like to talk to him.'

'Are you still considering going back to Tony then? Even after I told you about Noah?'

'I don't know, Mum. That's the point. I want to talk to Josh to see ... well, I don't know what but I just want to talk to him. He didn't exactly beg me not to when he told me yesterday that was the reason Tony was here. All he said was that Tony didn't deserve me.'

'You see! Everyone can see it except you. And Lucy of course, but he's her father so I wouldn't expect her to. I know you never take my advice but I really do wish you'd stay here and give this thing with you and Josh a chance. Tell Tony that you need time to think. If he loves you as much as he makes out, he'll give you the time you need. Just don't tell him why.'

'Mum! That's deceitful. I'm not doing that again. The bank account is bad enough.'

'Oh dear, he's taken you to task over that, has he?'

'What? Who? Tony? I haven't told him about it. I swore to you I wouldn't and I haven't. I keep my promises, Mother.'

'I know you do, darling. And I think that's half the problem here. You promised "until death us do part" and you meant it. Anyway, Tony knows about the account. He found the statements when he was looking for his passport. Hasn't he mentioned it?'

'No, Mum. He hasn't. How odd? What did he say?'

'Nothing much. Just that he'd found it and that he knew I would try to poison you against him. Which is true, of course. He also mentioned that he'd discovered you no longer work at the bank – which didn't make any sense at all because how did he think you could be working out here if you were still at the bank. I'll never understand the man. Not if I live to be a hundred.'

***

Verity stepped out into the early morning sunshine as it cast its golden cloth over the newly fallen snow. She heard birds rejoicing in the branches as the rays warmed their feathers. She watched an odd shaped, single white cloud as it raced across the powder blue sky like a little lost elephant chasing after its herd. She took a deep breath of alpine air and felt thankful to be alive. Hanging upside down in that gully made her realise just how precious that air was and she vowed right there and then that she would never take life for granted again.

As she walked to *Chalet Marianne* she noticed a dozen things she hadn't seen before, heard a dozen sounds she hadn't heard and she felt as if she were seeing life through new eyes. She felt more alive than she had in years and as fresh snow crunched beneath her feet, she remembered the day that she and Lucy had walked down Dunclutha Road avoiding puddles and sharing secrets. The day she'd found Tony with Daniella. The day her heart had broken like ice on a frozen lake, unable to bear the weight of the image of them together.

And doubts began to set in like ripples below the surface. Had it really been the first time he'd cheated? Did she really love him enough to spend the rest of her life with him? Would Lucy really be so unhappy if her parents divorced?

She raised her face towards the sun to savour its warmth and she wondered if she should take a chance. As she turned the corner of the road just a few hundred metres from *Chalet Marianne,* she saw Josh's car parked outside and her heart missed a beat – until she saw the chalet door open and Josh strolled out.

A beautiful woman linked her arm through his and leant into him as they walked towards his car, her face alight with laughter. Verity watched Josh run his hand through his hair and smile down at his companion as he opened the car door. Before she got in, she kissed him affectionately on the cheek. And Josh didn't seem to mind one bit.

The little cloud elephant had found its herd and they were gathering over Verity's head.

***

'Hello, Mum!' Lucy called out, sounding both surprised and pleased to see her mother at the chalet. 'You've just missed Josh. How are you feeling?'

'Fine, darling. Josh was here? On his own? I mean ... he didn't bring your father to see you?'

'No. He had a friend with him as it happens. Marie ... something.'

'Oh? He seems to have a lot of female friends, doesn't he?'

Lucy gave her an odd look. 'Are you jealous? That's not a good sign if you're thinking of going back to Dad, you know.'

'Don't be silly, darling. I'm just ... making a point. He does seem to have a lot of female friends. It's not jealousy – it's an observation. My near death experience seems to have done that to me. I noticed all sorts of things on the way here that I'd never noticed before.'

She was trying to make light of it but jealousy was coursing through her veins faster than her blood could carry it.

'They do say that happens, don't they?' Lucy said. 'Sit down and I'll make you some coffee. Christelle's gone to do the shopping so we've got some time for a chat.'

Verity pulled out a chair and sat down. 'How's that going? Working with Christelle, I mean.'

'Great! She's such a good cook and she's teaching me lots of time-saving tricks with the chores, too. She was a chalet girl for five seasons before she moved in with Louis, so she really knows her stuff. There's no need for you to worry about a thing, Mum, and I know that's what you're doing. We're fine, so you just take it easy.'

Oddly enough, that wasn't at all what Verity wanted to hear.

***

The more the day went on, the more Verity was beginning to feel that she was neither needed nor belonged in Meribel. She wandered aimlessly around the village, sat at a bar on her own and watched hordes of people having fun on the slopes. She tried to quiet the rising anxiety she felt as she looked at the mountains but it was impossible. It was as if they were taunting her. 'We'll get you next time,' they seemed to be saying.

Her head swam as she saw a river of snow thunder towards her. Josh was in the distance, laughing and dancing, first with Christelle, then with Marie and then with someone else she didn't know, and it was clear he wouldn't save her this time. As the avalanche got closer, she screamed and jumped to her feet. Strong arms encircled her and pulled her towards a comforting and familiar chest.

'Are you okay, darling?' Tony asked, holding her tightly in his arms. I saw you from a distance and waved but you seemed miles away. 'What happened? Bad memories?'

She nodded into his chest and wrapped her arms tightly around him.

'The sooner we get you home and safe, the better.'

She nodded again. 'Yes,' she said, sobbing quietly. 'Take me home, please Tony. Please take me home.' She thought she saw Josh in the distance getting out of his car with Marie. But it was probably just another of the hallucinations she'd experienced a moment ago.

CHAPTER TWENTY-NINE

'So it's true then?' Josh said, standing in the doorway of Verity and Lucy's tiny bedroom at *Chalet Marianne*. 'You're leaving. Were you planning on telling me? Or were you just going to sneak away?'

Verity's back stiffened as soon as she heard his voice; she continued her packing without looking round at him. She couldn't face him; she couldn't look into those incredible blue-grey eyes. If she did, she would be lost.

'Yes,' she said. 'I was going to tell you but I didn't know where you were and Tony managed to get us on a flight this evening. I've spoken to Christelle and she says she's happy to stay on here until you find a replacement. Lucy said that Jo may be able to come out in a week or two. I'm sorry, Josh but I need to go home. I shouldn't have come here. It was a mistake. And I'll be no great loss, will I? I mean it's not as if I can even cook.'

She was trying to sound light-hearted but her heart felt heavy and tears weren't far from the surface.

'I couldn't give a shit about whether or not you can cook! Verity, I ...!'

This time she did turn and face him. 'Yes, Josh?' she replied, watching him run his hand through his hair not once, not twice but three times.

'I ... I'm really sorry to see you go. I thought we ... Should you even be flying after your accident?'

Ever practical, she thought. 'Yes, we checked and it's fine.'

She was lying. She hadn't checked and she hadn't told anyone about her hallucinations. She was worried that they wouldn't let her go. And she needed to go. She needed to get as far away from Meribel – and from Josh – as she could.

'I'll miss you, Verity.' Far more than you could ever imagine.'

'I'll miss you too.' But it's for the best. For everyone concerned.'

'For Lucy and you and Tony perhaps,' he said. 'But not for me.'

What did he mean by that? Was he saying ...?

'Are you ready, darling,' Tony asked, joining Josh at the door. 'Sorry about this, Josh. But Verity wants to get home as soon as possible. As you can probably imagine, this last month hasn't been the happiest of times for her. We'll be home before the New Year. New Year. New start. Things are going to be wonderful for us from now on.'

'I'm sure they are,' Josh said without taking his eyes off Verity's face. 'I really hope they are. You deserve to be happy, Verity. Truly happy. But if you ever want to come back ... to be a chalet girl again, you know where to find me.'

He smiled half-heartedly and stepped aside to let her pass.

In the kitchen, Verity hugged Lucy and didn't even try to stop the tears from falling.

'You look after her, Etienne,' Verity said, looking him directly in the eye. 'And don't ever let her go off piste without you, you hear me. Never!'

'I'll make sure she's safe,' he said. 'Always.'

'Thank you for stepping in for me, Christelle.'

'My pleasure, Verity,' she said. 'I am just so sorry to see you go. You brought happiness where before there was none. I look forward to seeing you again.'

Verity shook her head. 'Thanks, Christelle. But I don't think I'll be coming back.'

'Not even for a long weekend to see me, Mum?'

'Oh! Well perhaps I'll do that.' She turned to Laura and tried to lighten the mood. 'Are you ready, Mum? And remember you two ...' She wagged a finger at Tony and her mother, 'play nice or I'll be very unhappy.'

226

Laura and Tony glared at one another but they both forced a smile.

'Anything for you, darling,' Laura said with a look of determination on her face as if she were about to run a marathon.

Verity took a deep breath and turned back to Josh. 'Goodbye, Josh,' she said, fighting back more tears. 'Thank you for everything. And I do mean, everything. Oh, I've left your cook book on the worktop there.' She pointed to it. 'I won't be needing it and you never know, you might get another chalet girl one day who can't cook.'

'There'll never be another chalet girl like you,' he said.

Tony smirked. 'You can say that again. I expect, deep down, you're very glad to be shot of her, aren't you?'

'That couldn't be further from the truth, actually, Tony. You take care of her. And remember, you're a very lucky man. A very lucky man indeed.'

Tony coughed. 'Let's go,' he said, ushering Verity to the door. 'We don't want to miss our flight. It was a nightmare to get tickets at such short notice especially at this time of year. I was certainly lucky on that score.'

Verity felt as if she were being dragged to Etienne's car. She thought Josh would offer to take them but he didn't. She wanted to look back but she knew that if she did, she would turn and run to Josh and beg him to let her stay. And she knew that was ridiculous. He didn't want her. Not really, even though the look in his eyes had pierced her very soul and his every word seemed to have formed a chain around her heart. She wanted to go home. To safety – to security. To her old life with Tony, the man she had promised to love until death do them part.

Lucy hugged her for some time and it was as if neither of them wanted to let go.

'We've got to go, darling,' Tony said. 'Don't worry, she'll be fine. I'll look after her.'

He eased his wife and daughter apart, their outstretched arms and fingers locking for just a moment before he separated them. Lucy couldn't speak. She just nodded her head repeatedly and her arms fell slowly to her side.

'Verity!'

Verity heard Josh call her name and it was like a foghorn to a ship lost on a murky night. She turned to see him run towards her. She wanted to run to him but Tony had his arm wrapped possessively around her and for some reason, her traitorous feet just would not move.

'Keep this,' he said, unzipping her oversized handbag and slipping *The Chalet Girls' Cook Book* inside. 'It'll remind you of here and ... you never know, it may come in useful one day.'

Disappointment coursed through her. She thought he was trying to tell her something but she wasn't sure what. Perhaps simply that she should learn to cook? No. He wouldn't be that facetious. Not at a time like this.

'Thank you, Josh,' she said, her voice cracking with emotion. 'I'll treasure it. Goodbye.'

He ran his hand through his hair. 'Goodbye, Verity. I truly hope you'll be happy ... but I hope I'll see you again.'

What an odd thing to say, she thought. Was he telling her she should come back if she wasn't happy with Tony? Is that really what he meant?

'Come along, darling,' Tony said, helping Verity onto the rear seat next to her mother before getting into the front beside Etienne. 'Airlines wait for no man ... or woman.'

As Etienne pulled away, it started snowing and Verity looked back to see Josh standing on the forecourt, running his hands through his hair as snowflakes kissed his forehead and the cold wind tugged at his jacket. She watched him until Etienne turned the corner and Josh was out of sight. Then she tucked her arm into her mother's, leant her head on Laura's shoulder and sobbed all the way to the airport.

***

Life in Dunclutha Road returned to normal. Or as normal as it could be when all Verity could think about was what time it was in Meribel, what the weather was like, what Lucy

228

and Etienne were doing ... and picturing Josh standing in the snow, watching her leave and not doing a damn thing to stop her.

The journey home had been exceptionally quiet – although far from peaceful with Verity's conflicting emotions waging war against one another the entire way. More than once, if she could have turned the plane around, she would have. But at least Tony and Laura had kept their promises. Although it meant they hardly spoke, at least they didn't argue and her mother didn't even give an indication that she thought Verity was behaving like a fool until the minicab dropped her at her home.

'I need to talk to you, darling,' she said. 'As soon as possible, please.'

Several times at the airport she had tried to get Verity alone but Verity couldn't face another lecture about her choices and she had resisted the attempts.

'Don't start, Laura,' Tony said, carrying her suitcase the few metres to the door and dumping it on the door step. 'Why can't you just allow me and Verity be happy?'

'I would, if I thought you could be.'

Verity shook her head. We're home, she thought.

Arriving at Dunclutha Road, Verity had felt like a new and nervous bride on her wedding night. Tony had even insisted on carrying her over the threshold – all part of their 'new beginning', he'd told her.

Inside, he was nothing but attentive and considerate and when he climbed into bed beside her and reached out for her, she didn't move away. She didn't even tell him it was too soon. Although she knew she should. She closed her eyes and told herself that if she loved him and she wanted this marriage to work, having sex again was a very important step. And a tiny part of her wanted to erase the memory of Josh. Having sex with Tony might just do that. Nothing else seemed to be working.

But neither did that. Had it always been that clinical? That quick? That ... unsatisfying? He'd kissed her and caressed her. He'd whispered that he loved her. He'd even told her that he couldn't remember sex with her being as good. But all she could think about were Josh's hands and Josh's kisses, and what little pleasure she did experience had nothing to do with Tony and everything to do with the memory of Josh.

***

'Finally!' Laura exclaimed three days after New Year when she and Verity were at last alone. 'That man is following you around as if you were a little lost sheep. How did you manage to get away from him?'

Verity laughed, although she didn't feel happy. 'He's not keeping me a prisoner, Mum! I'm there by choice. He's popped into the restaurant for half an hour. He's dropped me off and he's picking me up and no, it's not because he's my keeper, it's because he cares about me and wants to keep me safe.

'Yes. Well he should have thought about that before he screwed his little waitress.'

'Don't start, Mum. Please. We're together and we're going to make it work.'

'Make it work! You shouldn't have to 'make it work'. Love should be fun. Love should make you happy.'

'In your world perhaps, where you move on to the next one as soon as boredom creeps in. Most people work at their marriages to make them last. It's not all a bed of roses, you know.'

'I'm well aware of that, darling. And I've done my share of 'working at it', believe me. But it shouldn't be about fighting against the tide; it should be about going with the flow. And I think you're fighting against a massive Tsunami.'

'Mum! Stop! I mean it.'

Laura shrugged. 'I won't mention your marriage again. Have you heard from Josh?'

Verity glared at her. 'You just said you wouldn't mention my marriage again!'

'I'm not. I'm mentioning Josh. Have you heard from him?'

'Of course I haven't,' she snapped. 'Why would I?'

'Why would you?' Laura sighed. 'I love you beyond compare my darling, but sometimes I find it very hard to believe you are actually my flesh and blood. Because the man is head over heels in love with you, that's why!'

'Bullshit! To quote Etienne. Josh didn't seem very in love with me when he let me leave. Although I suppose he did say that I could have my job back if things didn't work out between Tony and me. At least I think that's what he was saying. I suppose that must mean he likes me.'

'Likes you!' Good heavens, girl. He loves you! I don't know how many times I have to say this. Mind you, I will accept that perhaps the man's as big a fool as you seem to be and that perhaps even he doesn't realise it. There is that.'

'Of course! That's it, Mum. *I* don't think he's in love with me. *He* doesn't think he is in love with me. *Nobody* thinks he's in love with me – except you, that is. You seem to know us all so much better than we know ourselves.'

'You may be sarcastic, darling but as it happens, yes I do, and unless you want to end up like me and make the biggest mistake of your life, you will get on the next plane and you will go back to Meribel – after telling Tony you want a divorce, of course.'

'For God's sake, Mum. Enough! I need a drink. In fact, I need several drinks.'

'Have as many as you want,' Laura said, passing Verity a bottle of wine. 'Just remember that having a broken heart is bad enough. Having a broken heart and a hangover is unbearable. Believe me I know. I've had both ... more times than I care to remember.'

'I don't have a broken heart! But I do have a headache from your constant jibes about Tony and your constant assumptions about Josh. He ... doesn't ... give ... a shit ... about ... me. Okay?'

'Do you remember that story I told you about Noah, darling?'

'Of course I remember.' Verity poured them both a large glass of wine.

'And you remember that I said Noah looked at me in a certain way? A way that Tony has never looked at you?'

Verity nodded and took several gulps of wine. 'I remember.'

'Well, on the day you left Meribel, Josh looked at you like that. I saw it with my own eyes and I've been trying to tell you ever since. I even thought about texting you but I suspect Tony would have seen it. Did Lucy tell you that she saw him check your phone?'

'Check my phone? Tony? Where? When?'

'In Meribel, of course. The day before you left. She asked him what he was doing and he said that he'd got the phones mixed up and thought it was his. But as your phone is bright purple and his is black, I doubt that very much.'

'But why would he be checking my phone?'

'For the same reason he's now following you around like some demented version of a love sick puppy! He obviously realised – clearly before I had, that Josh Calder has fallen in love with you. Why do you think he wanted to get you home in such a hurry? He didn't want to give Josh a chance to realise it for himself and ask you to stay.'

'Mum! This is so far-fetched that it could form the basis of a fantasy novel!'

'All novels have some truth in them, darling. Answer me one thing. And answer me honestly. Why didn't you want to stay in Meribel?'

'Because ... because ... I was confused, and frightened, and I knew I had to get away from Josh before he broke my heart too. It was just a matter of time. I saw him – the day we left – laughing and joking with another woman as if he'd forgotten I even existed. She had her arm through his and she kissed him on the cheek. They were happy and very much together.'

'Now who's living in a fantasy novel? Good heavens, darling. What has come over you? Men and women can be very good friends without being lovers – despite what everyone says – and lovers can love, deeply, passionately and completely but it doesn't mean they'll never smile at someone else or laugh with someone else or enjoy someone else's company. That sort of thing has never bothered you before. Why does it now? Unless of course, you are so eaten up with jealously because you love Josh with every ounce of your body.'

'No! I ...' But even as she said it, she knew that it was true and she refilled her glass, swallowing back the contents in several gulps. She placed the empty glass down on the table and looked into her mother's eyes. 'I have to leave Tony, don't I? Regardless of whether or not Josh loves me? May I come and live with you for a while. Just until I can sort out the house ... and everything?'

Laura gave a long, loud sigh of relief. 'At last! Thank God for that! Of course you may, darling. By the way, the woman you saw Josh with that day is called Marie. She's the wife of a very good friend of his. She and her husband live in Val Thorens ... and she's an architect. Did you know that Josh was having a new chalet built? Lucy knows all about it. And if you want my advice, darling, you'll find yourself a job. There's still a vacancy for a chalet girl in Meribel. Lucy told me so last night when I called to ask her.'

***

'Hello, Tony,' Verity said when he came to collect her from her mother's. 'Will you come in for a minute please? We need to talk.'

Tony looked anxious. 'Why? What about? Can't we talk at home darling?'

She shook her head. 'No. We need to do it here. And ... I'm not coming home. Well, not to stay at least.'

'What are you talking about? Of course, you're coming home! Verity, darling! We've started a new life together.

Please don't let your mother poison you against me with her nastiness and lies.'

'She hasn't, Tony. I thought I could forgive you for sleeping with Daniella, but I was wrong. I thought I still loved you enough to forgive you, but I don't. I'm sorry, but I've only just realised this. I'm in love with someone else and–'

'Josh! I knew it! Has he called you? Has he asked you to go back to him?'

Verity was taken aback by the anger in Tony's eyes. 'No, Tony, he hasn't. Please come in. I'd rather not do this on the doorstep.'

'Well, I'd rather not come in. Come home. Right now. We'll discuss it there.'

'No, Tony! It's here or nowhere at all. I am not coming back to you. It's over between us. I suspect the truth is that it was over between us years ago. I was just too foolish to see it. I want a divorce, Tony. I think we both need to start new lives. You're right about that. But not together.'

'Does Lucy know about this? Don't you care if you break your daughter's heart?'

'I care more than you did when you screwed your waitress and told us you were leaving! Yes, Lucy knows. And she's given me her blessing. It turns out that my happiness is far more important to her than us being a family. She said that she did miss you – and us as a family – but seeing me so happy in Meribel made her realise that I wasn't really happy here with you. Only problem was neither she nor I knew that at the time.'

'You weren't the only one who was unhappy! I was too. My restaurant was struggling but did you care?'

'That's not fair! I tried to talk to you about it and the extra hours you were working. Instead of sharing your problems, you told me that I didn't understand how hard you had to work to keep the place going, and that you were thinking of selling up. You refused to discuss it further.

You said that you had everything under control, so don't blame me for that!'

'But you didn't tell me that you had several thousand pounds stashed away in a secret account, did you? That money could have changed everything for me.'

Verity gasped in surprise. 'It's not my money, Tony. It's my mother's. Yes, it's in an account with my name on and yes, I'll admit that perhaps I should have told you but she asked me not to. She opened it because she thought you'd up and leave me and she wanted me to be secure, financially at least.'

'Well, I'm not the one leaving now, am I? And you'll definitely be secure, financially, what with that and your big redundancy payout? When were you going to mention that?'

'How do you know about that? It ... it was confidential.'

'Yes, well I know someone who works in HR at that bank and when you told me you'd left your job, I wondered if you'd been made redundant. You've been there for almost twenty years so I knew you'd get a big payout. I don't know how much but I do know you got more than everyone else. A lot more in fact. Why was that?'

'It's confidential, and I'm not having this discussion with you.'

'Well, you'll be having it with my lawyers because I'm entitled to half of everything you have and that includes the money in the account that witch of a mother of yours opened, and your big redundancy cheque!'

'Actually, Tony,' Laura said, marching towards the door. 'You'll find it may not be as easy as you think to get your hands on my money – or Verity's redundancy money for that matter. My lawyers are far better than yours and I'll pay them my last penny to stop you if you try to get even a pound from either accounts.'

'Mum, that's enough. I never thought it would come to this, Tony,' Verity said. 'I wouldn't try to cheat you out of anything but it does seem to me that you have a rather sudden and unhealthy interest in money. Is ... is that why you asked me to come back to you? Because you found out about my redundancy? Good God!'

'No! I missed you, Verity and I do ... love you, but the restaurant is struggling and money's very tight. It would certainly help–'

'I thought you were going to sell it. Oh, Tony, you can have the house. I'll transfer my share to you as part of the divorce. The mortgage isn't large and the house is worth a fortune now. As much as my payout, I should think. But that's it. You're not getting anything else. Let's not forget that if you hadn't cheated on me, we'd have still been together. This is your fault, not mine and there's a price to pay for our mistakes. I don't want Lucy to see us fighting though, so I sincerely hope you'll accept my offer and agree to end things amicably.'

Verity couldn't believe what she was saying. How could her life change so much in such a short time? How could she change so much?

'Fine!' Tony said. 'But I want that in writing. And I'm keeping my restaurant.'

'You're welcome to it. I never want to set foot in there again as long as I live.'

'I'll have my lawyers draw up the paperwork,' Laura said. 'Goodbye, Tony. You don't know what a relief it is for me to be able to say that to you for the very last time.'

CHAPTER THIRTY

Verity stood on the doorstep of Josh's home and took a long, deep breath. She knew he was home because she'd stopped at *Chalet Marianne* to see Lucy who had called him on some pretext, to check.

'Verity!' His blue-grey eyes opened wide with surprise and happiness. 'You're back!'

'Hello, Josh.' She smiled up at him. 'Yes, I'm back.'

'You ... you read my note?'

'Note? What note?'

'The note I put inside the cook book the day you left.' He glanced down at her oversized handbag and frowned. 'Isn't ... isn't that why you're here?'

She shook her head. 'No, I didn't see a note. There wasn't anything inside the cook book. I've been reading it so I'd have seen it if there was. What ... what did it say?' She was suddenly nervous. What had it said? And why hadn't she seen it?

He ran a hand through his hair. 'It said that if you ever need a job, just come and see me – amongst other things.'

'That's what you said when I left.'

He nodded, his eyes locked firmly with hers. 'And I meant it.'

'That's good because I do need a job as it happens. Er ... May I come in, please. It's very cold out here.'

They both grinned, remembering the last time she'd stood on his doorstep and uttered those words. He grabbed her by the wrist and pulled her inside but just like last time, he let her go immediately and they stood and stared at one another.

'I ... I've had a few cooking lessons. Not many, you understand. I've only been gone for two weeks. But a few.'

'Is that all it's been? It feels like a lot longer.' He ran a hand through his hair again. 'The job's yours anyway. You've obviously spoken to Lucy and you know that Jo doesn't want to come out and work. She's madly in love with some builder.'

'Rich,' Verity said.

He gave her an odd look. 'I have no idea whether he's rich or poor. Rich I would guess, knowing my niece but–'

'No. I meant his name is Rich.'

'Oh! Anyway, you can pick up where you left off. Er ... I do have a few new rules though,' he said, grinning at her. He coughed, looked serious and his hand went through his hair yet again. 'What ... what's happened with you and Tony? Is it over between you or are you just ... taking time out?'

'It's over. We're getting a divorce as soon as possible. I've been staying at Mum's to sort things out. One of her friends is the person who's been giving me cooking lessons. She's a brilliant home cook. I can now make crème brûlée, you'll be very pleased to hear.'

'I'm ecstatic,' he said, 'but not because you can make crème brûlée.'

'You ... you don't look ecstatic.' She cocked her head to one side. 'Aren't you pleased to see me? I rather hoped you would be.' She turned away from him, unsure now whether she'd been right to come back. He wasn't acting in the way she'd hoped. He seemed a little distant. Friendly, but distant.

'Verity!'

There was something in his tone, which gave her hope. She turned back to him and smiled provocatively. 'Yes, Josh.'

His mouth twitched into a half smile. 'I seem to remember we've done this before,' he said. 'When I said just now that you can pick up where you left off, I didn't just mean the chalet girl job.'

'No?' Her heart fluttered with hope.

'No. So let me be abundantly clear. The job is yours and you can start whenever you want but if you stay here any longer, you can't hold me responsible for the consequences. Unless you want a relationship with me, I suggest you leave right now.'

'Ah,' she said, smiling mischievously. 'Are we doing the "kitchen means I just want the chalet girl job. Sitting room means I want more – much, much more," scenario?'

He nodded slowly but his gaze never left her face.

She spun round on the spot, walked into the sitting room and popped her head back around the door, smiling seductively. 'Sitting room! Without any shadow of a doubt.'

She raised her eyebrows in a questioning look and seconds later, she was in his arms and he was kissing her, deeply, longingly and lovingly.

He half walked her, half carried her to the sofa and as he eased her down onto the cushions, her foot brushed against a pile of papers, knocking them to the floor. Mistral, who was curled up in front of the fire, barked, jumped up and nudged Josh with her nose.

'This isn't going to work,' he said, just like last time. 'Excuse me.' He got to his feet and called Mistral to him. 'I'll be back in a second. Don't move.'

Verity laughed and watched him go. She bent down and picked up the papers, putting them back on the coffee table. She noticed they were architect's drawings. And she also noticed a name. She took a closer look.

'Now,' Josh said on his return, 'Where were we?'

She glanced up at him. 'Josh?' She was holding the drawings in her hand. 'Chalet Vérité? You're ... you're naming your new chalet after me?' She couldn't believe it.

'Er. Yes.' He ran his hand through his hair and smiled sheepishly. 'I had to call it something and ...' The smile widened. 'I thought I could run a chalet girl cookery school there!'

He beamed at her and she knew then just how much he loved her.

'Josh? What else did the note say? The one you put in the cook book. You said it was the job ... amongst other things.'

'Does it matter now?'

'Yes, I'd like to know.'

He sat beside her and took her hands in his, looking deeply into her eyes. 'It said: 'I want you to be happy, but if you ever change your mind, come back to me. I love you more than I thought possible. And I'll be here for you. Always.'

She gave a little gasp. 'Oh, Josh!' Tears welled up in her eyes. 'Why didn't you just tell me that?'

'Because I didn't know it myself until you were leaving! I know this sounds ridiculous but the moment I saw you I ... I felt as if we were connected in some way. I couldn't stop thinking about you – and believe me, I tried. My last relationship ended badly. I'll tell you about that later. But as hard as I tried, I just fell deeper and deeper in love with you, even though I didn't realise it was love. I thought it was just ... lust, I suppose. The image of you in that T-shirt is still with me even now. Verity, please don't cry!' He searched his pockets. 'I can't find a handkerchief. Hold on, I'll get some tissues.'

She sniffed. 'I've got some tissues in my handbag.'

He passed her her bag and she rummaged around in it for some time before tipping the contents onto the coffee table, in frustration. The packet of tissues flopped onto the floor as her belongings tumbled out – and so did a piece of folded paper.

'The note!' They said in unison.

Verity picked it up and read it; it said everything Josh said it did.

'I really *must* get a smaller handbag!' She was laughing and crying at the same time as she wiped her eyes. 'I ... I love you too, Josh. And I felt the same as you did when I

240

saw you but I didn't realise it was love, either – until I'd left.'

He kissed her deeply and when he let her go, he grabbed her hand and led her towards the door. She was rather disappointed that he headed for the front door and not his bedroom.

'Oh! Where are we going, Josh? I was rather hoping that ...' She nodded towards the stairs.

He grinned. 'And we will, but there's plenty of time for that later. We've got to get to the shops before they close.'

'The shops? Why? What shops?'

'The handbag shop, for one. To get you a smaller bag.'

Verity chuckled. 'Oh! Okay. But can't that wait? I'd rather have passionate sex with you than buy a new handbag.'

He raised his eyebrows and turned to face her, pulling her back into his arms. 'I bet that's a sentence that men the world over long to hear. And as much as I'd love to do the same, the handbag shop isn't the only place we're going.'

'Oh?'

'We're going to the jewellers to look for a ring. I know it's sudden. I know you're still married. But I've never been more certain of anything in my life. I love you, Verity Lawton. With all my heart. And I want the world to know it. I want the world to know that this chalet girl is here to stay.'

'Josh! I love you so much!' She was overcome with happiness and kissed him passionately to prove it. Several minutes later she looked into his eyes and said: 'But ... don't you think you should *ask* me?'

'No. I'm your boss and you'll do as I say.' He ran a hand through his hair. 'If ... if you want to, that is. You do want to ... don't you?'

The look he gave her was so desperate, so worried, and so full of love. Even though this *was* rather sudden, she knew she wanted it too.

'More than I've ever wanted anything in my life!' She pulled him towards her so that she could kiss him again. 'Although a smaller handbag would be nice.'

THE END

Thank you so much for reading, A Slippery Slope. I do hope you enjoyed it. I'd really appreciate an honest review, on Amazon, if you have the time. To see details of my other books, please go to http://www.emilyharvale.com/books.

Scan the code above to see all my books on Amazon

To read about me, my books, my work in progress and competitions, freebies, or to contact me, pop over to my website http://www.emilyharvale.com. To be the first to hear about new releases and other news, you can subscribe to my newsletter via the 'Sign me up' box.

Or why not come and say 'Hello' on Facebook, Twitter, Google+ or Pinterest. Hope to chat with you soon.

Emily xx

COMING SOON

Please take a look at the WIP (work in progress) page on my website for details.
http://www.emilyharvale.com

***

Author contacts :
http://www.emilyharvale.com
http://www.twitter.com/emilyharvale
http://www.facebook.com/emilyharvale
http://www.facebook.com/emilyharvalewriter
http://www.google.com/+EmilyHarvale
http://www.emilyharvale.com/blog
http://www.pinterest.com/emilyharvale
http://www.amazon.co.uk/Emily-Harvale/e/B007BKQ1SW

Printed in Great Britain
by Amazon.co.uk, Ltd.,
Marston Gate.